"Is your business do

Steed returned to hi

said.

"Good. Perhaps now you can give Kenny's case the attention it deserves."

"Look, Ms. Clark, I've done my job. Mr. Warwick is not and was not the only citizen of Sterling."

"But he's the only citizen of Sterling who was my best friend and is suspected of killing himself."

"It's not a suspicion, it's a fact." Steed's eyes, a striking combination of cobalt blue and teal, flashed irritation as they fell upon her. His mouth twisted into an annoyed frown. "Warwick being your best friend won't change any of that."

Darci glanced at the golden shield clipped to the pocket of his coat before fixing him with a hard glare. How could such a hot man be so cold? "Tell me, Detective, did you get that shiny badge out of a Cracker Jack box?"

—◆◆◆—

remained in his desk. "For the time being," he

NOT QUITE RIGHT

TAMMY WILLIAMS

Genesis Press, Inc.

INDIGO LOVE SPECTRUM

An imprint of Genesis Press, Inc.
Publishing Company

Genesis Press, Inc.
P.O. Box 101
Columbus, MS 39703

Copyright © 2010 Tammy Williams

ISBN: 13 DIGIT : 978-1-58571-410-0
ISBN: 10 DIGIT : 1-58571-410-0
Manufactured in the United States of America

First Edition

Visit us at www.genesis-press.com
or call at 1-888-Indigo-1-4-0

DEDICATION

This story is dedicated to my parents,
Rev. Willie and Betty Williams, and my siblings,
Willesa, LaWanda, and Derrick

ACKNOWLEDGMENTS

I would like to acknowledge my Lord and Savior Jesus Christ for making anything possible.

I would like to acknowledge my family for their unflagging support. Your confidence and belief means more to me than I could ever say.

There are quite a few others I would like to acknowledge for their assistance with certain details in the writing of *Not Quite Right*. To my brother-in-law, Senior State Transport Officer Steven Hallinquest, thank you for entertaining my numerous questions on any and everything law enforcement related.

Chief Leroy Grimes, Coroner Willard Duncan, and Coroner Gary Watts, thank you for answering the many questions I shot your way. Your willingness to help was truly appreciated, and your help invaluable.

To my faithful readers, thank you for your continued support. You make it all worthwhile. I now introduce Darci Clarke and Steed McGraw.

CHAPTER 1

"I need to report a murder."

Murder? Steed McGraw lost all interest in the file on a rash of convenience store robberies and turned his attention to the troubled female voice. "Excuse me, ma'am?" He waved over the statuesque, dark-haired beauty who seemed strangely familiar and a bit out of sorts. "Did you say a murder?"

"Yes, my best friend was murdered. The officer at the front desk told me come on back. Are you Detective McGraw?"

Steed nodded as she approached, his train of thought centered on the knee-high skirt of her black halter dress and her shapely, seemingly endless mocha legs. Stiletto heels added several inches to what he gathered to be nearly six feet of height, but she had no trouble keeping her curvaceous form upright as she closed the distance from the door to the empty chair in front of his desk.

She crossed her legs, exposing more of her gorgeous limbs to his female flesh-loving eyes, and eliciting reactions in his body that were anything but professional for an on-duty law enforcement agent. Steed shook off his lust. It was time to be a cop first and a man second.

He added the robbery file to the growing stack next to his computer and gave his complete, all-business attention to the upset woman. "Your best friend was murdered?"

"Yes." She nodded. "Somebody shot him."

Him? Why did so many beautiful women have male best friends? Steed reached for a pen and his notepad. "What is the victim's name?"

"Kenneth Warwick."

Oh, boy. Steed dropped his pen. Even in September, with the countdown to fall well under way, that summer sun was doing its damndest. That lady definitely had too much heat today. *Murder.* Sterling, like most growing small cities in the country, battled a rising drug problem, which led to more robberies and assaults, but the people here didn't kill each other, they just drew blood.

Steed closed the pad and dragged his fingers through his hair. After he explained things to this lady, getting a trim would be the next item on his "Things to Do" list. The dismissal of one detective and the resignation of another over the last two months had left him carrying the workload alone, but a few minutes for the barbershop had to be found. He had no desire to look like the brunette twin of that guy on the cover of romance novels.

"Look, ma'am . . ." Steed began.

"Darci. Darci Clarke."

Darci Clarke. She was familiar. The Sterling native who had made it big in New York with her hard-hitting journalistic approach and contributing reports for the high-rated TV magazine show *Heart of the Matter* and the network news. In the nearly three years he'd lived in the town, he'd heard her name enough, but the pictures he'd seen around the local eateries, and even at Warwick's house, didn't do her justice.

He'd spoken to her on the phone after Warwick's death. Her upset had been obvious, and her information the same as Warwick's family, co-workers, and acquaintances—he was happy and everything seemed fine. The man's funeral was today. That would explain her being back in South Carolina, but it wouldn't explain her complaint.

"Ms. Clarke, Mr. Warwick's death was a suicide."

"Kenny wouldn't kill himself."

"According to the coroner and M.E. he would and did." Why a young, healthy man with financial success, scores of women, an incredible house, and no enemies to speak of would do himself in remained a mystery, but it wasn't Steed's job to read Warwick's mind. He was an investigator, and he'd done that. "Ma'am, Mr. Warwick shot himself in the head at point-blank range. I'm sorry, but this case is closed."

Darci sniffled. "It shouldn't be." She pulled a tissue from her purse and dabbed her teary black pearl eyes. "Something's not right here. I know Kenny wouldn't kill himself. This needs further investigation."

Steed winced. He was never good with tears. Making his way to the corner water cooler, he filled a small plastic cup and offered it to Darci. "Here, take a drink of this."

Their fingers brushed. A strange fluttering, like a million butterflies juggling for space to expand their wings and take flight, filled his stomach. Darci smelled of fresh summer peaches, with skin just as soft. It took everything he had to not bury his head in her neck and inhale. What was that strange fluttering about? And why was his body tingling?

Darci cleared her throat. "Thank you," she said, taking a drink.

Her voice broke his reverie. Since when did perfume and soft skin get him off track? Steed shook the cobwebs from his head and returned to his chair. "You're welcome."

Darci's tongue brushed the glistening water droplets from her full lips. The weird tingling shot down his spine. What was going on with him?

"When will you continue the investigation?" she asked.

Steed grimaced. Maybe he should have offered her a shot from his private stash. Jack Daniel's would probably do her more good than water. And after his reaction just now, him, too. "Ms. Clarke, I can see you're upset, and you have my deepest sympathies, but there's nothing more to investigate. I am an investigator, and I have done just that. I have been doing it for a lot of years."

"But—"

"Mr. Warwick was a television newsman. He was a celebrity around here. Not nearly as celebrated as you, but famous enough. I gave his case the time it merited and then some. If you look around," he jutted his head in the direction of the two empty desks along the front and side walls, "you'll notice things are a bit thin in the way of detective personnel. I can't afford to waste time on a case that was practically solved the moment after it happened."

"I understand, but . . ."

"Look, I hate to be blunt, but your friend blew his brains out. I'm waiting for final results from his autopsy, but cause of death is not in question. The point of entry rules out anything other than self-infliction, his fingerprints were the only set on the gun, the gun was his, and powder residue was found on his hand. There were no signs of forced entry or foul play. It's pretty much open and shut. My investigation and all reports confirm Mr. Warwick committed suicide."

Darci took another sip of the water and placed the cup on the desk. "Then you and all the reports are wrong."

Steed sucked in a breath. Now she was starting to irritate him. "Ms. Clarke, what would you have me do differently?"

"I would have you find who killed my best friend."

Before he could comment, Jackson, the front desk officer a month into his rookie year, entered. "Detective McGraw, the chief wants to see you," he said.

Steed welcomed the interruption, but this momentary reprieve from the gorgeous but pushy woman wouldn't keep him from giving Jackson a piece of his mind for sending her back here in the first place. *Find the killer of a man who committed suicide.* His time was too precious for this.

"I'll be right there."

Jackson nodded and left.

Steed gave Darci a tight smile. "Sorry, I have to go."

"Fine." She crossed her legs and settled into the chair. "I'll wait."

"Great," he mumbled, pulling his sports coat from the back of his chair and making his way to the office of his ranking superior. He gave Jackson a harsh stare as he passed the front desk. "Why did you send her to me?"

"She had a question about the Warwick case, and you're the lead investigator," Jackson explained.

"I'm the only investigator."

Jackson looked in the direction of the detective's office. "That's Darci Clarke, sir." He smiled brightly.

Steed frowned. "I know who she is."

"Sorry, sir."

Steed drew a deep breath as he continued eyeing the young officer who reminded him of his younger brother. Blonde and clean-cut, Lucas Jackson looked every bit of his twenty-two years. Fresh out of the academy and green as a string bean, he was eager to please and anxious to learn. Too bad he was starstruck, too.

"Did Rogers say what he wanted?" Steed asked, slipping on his coat. Rogers always dressed as if he'd just stepped off the cover of *GQ*, so wearing a sports coat in his presence made Steed feel less underdressed. A black modern-day Kojak. That was Chief Rogers.

"No, sir, he didn't," Jackson answered.

Without another word, Steed continued to Rogers's office. Outside the door, he did a mental checklist of his last cases and found no problems, but that wouldn't stop Martin Edgar Rogers from finding something to criticize. Rogers's drill sergeant mentality, a holdover from his Marine days, peppered his tone and demeanor with a "don't test me" edge, and his imposing six feet-five, 250-pound frame reinforced it.

Though he didn't like hearing about his shortcomings, Steed held the chief in high esteem. Rogers was a great cop, and every meeting helped Steed in his pursuit of being the best cop he could be. The kind of cop his father had died trying to be.

A hard shove jostled Steed. "Out of my way, McGraw!"

Paul "Fritz" Fritzano, a Sterling officer of eighteen months who had wanted to be a detective since his first day on the job, zipped past Steed and burst into the chief's office.

Steed had spent two years in New York walking the beat, and another five on patrol, before leaving for patrol duties in Texas and getting appointed detective. After four years in Texas, he relocated to Crider County, South Carolina, and settled into the city of Sterling. Career movement didn't happen here overnight, so he'd worked hard and harder to get recognition. After almost three years, he'd gotten a lot of experience, plenty of pats on the back, and a couple of raises, but no promotion in title.

For Fritz to expect to be made a detective after less than two years made no sense. Fritz was older than Steed and had been an officer elsewhere for years, but he wasn't as experienced in matters of investigation. In Sterling, you weren't appointed detective, you had to prove yourself worthy of the job, and then pass a written and physical test. Coming in as detective precluded Steed from the tests, but in his quest for advancement, he'd found proving yourself didn't come easily.

Loud voices emanated from within at the slam of the door. Fritz's insistence it was high time Rogers made him detective was followed by Rogers's even louder declaration that Fritz was in no way ready to be one. Rogers followed his edict with a demand Fritz get out of his office before he made him wish he'd never come in.

"Oh, I'm out, Rogers! I quit! You and this whole department can go to hell!"

Steed received another hard shove as Fritz barreled out of the office, red-faced and steaming. There was something about the man Steed had never liked. Physically fit with good knowledge of procedure, Fritz seemed like ideal cop material, but the shiftiness and cat-that-swallowed-the-canary look in his dark eyes put Steed on edge. He was glad the man had quit, although losing more personnel was not something Rogers needed.

Steed stuck his head in the office door. "I know you wanted to see me, sir, but I can come back a little later."

"No." Rogers waved him in. "Fritz was just . . . being Fritz. The bad thing is his quitting robbed me of the pleasure of firing him. I need more officers, but I don't need him."

"You won't get an argument from me," Steed said, entering and closing the door.

"I've had enough of Fritz's know-it-all mentality, but what's your beef with him?"

"Nothing I can put my finger on. There's just a taunting way about him." Steed shrugged. "What's on your mind, sir?"

Rogers raised a steaming mug to his lips. "I understand Darci Clarke came in."

Steed stuffed his hands in the front pockets of his jeans. "Yeah, she did that." Into the office and into his head.

"What's with the tone?" Rogers motioned to the chair in front of his desk. "Aren't you helping her?"

"There's not much I can do to help her, sir." Steed sat. "She's upset about Warwick's death and not thinking clearly."

"How so?"

"She's certain somebody killed him."

"That's not what your investigation shows."

"And neither do the reports from the coroner and medical examiner, but that lady's not hearing it. She's convinced he was murdered. It's why she's here. To report his *murder*. She's still here."

"Hmm." Rogers trailed his thumb and forefinger along his dark goatee. "They were very close friends growing up."

"According to her, he was her best friend."

"Is that all she said?"

"Are you asking me if she said they were more?"

"Did she?"

"No. Why?"

"Before she left, people talked. Sterling's a progressive little city, but it's still the South. Darci's father and I were schoolmates, and he never suggested they were anything more than good friends. But a black woman and white man always joined together at the hip . . ." Rogers clicked his tongue. "Makes you wonder."

"Not me. She's a beautiful woman. A bit pushy, but beautiful. Any man with a pulse would be attracted to her."

Rogers cocked an eyebrow. "You find her attractive?"

"Last I checked I still had a pulse." Steed grinned.

"I didn't think she'd be your type."

"She's female and beautiful. That's always my type."

"Thanks for sharing, McGraw. What else did she say?"

"Not much. She's just adamant Warwick wouldn't kill himself."

"What did you tell her?"

"What could I tell her? I said the case was solved and the final results from the autopsy are just a formality. The guy shot himself in the head. There's not a shred of evidence that says differently."

"When did Dr. Kellogg say those results would be in?"

"Two weeks, more or less."

"Think you can humor Darci until then?"

"Humor her?" Steed grunted. "How am I going to do that?"

"Listen to her, tell her you'll look into it, and when the final results come in, show them to her and then she'll head back to New York. You know these news types need facts before they let anything go."

"What?" Steed leaned over the desk, pushed aside a half-eaten banana nut muffin, and rifled through the chief's neatly stacked files. "Okay, where is it?"

"McGraw, what are you doing?"

"I'm searching for the script you memorized before I got in here. I'm surprised that run-in with Fritz didn't erase it straight from your memory." Steed sat back in the chair at the unhappy scowl on the chief's face. Rogers was not one to abide frivolous pursuits, and nothing was more frivolous than this. "What's going on?"

"I got a call from the mayor. It seems Darci went to see him before she came over."

"And?"

"She intimated Sterling law enforcement would not be painted in a favorable light if she didn't see some real action taken with this case."

"Real action? Warwick killed himself. Only God knows why."

"We know that, but apparently she doesn't."

"And you expect me to convince her otherwise?"

"I expect you to show the mayor and me why you should be promoted to sergeant."

"Sergeant?" Steed eyed his superior. He'd been working hard out of dedication and necessity, but also to prove a point. He wanted to be promoted. It wasn't so much the responsibility that came with the title, he had plenty of that, it was the idea of it. Sergeant. He wanted to achieve that goal, and the chief knew it. "I'm getting the promotion?"

"That depends on you. I'm having enough problems with personnel, so I don't need new problems. Just keep Darci calm and quiet until those test results come back. You said she's attractive, and . . ."

"Pushy. She's pushy."

"Find a way to keep her occupied. She told Mayor Benjamin she wanted our full cooperation, so you make sure she gets it. It's only going to be for a couple of weeks." The chief shooed him off. "We're done."

Steed stood in one fluid motion. Halfway to the door, he turned around. "I've earned this promotion, Chief."

"Show me," was all Rogers said before biting into the muffin and chasing it with a loud swallow of coffee.

Knowing there was nothing more he could say, Steed made his way back to his office, wondering how he was going to handle Darci Clarke—the one person standing between him and his promotion.

"All right, Kenny, what trouble did those smoky eyes and silver tongue get you into that you couldn't get out of?" Darci brushed her finger against the smiling face in the wallet-size picture. "I promise, I'm going to find out what happened to you, that bonehead cop be damned."

Steed McGraw. Darci rolled her eyes. What kind of woman would name her child after a horse?

She recalled the detective's long powerful legs, broad shoulders, and dusting of fine dark hairs leading to the imprint of muscles hidden beneath a white dress shirt. Heat rushed to her cheeks. If the horses her childhood summer camp counselors tried to force her to ride had looked anything like him, she would probably be a world-class equestrian by now.

"You're still here."

Steed's voice, a reluctant Southern drawl with a dash of the North, startled her, but lately almost everything did. She might have had ten hours of sleep total in the three days since she'd heard about Kenny's death. The next day Detective Stud called, asked several questions, extended his condolences, and then said he'd be in touch if he had more questions. He didn't have any more questions, but she had plenty.

"I said I would be," Darci answered, stuffing the photo in her purse. "Is your business done?"

Steed returned to his desk. "For the time being," he said.

"Good. Perhaps, now, you can give Kenny's case the attention it deserves."

"Look, Ms. Clarke, I've done my job. Mr. Warwick is not and was not the only citizen of Sterling."

"But he's the only citizen of Sterling who was my best friend and is suspected of killing himself."

"It's not a suspicion, it's a fact." Steed's eyes, a striking combination of cobalt blue and teal, flashed irritation as they fell upon her. His mouth twisted into an annoyed frown. "Warwick being your best friend won't change any of that."

Darci glanced at the golden shield clipped to the pocket of his coat before fixing him with a hard glare. How could such a hot man be so cold? "Tell me, Detective, did you get that shiny badge out of a Cracker Jack box?"

He returned her stare-down. "No, I got it from the same street vendor in New York who sold you that smart mouth."

With anger burning through her veins, Darci jumped to her feet, prepared to give the sinfully handsome but inept detective a big piece of her mind.

Steed stood and placed his hands on her shoulders. Suddenly the angry fire became a flame of a very different sort, radiating from the point of Steed's touch and spreading throughout her body. Darci sucked in a breath, wanting to gaze into the blue eyes staring down at her but afraid to. His masculine scent rendered her weak in the knees. She didn't like this man, so why did she enjoy his touch so much? She shrugged away.

"Look, I—I apologize for saying that." Steed shoved his hands in his pockets. "I was out of line," he said.

"Finally, something we agree on." Darci sat before she fell. "I'm sorry, too. I'm just very upset, and I know Kenny wouldn't kill himself. There was no note."

"Not all people who commit suicide leave a note. There's no etiquette for situations like this."

"Maybe not, but if Kenny had killed himself, he would have left a note. He'd have to explain himself; otherwise, no one who really knew him would believe it. I talked to him the day before this happened, and there was nothing wrong. He was excited about an upcoming trip to Rio. He had no reason to kill himself."

"Ms. Clarke, Warwick's family still lives here. His parents aren't questioning this, neither is his sister, and she found his body. They are surprised and saddened, but they have accepted the facts. I suggest you do the same."

"I'll never accept this. I knew him better than anyone, and Kenny would not kill himself. As a reporter, I have seen and done dozens of interviews with loved ones of people who have committed suicide or homicide and they always say, 'He wasn't that kind of person' or 'She seemed just fine.' Well, I'm certain Kenny wouldn't kill himself and he was fine, and it's not just grief I'm feeling. It's knowledge of my friend."

"Knowledge of your friend? So, you're not like those people you interview?"

"No!" Darci said emphatically. "Something is not right here. I know that. I can feel it in my bones."

"Okay, fine." Steed smoothed his hand over his sun-kissed face and days-old stubble. "Who would want him dead and why?"

Darci frowned, not happy with his condescending tone and dismissive attitude. "You're the investigator, Detective, it's your job to find that out." She stood. "I have a funeral to attend, but know when I come back, I'll expect some answers from you."

CHAPTER 2

Through a haze of tears, Darci stared at the glossy mahogany coffin blanketed with roses, daisies, carnations, and wildflowers. Her best friend. A man who loved himself more than he did his many women, dead at thirty-two from an apparent self-inflicted gunshot wound. She closed her eyes, wanting to block out this horrible moment. To drown out the sobs from the nameless beautiful blondes and brunettes who filled the pews and the sorrowful strains of "Just a Closer Walk with Thee" from the organist.

Darci sniffled as she gazed at the large color picture to the side of the casket. "Oh, Kenny."

A hand closed over her shoulder. Darci turned with a start to find Kenny's parents.

"Suzette, Thomas." Darci brought Kenny's grieving mother into the circle of her arms. Darci's tears returned as Suzette softly sobbed. "I'm so sorry." She hugged Thomas, who didn't look much stronger than his wife. "I just can't believe this."

"I know." Suzette dabbed her eyes with a crumpled tissue. "I'm sorry this is why you had to come home, but I'm glad to see you. We've missed you."

"Me, too." Visits to Sterling had been few and far between since she moved to New York seven years earlier and got caught up in her career. But she kept in constant contact with Kenny, and he visited her all the time. Seeing so much of Kenny in his parents, with their dark hair and light eyes, gave Darci some comfort, but she still couldn't believe she'd never see him again. "I spoke to Kenny the day before he . . . the day before this happened." Darci sniffled. "It doesn't make sense."

Thomas wrapped his arm around Suzette's shoulders. Fresh tears shone in his eyes. "So, he didn't say anything to you that would—" he began.

"No. He was being Kenny. Bragging about his women and the trip to Rio he was taking next month. He was excited about life. To believe he . . . This is very hard for me to understand."

"It's hard for all of us," Suzette said. "I wish we could show him, but . . . I don't want him to be remembered like this."

"I understand. Is there anything I can do for you?"

"No, Darci, thank you. You being here is comfort enough."

Darci brought Suzette into another embrace. She couldn't begin to understand the pain of losing a child, but she wouldn't rest until she knew for sure, in her own heart, how Suzette lost hers.

Thomas draped an arm around each woman. "Let's go take our seats. It's time for the service to start."

Suzette looked around. "Shouldn't we wait for Eva?"

"She's still resting in the choir room, and I think her staying there would be for the best." Thomas turned to Darci. "Eva found Kenny, and it's been especially hard for her."

"I see," Darci murmured. She tolerated Eva, the Warwicks' oldest child and Kenny's only sibling, because of Kenny, but she'd hardly call the woman a friend. Eva was an awkward thirteen-year-old when Kenny and Darci met, and taking her teen angst out on the young friends seemed her favorite summer pastime. Over the years, Eva's taunting had grown into downright hostility. Darci didn't understand it, but with few interactions with Eva, she didn't really care. Darci motioned to the pews. "Let's sit."

Two hours later, Darci and the Warwicks stood alone in the church cemetery staring at Kenny's coffin. Their deafening silence screamed all the unanswered questions.

"This is so unbelievable."

Darci looked up when Thomas's voice broke the quiet. The man clutched his wife's hand as his gaze stayed fixed on his son's bloom-covered casket.

"What caused this to happen?" He sighed. "Not having Kenny around is bad, but living with not knowing why he did this to himself . . . How are we going to do that?"

"I don't think I can," Darci murmured.

Suzette lifted her head from Thomas's chest. "What?" the grieving woman asked.

Darci rubbed the back of her neck as the beating rays of the summer sun and the tension of the situation pounded her body. It wasn't right for her to share her belief that Kenny didn't kill himself with them now. Their pain was too fresh. If she was wrong, a thought she didn't want to entertain, she couldn't allow them to believe otherwise. "It's nothing," she said. "I just—I don't think I'll ever be able to accept this."

Loud, broken claps interrupted the awkward moment. "A public gathering just isn't complete without Darci Clarke making a grand declaration." All eyes turned to Eva's staggering form.

Darci rolled her eyes. Barely two-thirty and the woman was already lit up.

Suzette shook her head in dismay. "Eva, don't do this. This day is to remember your brother. Don't ruin it."

"Ruin it, Mom?" Eva stumbled over to her parents and slung her arm over her mother's shoulder. "This day was ruined right after Kenny did what he did. You saw him!" She whipped her head to look at Darci. Locks of her thick, dark mane stuck to her face. "But there is a good side to this. Your sweet Darci, the one you wish was your daughter, came home. The black sheep of this family has white wool. You get it? White wool. That's me." She laughed at the statement no one else found funny.

"I'm sorry about this, Darci," Thomas apologized. "She's grief-stricken."

"No, she's drunk," Eva countered. "And don't apologize to her for me, Dad." Eva nudged her head toward the coffin. "That thing was closed for a reason. I think I have every right to be drunk. Good and drunk."

Darci read the pained expressions on the Warwicks' faces. Eva was always hostile towards her, but liquored up, she seemed even more cutting. With two divorces and several business ventures gone bad under her belt,

Eva Jasper looked closer to retirement than her thirty-eight years indicated. The constant failures she'd endured had hardened her, and led her down a road that had found her in and out of rehab battling addictions to hydrocodone, cocaine, and alcohol.

Kenny's success had been a sore spot for Eva, but he'd loved his sister in spite of her animosity and envy, and did whatever he could to help her whenever she'd asked. He'd even managed to keep Eva's substance abuse from their parents, calling her stints at rehab much-needed vacations.

As hard as it was, Darci felt Kenny would want her to look out for Eva. *'She's lost, Darci,'* he would always say. Helping Eva as best she could was the least she could do for the people who were like second parents to her. Even if she thought a swift kick and tough love would do a lot more good. "I heard you found Kenny. I'm sorry you had to go through that, Eva," she said. "I'm sorry we all have to go through this."

"What *we*? It's my parents and me who'll have to deal with this mess. You'll be heading back to your cushy job in New York."

"Yes, eventually, but I plan to stay on for a while. There are some things I need to take care of." Dealing with a headstrong police detective the first of many.

Eva raised a curious eyebrow. Even in her sloshed state, she didn't look too happy with that announcement. "Things?"

"Yes, things," Darci said, feeling a more detailed explanation was unnecessary. She gave Thomas and Suzette a big hug. "I'll stop by the house later."

"Thank you for coming, Darci." Thomas kissed her cheek.

"Don't thank me. I had to be here." She stopped in front of the swaying Eva. She wouldn't want to be her in the morning, or any day for that matter. "Take care of yourself, Eva." Darci reached into her purse and pressed a business card into Eva's hand. "My cell phone number is on the back. I'm staying with my cousin Jackie and her husband while I'm here. Please, call me if you need anything."

Eva tore the card into tiny pieces that she showered on the ground. "I won't be needing anything from you."

"Eva!" Suzette admonished.

"It's okay, Suzette," Darci replied. She wondered how Kenny took this grief from his sister, and if she could. Fighting the urge to be snippy, she extended a smile as cordial as she could muster. "If you change your mind, Eva, you know how to find me."

Darci made a final stop at the coffin. The scent from all the floral arrangements hung in the humid air like a suffocating fog. Petals wilted and fell to the thick green grass as they lost the battle against the oppressive heat. This day was hellish in so many ways.

Darci laid her hand atop the coffin. Tears slipped down her cheeks as she softly whispered, "I'm going to do what I think you want of me, Kenny, and get to the bottom of what happened to you. I won't leave Sterling until I do. I promise."

—∾∾—

A bright smile and tall glass of lemonade greeted Darci as she stepped into her cousin's house. She accepted the glass and returned Jackie Pierce's smile. "You always know what I need, huh, Jackie?" she said, kicking off her shoes and plopping onto the couch.

"As your older, more brilliant cousin, I'm supposed to know these things." Jackie joined her on the couch. "You look beat. I could have come with you."

"I appreciated the offer, but I know you're not big on funerals."

"True enough. Still, I know that had to be hard on you."

"Jackie, I have so many questions. I know I won't be able to rest until this makes sense. I just went to the funeral of my best friend, but I can't accept he killed himself. Kenny wouldn't do that."

"You keep saying that, Darci, but Kenny obviously had some demons he didn't tell you about."

"No." Darci shook her head. "Kenny didn't have any demons. An almost unhealthy preoccupation with his looks and the opposite sex, yes, but no demons." She took several swallows of the drink. Jackie made the best lemonade, just the right combination of tangy and sweet. She finished the glass and stood. "I'm going to get to the bottom of this. I won't rest until I do."

"Where are you going?"

"To shower and change before heading back to the police station."

"Back to the police station? Did you really go there before the service?"

"Yes."

"And you filed a report?"

"Yes. Well, at least I tried."

"Darci!" Jackie pulled her back to the couch. "I know Kenny was your best friend and you have lots of unanswered questions, but the police can't help you find them. No one can. He killed himself, sweetie."

"I don't believe that."

Jackie groaned. Her full lips thinned to a line. Darci shuddered. With her dark brown eyes and golden brown skin, Jackie looked more like Darci's mother than Darci did; it was almost frightening.

Twelve years younger, Darci looked up to her older cousin as the sister she'd never had, but when Jackie got like this, Darci knew a lecture was forthcoming. As head of the math department at Sterling University and mother of two, Jackie was great at lecturing, and Darci wasn't in the mood for listening.

Darci glanced at the clock on the wall. Five after three. Jackie's teen sons would soon be home from school. With any luck, they would arrive before their mother got too far into her spiel to turn back. "I know what you're going to say, Jackie. You're going to say what that idiot cop at the station said."

Jackie's perfectly arched brows furrowed. "Idiot cop?"

"The investigator in charge of the case. He's named after a horse." *A six feet-two inch stud.*

"Ah, Steed McGraw." Jackie smiled.

"You know him?"

"I think every woman in Sterling knows of Steed McGraw. He's very attractive."

"I didn't notice."

"Liar." Jackie laughed.

"Okay, he's kinda cute, but he isn't exactly the warm and fuzzy type. He practically called me crazy to my face."

"Can you blame him? You asked him to find the murderer of someone who killed himself. What reaction did you expect?"

"Consideration is what I expected. Before I went by the station, I stopped at the mayor's office." Darci smiled. "Jacob was happy to see me."

"No kidding. He's always asking about you. One would think the man's not married, the way he's so intrigued with what's going on in your life."

"Well, he is married, and even if he wasn't, it wouldn't matter. Things never progressed from the prom for a reason. Still, it's good to have someone to call upon when you need a favor."

"What did you ask of him?"

"To get the investigating officer to keep investigating."

"And?"

"And nothing."

"Darci?" Jackie said incredulously.

"Okay, I told him if I didn't get some satisfaction I would write a report that would not shine a favorable light on the Sterling Police Department."

"You didn't?"

"Yes, I did, and I meant it. Something's not right about this, and I'm determined to find out what it is. My contract with *Heart of the Matter* is up for renewal. I don't think I'm going to re-up. I need to be here. Kenny had been badgering me to move back. He said I was staying in New York, but I wasn't living there, because all I did was work. He said I had no life." A humorless chuckle fell from her lips. "No life. That's ironic, huh?"

Jackie sighed. "Darci, I think you moving back would be great, but this finding what happened to Kenny . . . You say something's wrong and you're determined to find out what it is. I can tell you what it is. It's you being too close to this to let it go. Your dearest friend in the world put a bullet in his head. The cops may not be able to tell you why he did it, but there's no question that's what he did, and for whatever reason, you refuse to accept it."

"I refuse to accept it because it—"

"Doesn't make sense," Jackie finished for her. "I know."

"Kenny wouldn't kill himself." Darci groaned. She was getting really tired of saying that over and over again.

"I have news for you, Darci. That's exactly what he did." Jackie stood from the couch. "The sooner you accept that, the better off everyone will be. I have dinner to cook."

"I'll never accept that, Jackie," Darci said to her cousin's retreating back. "Never!" Somehow she would find out what had happened to Kenny, and that horse-named detective was going to help her do it.

CHAPTER 3

Grumbling, Steed flipped through the pages of the Warwick file. *Investigating a confirmed suicide.* Who did Darci Clarke think she was, anyway? Long legs and full breasts came a dime a dozen. Because she had some nationwide celebrity, he was supposed to bend to her will? *Hell, no!* He slammed down the file.

"Problem, McGraw?"

"Chief Rogers." Steed slid the folder to the far side of the desk. "I didn't hear you come in."

"Clearly." Rogers took the seat in front of Steed's desk. "An attitude like that won't help with your promotion."

The promotion. Now he remembered why he was humoring the beautiful walking headache.

"About that, sir. I think it's asking a bit much for me to placate a grieving woman in order to receive a promotion I've already earned. I'm a great cop. I've closed every case I've worked, including this one, and I'm here. I've been here through all the comings and goings, through all the everything. Working long hours, proving myself, doing the job. But this . . ." Steed tapped the folder on the desk, "this is a waste of my time."

"No, what it is, McGraw, is a test of your people skills."

"What?"

"You said it, you're a great cop, an amazing investigator, but you're not the most approachable guy in the world. In fact, I'd go so far as to call you gruff."

"Gruff?"

"You're monosyllabic, which tells me you know I'm right."

"Actually, I disagree with your assessment, sir."

"You can disagree all you want, but until I see differently, what I think is all that matters." Rogers sat back in the chair, propping his right ankle on his left knee. "Now, how do you plan to deal with Darci?"

"I don't know," he answered truthfully, bringing the file back to the middle of his desk. If she wasn't such a monumental pain in the ass, he would probably ask her out to dinner, maybe find out if those full lips were as soft as they appeared. Unfortunately, the lady's determination to prove her best friend didn't commit a mortal sin made wanting to get close to her as appealing as getting a shot of the Ebola virus.

"You're reviewing the file. That's a start. What else?"

"I called the M.E. over. Since she lives in town, I thought maybe she could drop by and tell me something I can tell Ms. Clarke that will end this ridiculous notion. She's so single-minded in this, I almost feel sorry for her."

"I don't need your pity, Detective."

Steed couldn't say he was surprised to find Darci standing in his doorway, but he was surprised at how happy it made him feel. Dressed in a hot pink and orange floral sundress, with her dark hair pulled back in a ponytail, Darci looked summertime cool and scorching hot at the same time. One woman should not be this gorgeous. "How long have you been standing there?"

"Long enough to hear you say I'm being ridiculous and you feel sorry for me." Darci walked to the desk. "Did I miss anything else I shouldn't have heard?"

Steed clicked his tongue. "No, that's about it."

Rogers stood and extended his hand to her. "It's been a while, Darci," he said, with a warm smile.

"Yes, sir, over three years," she answered. "How have you been, Chief Rogers? How is your wife?"

"Ellen is just fine. She's visiting some family in Charlotte. And what's this Chief Rogers business?" He clasped her small hand between his big ones. "Call me Martin."

Call him Martin? Steed sat up in his chair. He couldn't remember a time he'd seen Rogers so pleasant, and giddy.

"Okay, Martin it is. Daddy asked that I say hello to you."

"How is Chuck?" he asked, releasing Darci's hand. "Enjoying that Florida sunshine?"

"A little too much." She giggled.

Steed sat up more. Darci Clarke laughing? She had a nice laugh, and a smile as gorgeous as the rest of her. She needed to display those traits more often.

"Last week he bruised his ribs playing an intense game of touch football with the neighborhood kids," she went on to explain. "He's trying to be stoic, but he's still in a bit of pain. Mama's keeping a watchful eye on him. Otherwise, they would be here."

"Aw, yes." Rogers' face lost its happy glow. "I'm sorry it took such a tragic event to bring you home."

"Me, too. It is tragic, but I'm sure you're aware of my feelings on this situation." She glowered at Steed.

"Yes, I've heard some rumblings." A loud clap, Rogers's "all righty then," signaled he was ready to leave. "On that note, I'll leave you two to confer. If you need anything, Darci, anything at all, you just ask, okay?"

"Thank you, Martin, I'll do that."

"Think I'll see you in church this Sunday?"

"Absolutely. Bye now," she said with a wave and smile.

Darci's smug grin turned Steed's stomach. He definitely didn't want to deal with her right now.

Darci claimed Rogers's vacated chair. "So, you have any information for me?" she asked.

"Other than the same information you had before you left? No," Steed answered. "Your friend is still dead by his own hand with the aid of a semi-automatic weapon."

Anger flamed in Darci's dark eyes. "You are such a heartless bastard."

"No, ma'am, what I am is a realist." Feeling his own righteous anger, Steed grabbed the folder and shoved it toward her. "Look at this!" He flipped the file open. "Go on, look!"

She leaned forward in the chair and peered at the open folder. Her lower lip quivered. Tears filled her eyes.

A stinging stab of regret jabbed Steed in the gut. Maybe this in-your-face approach wasn't his swiftest move. Face on, Warwick looked asleep, but the left side profile . . . Those pictures would disturb the sensibilities of the most seasoned of crime scene investigators, but to show them to a grieving friend was pretty heartless, and Darci was clearly shaken.

"I'm sorry," he apologized. "I thought you should see that, but—I'm sorry."

"You're not sorry." Darci swiped at the tears sliding down her cheeks. "I suspect you thought I would collapse in a fit of hysterical tears and declare your way of thinking as correct, but that's not what you're going to get. I understand Kenny died from a gunshot wound. My concerns come in how it was delivered. You can't shock me into changing my opinion on this, Detective!" She shoved the folder back at him. "I want to know what you're doing to find out what really went down in Kenny's house that night."

Steed hung his head. Darci read him like his preconceived ideas were displayed across his forehead. He wanted her to see things his way, but he didn't want to hurt her more, and he couldn't stand the tears.

"Again, I'm sorry, Ms. Clarke. I could have handled that better." He closed the folder and set it to the side. "I'm expecting the M.E. to arrive at any minute. I was going to ask her to give me a verbal overview of her findings. If you're interested, maybe you can stick around and ask some questions."

Darci nodded between sniffles. "I think I'll do that."

Steed reached into the pocket of his sports coat. His grandmother had taught him a gentleman always carried a handkerchief. He didn't feel like much of a gentleman right now, but he was glad to have the pressed piece of cloth on hand. "Take this," he said.

"Why?"

"Because you're crying, and it's my fault. I don't like to see ladies cry. Please, take it. I promise, it's clean."

Steed felt the tiniest bit better as Darci accepted his offering and dabbed the corners of her eyes.

"You know, if you stopped being so unfeeling and impersonal, you wouldn't have to worry about making ladies cry."

"In my line of work, you can't afford to get too close. Keeping a conservative distance keeps you alive and helps you get the job done effectively."

"I guess that's true, but you can't convince me a cop has to be an ass to do his job effectively."

A knock at the door prevented Steed from commenting on her dig. "You wanted to see me, Detective?" said Dr. Lorene Kellogg, the medical examiner.

"Yes, come in." Steed made his way around the desk and positioned a chair beside Darci's. "Please, have a seat."

"Thank—" The woman gasped. "Darci Clarke!" Lorene grabbed Darci's hand from the armrest. "I watch you all the time. It's a pleasure to meet you."

Steed looked on in surprise. Lorene had been the M.E. for five years, and in his dealings with her he'd never pegged her as starstruck. She seemed too serious to be caught up in celebrity, but she was falling all over herself with Darci.

"Thank you," Darci said with a wee smile, returning her hand to the armrest.

Steed noted a ruby glow to her flawless brown cheeks, a show of modesty he found endearing and surprising. Darci Clarke humble. He would have never thought it possible.

"Since you know of Ms. Clarke, I guess I should introduce her to you, Lorene," Steed said. "Darci Clarke, this is the medical examiner, Dr. Lorene Kellogg."

"Nice to meet you," said Darci.

"I wish it could have been under better circumstances." Empathy tempered the excitement that moments earlier had brightened Lorene's eyes. "I understand you and Mr. Warwick were very close. My husband and I belonged to the health club where he was a member. He seemed like a nice man."

"Actually, Mr. Warwick is why I called you over," Steed said.

Lorene took a seat. "Mr. Warwick?"

"Yes. Do you think you can explain to Ms. Clarke the findings from the autopsy?"

"I don't have a copy of my report."

"You can use mine," he said, handing her the file.

Lorene turned to Darci. "These details are a bit grisly, Ms. Clarke."

"She knows," Steed said, settling into his chair. He would enjoy being proven right, but in respect to Darci's feelings, vowed not to say "I told you so" when Lorene finished. "Try and give her the condensed, less gruesome version if you can. We wouldn't want to disturb Ms. Clarke's sensibilities more than we have to."

Darci frowned at him. "Thanks, Detective."

Lorene fiddled in her purse and produced a pair of glasses she rested on the bridge of her nose. With flowing blonde hair and sparkling green eyes, she looked more like a model than a doctor who dug into dead bodies for a living. But as with most model types, Steed thought she was a bit too thin.

Lorene opened the file and began her summation. "The victim succumbed to head injuries sustained from a single shot fired from a semi-automatic handgun. Findings show the bullet entered at the right temple, traveled through his right frontal lobe, and exited at the left temple where it lodged into the living room wall. The force of the bullet in conjunction with the firepower of the weapon caused what is tantamount to a mini explosion that . . ."

Darci held up her hand, breaking into the very clinical summary. "Thank you, Dr. Kellogg—"

"Please, call me Lorene."

"Lorene, I appreciate you sharing these details, but as I told Detective McGraw, the nature of Kenny's death is not what I have questions about, it's how the injuries happened."

"The victim shot himself."

"So I've been told," she said, taking a sideways glance at Steed. "Explain to me how you know that. It seems Detective McGraw has a little trouble doing so."

Steed scoffed. Was she calling him dense?

"I don't understand," Lorene said.

"It's simple. How do you know Kenny shot himself in the head? I don't need to see pictures of after the fact or hear chilling details of how the bullet did its damage. I want to know how you know beyond a shadow of a doubt Kenny shot himself?"

"The burn marks on the victim's hand and the point of entry of the gunshot are consistent. From my crime scene and professional experience, and the findings from the autopsy, the only deduction is a self-inflicted gunshot wound."

"Fine," Darci said, annoyance and sadness apparent in her clipped response. "I guess that's that." Tears streamed down her cheeks.

Steed's chest tightened. Why did this woman's tears affect him so? He grabbed her hand as she stood to leave. "Ms. Clarke, please stay a few minutes."

Darci sniffled. She eyed Steed for a long moment before easing back into the chair. "All right." She dabbed her tears with his handkerchief. "Five minutes."

"Thank you for coming by, Lorene," Steed said, making his way to the doctor and escorting her to the door.

"I was glad to be of help." She looked over her shoulder at Darci. "Ms. Clarke, it was a pleasure meeting you. Again, I'm very sorry for the circumstances."

Darci met the woman's gaze, but said nothing.

"I'll get back with you when the rest of the test results come back," Lorene said.

"Thank you." Steed showed Lorene out and returned to his chair. "You want to tell me what's on your mind, Ms. Clarke?"

"Are you going to give me a choice?"

He chuckled. "Lady, in the few hours I've known you, I've learned I can't make you do anything and would be foolish to presume I could."

"Good, that's smart. I need to get out of this cop shop." She walked to the door and turned around. "You coming or what?"

CHAPTER 4

The last of the late lunch crowd streamed out of Sophie's Soul Food Restaurant as Darci and Steed made their way in. The smell of fried chicken, macaroni and cheese, collard greens, and peach cobbler hung in the air. Darci drew a deep breath. How she'd missed Miss Sophie's delicious cooking. Food for the soul. Her soul was in a world of turmoil. Perhaps Miss Sophie's peach cobbler could help calm that raging storm, or at the very least help her put what she felt into perspective.

"Have a seat anywhere," said a young woman behind the counter, not bothering to look away from the tips she counted. "I'll be right with you."

Darci slid into the red vinyl upholstered booth to her immediate right, and Steed got in across from her. Her eyes darted about the room. Not much had changed about the place in the three years since her last visit to town, and for that she was grateful. Sophie's didn't have a lot of fancy decorations: a nineteen-inch color television in one corner, a few family pictures sprinkled about the wall, two ceiling fan lights, and a jukebox she remembered from when she and Kenny were kids. Everything else was strictly for servicing the clients. Five booths, six tables, and a counter with five stools. Sophie's wasn't like the fancy restaurants in New York, but nothing beat the ambiance. Miss Sophie made you feel like family, and the food was out of this world.

The sense of being watched ended Darci's re-acquaintance with the room. When she met Steed's gaze, he didn't even attempt to look away. She frowned. "Your mother didn't tell you it was impolite to stare?"

"Actually, she did," he answered. "Unfortunately, when I have a hard time reading people, the cop in me has to study the subject until I can get some understanding."

"An easier and perhaps more effective way would be to ask the subject what she is thinking. I don't like people staring at me."

"No? Then I think you went into the wrong line of work."

"When I'm on television, I don't know people are staring."

"But when you're not on television and they recognize you, I'm sure they do."

"That's different," she said, perusing the one-page laminated menu.

"How's it different?"

"Because when I feel people staring and it's out of recognition, they have the decency to look away and not continue to stare when I look back. It is very unnerving to be scrutinized like that."

"Are you saying I unnerve you?"

"No, you annoy me." The fact she found him so attractive annoyed her even more.

"Okay. I'll do things your way. What's on your mind?"

"I think you know the answer to that."

"Lorene explained her findings to you. You can't tell me you still haven't accepted the truth behind Warwick's death."

Before she could answer, the young woman from behind the counter approached with two glasses of ice water. She set one before each of them, dropped two straws on the table, and then pulled an order pad from her apron pocket. "May I take your order?" asked the woman whose nametag read "Tina."

"Yes," Darci readily answered, happy for the break in conversation. "I'll have an order of peach cobbler with vanilla ice cream, and a large sweet tea."

Tina scribbled Darci's order onto the pad. "And you?" she asked Steed, never once looking at either of them.

"I'll have the rib plate with string beans, macaroni, sweet potatoes, and tea," Steed answered.

"All right, I'll put this in and it'll be right—" Tina's words ended when she finally made eye contact with Darci. The pencil dropped to the floor. "Oh, my goodness, you're . . . Do you know who you are?"

Darci laughed. She didn't think the waitress was capable of this much excitement. "Yes, I do," she answered. "How are you, Tina?"

Tina's brown eyes widened. "You know who I am?"

"It's on your shirt," she said, motioning to the nametag.

"Oh."

"I guess you all have been busy today," she said, reaching to the floor and handing Tina her pencil.

"Very. I apologize for not noticing you sooner."

"Please, don't apologize for that. I'm just me. I don't need special treatment because I report the news. Is Miss Sophie around?"

"She's in the kitchen. I'll get her for you."

"Thank you, Tina."

"Thank you." Tina's smile grew wider, her face the picture of awe. "I'm a communications major at the university, and my friends won't believe it when I tell them I met you. You're even nicer in real life than you seem on TV."

"That's very nice of you to say." Darci couldn't help smiling back. She worked in the TV news industry, so she wasn't acting, just being herself. For Tina to say she seemed even nicer was a pretty good compliment. Especially when the cop sitting across from her had all but called her a pain in the butt to her face.

"I'll place your orders and tell Miss Sophie you're here."

Darci placed her straw in the water and drew a sip as Tina made tracks to the kitchen. "She seems like a nice girl."

"And you wonder why I stare," Steed remarked.

She took another sip and met Steed's gaze. "What are you talking about?"

"You. Lady, you are a walking contradiction. You've been on my back all day, but in between all that, you have time to be pleasant to the chief and make the day of one of your adoring fans. Why can't you be easygoing like that all the time?"

"I am like that all the time."

"The hell you say! You've barely been civil to me."

"I haven't been unkind to you. If anything, I've just been responding to your lack of warmth. I happen to have a lot on my mind."

"And whose fault is that? You heard what Lorene said. You know how Warwick died. You were just about to explain yourself when Tina came over. I would very much like to hear what's going on in that mind of yours."

"You think you do, but you don't."

"I said so, didn't I?"

"You also said I was crazy—no—ridiculous to think what I'm thinking. So, maybe I should keep my thoughts to myself. I don't need you to humor me."

"Have you taken a moment to think that maybe I need me to humor you?"

Darci frowned. Why was he speaking in riddles? "What?"

"I need to understand why you feel the way you do. All signs say Kenneth Warwick committed suicide, but you want to call it a murder, and you're determined to do so regardless of what the facts show."

"I'm a reporter, Detective, facts are important to me, too. However, unlike you, I have another fact. A fact you are unwilling to take under consideration. That being, Kenny wouldn't kill himself. You know, if I were given a dollar for the number of times I've said those four words today, I would be able to pay for your lunch and mine several times over."

"Perhaps you should use that figurative money for some sessions on a psychiatrist's couch," he mumbled.

Darci's jaw tightened. Her fingernails tapped an anxious beat against the tabletop. "You know, it's those kinds of comments that make telling you what I think impossible."

"I'm sorry."

"Stop saying that!" She sucked in a breath. "What are you apologizing for, huh? Being a smart-ass or just lacking tact?"

"Well I'll be!"

"Miss Sophie!" Darci set aside her hostility toward the irritating detective as the owner/operator of the restaurant approached with two glasses of tea and her megawatt smile. Darci set the drinks on the table and slid from the booth to greet Miss Sophie. "It's so good to see you again," she said, giving the woman a bright smile and big hug.

Darci pulled back to take a good look at the woman. Seventy if she was a day, Miss Sophie looked at least fifteen years younger, and at about five feet-four, carried her twenty extra pounds like a medal of excellence for her culinary expertise. Her milk chocolate complexion glistened from the heat of standing over a stove all afternoon, and per the norm, a hairnet covered her shoulder-length wavy mane.

"You look good, child." Miss Sophie clasped Darci's hands and pulled her downward to kiss her cheek. "Tina told me you were out here." She shook her head. "It's a shame about that poor boy."

Darci nodded. "Yes, ma'am, it is."

"Steed!" Miss Sophie held her hand out to the abrasive detective. "Come give me some sugar, baby."

Darci watched in stunned silence as Steed happily slid off the seat and brought Miss Sophie into his arms. He seemed more like a steak and potatoes kind of guy, with the hint of a Texas accent and cowboy boots, not someone who'd frequent Sophie's.

"It's good to see you, Miss Sophie," Steed said, pressing a kiss to her cheek and then releasing her.

"Where have you been keeping yourself?"

"At my desk." His eyes cut to Darci. "There's been a lot keeping me busy."

Not missing the visual dig, Darci returned his evil eye before taking one of the two glasses of tea. Iced tea you got in the North, sweet tea you got in the South. And nobody's sweet tea could beat Miss Sophie's. Darci savored a long sip. Lemony sweetness blended with perfectly brewed tea. She drank more. It was like rapture in a glass.

"Well, I'm just glad to see you." Miss Sophie patted Steed's muscular upper arm. "It's not good to work too hard. I'm glad to see you out and about, and with such a nice girl, too." She smiled brightly. "You two look real good together."

Darci almost strangled on the tea. "Miss Sophie, you couldn't be more wrong," she said in the midst of her coughing fit. "We are *not* together."

"Of course you are, baby."

Steed shook his head. "No, ma'am, we're not," he said. "I was in charge of Kenneth Warwick's case, and Ms. Clarke is having a little trouble accepting the facts behind his demise."

"You telling me you don't think she's a pretty girl?"

Steed poked around the shell of his ear. Darci couldn't help wondering about his strange reaction as she waited for his reply.

"No, ma'am, I'm not saying that," he said.

"So, you think she's pretty?"

"Yeah, I guess she's pretty, sure," he mumbled.

Darci's eyes widened. Did Steed McGraw admit, half-heartedly, he thought she was pretty? The smile encompassing Miss Sophie's face said he did. Why did that make her feel so good?

"And what about you, Darci?" said Miss Sophie.

Darci blinked. "Me?"

"Uh-huh." Miss Sophie nodded. "Steed is a handsome young man, don't you think?"

Darci took a sideways glance in his direction and noted the wide grin on his face. She didn't like lying, but she definitely didn't want to answer that question right now.

"Well, baby?"

"Miss Sophie, if you think so, is there any way I can disagree with you?"

The smug grin on Steed's face vanished. Darci smirked, pleased with her quick thinking and Steed's unhappy response to it.

"Anyway, I'm not looking for romance," Darci said, "just some insight as to what happened with Kenny."

"When you look for love, you never find it. I'm just telling you young people to keep your eyes open. Sometimes you find things staring you right in the face when you think you're looking for something else. Now,

I'm gonna go on back and get your food. I'm bringing out more than peach cobbler for you, Darci." She gave Darci's hip a pat. "Baby, you're just about skin and bones."

Skin and bones? At five-eleven and a size ten, she was straddling the obese line in terms of female television newswomen, but hearing someone call her skin and bones made her feel good. Miss Sophie and her staff were just full of compliments today.

"You two sit on down." Miss Sophie pushed them back into the booth. "I'll be right back."

Steed gave Darci all his attention when Ms. Sophie disappeared into the kitchen. "You are quite the evasive one, aren't you?" he said, taking a drink from his sweating glass of tea.

"Am I supposed to know what that means?"

"Yes, you are, but I don't expect you to own up to it. It would go against your nature."

"Speaking of going against nature," she said, ignoring his little crack, "I didn't know you knew Miss Sophie."

"You didn't ask."

"You don't seem like the soul food type to me."

"Lady, I think you'll have a better chance at proving Kenneth Warwick didn't kill himself, which is impossible, than you'll ever have at trying to figure out what type I am. I'm an open book to no one. Now, why don't you tell me about your reaction to Lorene's report."

Darci shook her head. After roughly ten minutes with Steed McGraw, she'd had enough. Looking at a handsome face and buff body could keep one entertained for only so long, and fun time was long over for her.

"Fine, you want to know, I'll tell you. I can't refute what Dr. Kellogg's report shows, but I still don't buy it. You can call me crazy, in fact, you can call me whatever the hell you want, but I cannot accept this." She grabbed her purse and eased out of the booth. "Thank you for your *invaluable* help, Detective, but I'll no longer be needing your services. I'm the only one in this town who doesn't believe Kenny killed himself, and I'll be the only one who proves it."

CHAPTER 5

Steed considered letting her leave, with a suggestion she not let the doorknob hit her on the way out. But he couldn't do it for two reasons. One, he didn't want to lose his promotion, and two, he truly felt bad for her and didn't get any pleasure in seeing her in so much pain.

"Ms. Clarke, wait." Steed slid from the booth and took her hand. Electricity crackled in the air from the sizzle of the simple touch. He met her gaze. "Don't leave in haste."

Darci looked at their joined hands, and after a fleeting moment pulled hers away. Her dark eyes shone with equal parts fascination and frustration. Steed laughed to himself. He could definitely relate to her feelings. No woman had ever stirred up such conflicting emotions in him all at the same time. Half the time he wanted to take her in his arms and kiss her senseless, and the rest of the time he wanted to take her over his knee and spank her until she started thinking like the rational woman he knew she was.

"Haste?" she repeated. "This is not hasty. I'm just really tired of explaining myself."

"I understand that." Steed sighed. "I've not been very understanding of your pain and I want to try to rectify that." He slid back into the booth and gestured to the other side of the table. "Let's start over. Tell me every-thing you think I should know, and I promise not to judge or make snide comments."

She folded her arms over her full breasts. Her mouth twisted into a dubious smirk. Steed bit back a grunt. Darci was just too sexy, even more in this case, when she wasn't trying to be.

"I think a snowball has a better chance in hell than you do of keeping that promise."

"I'll be on my best behavior, and if I don't keep my word, I'll pay for your lunch." He smiled. "Deal?"

After what seemed like forever, she returned to the booth. "What do you want to know?"

Why I can't stop thinking about you. "I think I mostly want to know why you won't believe Warwick didn't kill himself," he said. "You've heard and seen the evidence and you've seen pictures of after the fact. Why do you still question it?"

"Because I know Kenny."

Steed fought hard not to roll his eyes and practically bit his tongue to keep from being curt with a response. How well could she have known Warwick if she didn't know he was capable of killing himself? "Go on," he said.

"Kenny and I met when we were seven. Thomas, Kenny's father, got hired as plant manager at Sterling Steel, and they moved to town during the middle of the school year. Kenny was the new kid, braces and over-weight, and I was the smart girl, the nerd of the class."

"I'd heard about Warwick overcoming his chubby years, but you a nerd?"

"It's true. My parents instilled the importance of education and hard work, and it became important to me." She smiled. "My folks. A stay-at-home mom who baked cookies for school functions and helped me with homework, and a dad who worked hard to give Mama and me everything we needed and most of the things we wanted. I was an only child, and they gave their all to me, so I figured I could do the same for them."

"Your parents sound like good people. Chief Rogers seems to think a lot of your father."

"They've been buddies since high school, and Daddy is a wonderful man. He just needs to remember he's not twenty-five when he gets the hankering to play football." She chuckled and took a sip of tea. "Anyway, I think being isolated drew Kenny and me together, because we became fast and very close friends and stayed that way for twenty-five years." Her expression became more serious. "Twenty-five years of laughter and tears, triumphs and tragedies, successes and failures. There was nothing we couldn't and didn't tell each other. Nothing. I talked to him almost every day, and saw him more than my folks. We were like this," Darci crossed her fingers, "until three days ago. I think that gives me a pretty good idea of the person Kenny was," she said. "He wouldn't take his own life."

Steed almost wished he hadn't asked the question. The passion in Darci's voice and the determination in her eyes made it clear anything he said contrary to what she believed would go in one ear and out the other. But facts didn't lie, and the facts showed Kenneth Warwick had killed himself. Somehow, someway, he had to get her to see reason.

"I hope you two are ready to eat," chimed Miss Sophie, exiting the kitchen carrying two full, steaming plates of food.

Steed waved her over, welcoming the interruption. "I am," he said, filling his lungs with the mouth-watering aromas Miss Sophie set before them. Maybe a little food and a break from talking about Warwick and his death would do them both some good. At the very least, it would give him time to figure out how he could get Darci off this path that would otherwise lead to more pain.

"You don't mind if we stop talking about death, murder, and suicide for a little while, do you?" Steed slipped on his puppy dog look. He'd been told by his grandmother and a couple of ex-girlfriends that casting down his eyes and pouting the slightest bit made telling him no impossible to do. He sure hoped that worked now. "I'm starving," he said.

Darci looked at him for a moment before gazing at the chopped barbecue plate—Miss Sophie's signature dish. Steed watched her closely. It would be just his luck she'd be immune to his charms.

After what seemed like forever, Darci shrugged. "I guess I could eat a bite or two," she said, unwrapping the paper napkin holding the silverware.

Steed smiled. She wasn't immune. "Good," he said.

"I'm goin' on back to the kitchen now. It's usually real quiet here until dinnertime, so y'all will have the place to yourselves." Miss Sophie flashed a grin that said as much as the gleam in her eyes. The woman was about as subtle as a boulder. "If ya need anything, just holler."

"We will, Miss Sophie, thank you."

"All right. Don't y'all worry about paying for this. Your money ain't no good today. Just enjoy yourselves." She gave each a pat on the shoulder and returned to the kitchen.

Darci stuck her fork into the chopped barbecue meat and mixed it with the small mountain of hash and rice on her plate. "Miss Sophie has got the wrong idea about us," she said.

"Ya think?" Steed laughed, biting into a rib.

"How is it she knows you so well, Detective?"

He chewed and swallowed. "Since we're not talking about the case right now, you think we can drop the formalities? You can call me Steed."

Her face scrunched. "About that," she said. "Is Steed your real name? I've never met a man named after a horse."

He laughed. "Yes, Steed is my real name."

"There's got to be a story behind that. I'm named after my parents Darlene and Charles, at least the 'C' in Charles, but I don't understand how you could get a name like Steed."

"Allow me to explain. When my mother was pregnant, she and Dad made a friendly wager on a horse race. If he won, he got to name me on his own, and if she won, she would get to name me Francis—as in Old Blue Eyes." He chuckled. "Dad did not want me to be named Francis."

"I take it your father won the bet."

"Yeah. But he was a sport about it. He let Mom use the letter "F" as my middle name. It's an initial, but it worked to keep things harmonious."

Darci laughed. Steed wondered where she kept this fun side hidden when she wasn't making his life miserable. If the nerve-wracking Darci hadn't been in his presence minutes before, he would swear she was a twin or had a clone running around town.

"So, your father a tough as nails cop, too?" she asked.

Steed's happy feeling slipped away. Even after all these years, nothing brought on his melancholia faster than somebody asking about his dad being a cop. Silence hung over them.

"Did I say something wrong?" Darci asked.

"No." Steed cleaned the sticky barbecue sauce from his fingers with the provided warm towelette. "My dad was a cop. He got killed in the line of duty when I was twelve."

"Steed."

Darci dropped her fork and covered his hand. Her touch, like fire shooting through his veins, with the effect of a heavy blanket on a cold winter day, was as much a contradiction as the woman herself. It excited him, calmed and soothed him, and it made him feel safe. What was it about this lady?

"I'm sorry," she said.

Darci's beauty captivated him, but the caring in her dark eyes overwhelmed him. Steed found himself fighting an irresistible urge to lean over the table and kiss her until she begged for more. His fingers squeezed around hers. She returned the action. He was going to lose this battle, and he got the distinct impression Darci wouldn't mind. He leaned forward as she did the same.

"Ahem!"

They both flopped backward. Darci took back her hand, confirming the break in the magical moment.

"I'm sorry," Tina said, extending a bowl of peach cobbler a la mode and wearing a goofy grin. "Miss Sophie forgot this."

Darci set the bowl on the table. "Thank you," she said.

With a quick nod, Tina dashed back into the kitchen. Muffled tones reached the table as the door swung back and forth. Boisterous laughter erupted.

"Uh-huh, I told you, didn't I?" Miss Sophie boasted. "They weren't foolin' me none."

Steed met Darci's gaze. So much for playing it cool. "About what just happened," he said.

Darci picked at her food. "Nothing happened."

"Not from—"

"How is it again you know Miss Sophie?" she asked.

Not needing a block to fall on his head, Steed left his path and walked on hers. "Rogers brought me here soon after I came on board at the station," he answered. "Miss Sophie learned I was single and without family in town, so she took me under her wing. She's a good woman and a great cook. No one can do to a sweet potato what Miss Sophie can."

"On that we can agree." Conversation continued while they ate. "How long have you been in Sterling?"

Steed devoured another rib and licked his fingers. "You are a reporter, aren't you?" he said, before shoving his fork in the macaroni.

"My parents always told me if you want to find things out, you gotta be willing to ask questions."

"Considering your career, you took those words to heart."

"I did. So, how long have you been in Sterling?"

"About three years."

"And law enforcement?" she asked between bites of coleslaw.

"Almost fourteen. I joined the NYPD soon after college. And before you ask, it was NYU."

She pushed aside the remnants of her meal and brought over the bowl of cobbler. "You were in New York the whole time?"

Steed shook his head.

"Texas?" she asked between spoons of dessert.

"What gave me away?" he asked.

"The boots and blue jeans were a hint, but the slightest detection of an accent sealed it. How did a Texas boy get to New York and end up in South Carolina?"

Steed grinned. Darci definitely didn't believe in not asking questions. He finished the last of his lunch and drained half of his tea. "Your order isn't quite right." He wiped his mouth and pushed away the plate of dry bones. "I started in New York, moved to Texas, back to New York, Texas, and, well, you know the rest." He held up his hand, feeling another question coming. "My mother remarried when I was fourteen, and that's when we left

Brooklyn to live in Fort Worth. I have an older sister, Lori, and a half-brother named Brett. Now, what about you, the toast of Sterling?"

"I'm hardly the toast of Sterling."

"C'mon, you're the town's little sweetheart. I mean, you've got the mayor doing your bidding. That's something."

Darci held the spoon in her mouth long after she emptied it. A flash of irritation sparked in her eyes, and the easy atmosphere took a sudden chilly turn.

She dropped the spoon to the bowl. "I have the *mayor* doing my *bidding*? Is that what you said?"

"Look, don't flip out. I happen to know you went to him earlier and made a not-so-veiled threat."

"What I made to the mayor, Jacob, an old friend, wasn't a threat."

"No?" He picked up his spoon and motioned to her bowl. "You gonna eat the rest of that?"

She sprinkled salt on the dessert and shoved it toward him. "As a matter of fact, I'm not."

Steed frowned. He'd really wanted some of that cobbler. "Real mature, Darci. Is that what you do when things don't go your way? Act out?"

"Act out?"

"Lady, I didn't stutter. You went to the mayor and told him if you didn't get the answers you thought you should have in regard to this case, you would do a scathing exposé on the Sterling Police Department. Is that a lie?"

"Mostly!" she fired back. "I went to a friend to get help with details surrounding the death of another friend."

"My, you have a lot of *friends*."

Her eyes narrowed. "What are you insinuating?"

"I'm not insinuating anything, I'm asking right out! How close were you and Kenneth Warwick? Were you two lovers?"

"What does that have to do with anything?"

What did it have to do with anything? Besides just wanting to know the answer, not a lot. But Darci's evil clone was back and she made him so crazy, he said things without giving it a lot of thought. *Damn!* Was Rogers right? Was he gruff? *No!* If Darci shared an intimate relationship with Warwick, it might explain her inability to accept his suicide. "You gonna answer the question?"

"No, but I have one for you. If Kenny were a woman, would you have asked me that question?"

"In this day and age? Probably. But since Warwick wasn't a woman, what's the point in being hypothetical? I need to understand why it is you can't accept what is a clear case of suicide. And I'll ask whatever questions necessary to find that answer. I get you don't believe a word I say, but why not Lorene? Do you have a problem listening to the opinion of a woman who's almost as beautiful and intelligent as yourself?"

"Almost as beautiful?"

"Get off it, Darci, you know you're a very beautiful woman. As beautiful as you are a pain in my butt. But you have got to get over this obsession with proving

Warwick's death is anything other than what it is. The man killed himself."

Darci squared her jaw and slid out of the booth. "You know what, Steed, I'm not going to argue with you anymore."

"No, you're just gonna leave."

"I think that's best. But before I go, I want you to think about someone you know inside and out. Someone you know as well as yourself. And then ask yourself what you would think if someone told you that loved one had done the impossible. Would you just accept it if you knew without a doubt in your heart that person wouldn't do such a thing? That something wasn't right?"

Thoughts of his father and his tragic death filled Steed's head. He still had questions, and felt like he always would, but the truth was the truth. "If I had evidence like I'm showing you, I would have to accept it, yes."

"Well, that's your answer. Mine is no way in hell!"

"Darci, stop making Warwick's suicide about you. He's gone because he chose to be, and you don't want to accept that, so you've dreamed up a scenario that can make his death palatable. Murder trumps suicide, right?"

"It's more than that. Kenny loved his face too much to blow it off, and he loved his life too much to end it. I don't care what the M.E.'s report or your, I suspect lax, initial investigation shows. Call me ridiculous, call me crazy, but I'm not dropping this until I get answers that make sense, because Kenny killing himself does not." She opened her purse and placed a $20 bill on the table.

Steed pushed the money back. "Miss Sophie said it was on the house."

"Tell her it's a tip, or the charge for her services."

"Services?"

"Yes." Darci's derisive laughter echoed in his ears. "Miss Sophie is fantastic woman, salt of the earth, but she sucks as a matchmaker." Angry dark eyes fixed on him. "What I said the first time I tried to leave still stands. I don't want your help. I'll get justice for Kenny by myself."

Steed's gaze stayed on the door long after Darci walked out of the restaurant and even after he heard the swoosh of the kitchen door and the soft shuffle of footsteps on the shiny linoleum floor. "You took your time coming back out, didn't you?" he said, meeting the disappointed gaze of the shameless matchmaker.

Miss Sophie frowned. "Why'd you let her leave?"

"I couldn't make her stay."

She fanned her hand at him. "You could have." She plopped down on the edge of the vinyl seat. "You almost kissed her."

"Yes, and then I came to my senses. That woman is . . ."

"All in your head, and she's grieving. I watched her and Kenny Warwick grow up. I saw how close they were. Maybe her grief's got too strong a hold on her, but what if she's right?"

"Right? About Warwick's death?" Steed shook his head. "Miss Sophie, there's no way. The man buried today killed himself. For Darci's sake, I wish the facts were wrong, but they're not. She's going to spend what's going to be a lot of wasted time like a hamster on a wheel—spinning around and around and getting nowhere." He took the old woman's hands and kissed her cheek. "Thank you for trying earlier, and thank you for lunch." He matched Darci's $20 and walked out the door, silently wondering why fate was so cruel as to have his promotion tied to this crazy case and a maddening woman he couldn't stop thinking about.

CHAPTER 6

Darci took the scenic route back to Jackie's, trying to forget the fact she'd almost kissed a man she found totally insufferable and who thought she was a loon. Humph. How could she think a decent guy lived inside Steed McGraw? Was it his bewitching blue eyes, coal black hair, and intensely masculine form that did it? Probably. But it didn't matter how her body responded to Steed. She was human, and he was an attractive man, but she wouldn't allow her swimming head and tingling body to override what she knew was right in her heart.

She missed Kenny so much. She missed talking to him. Several times over the last couple of days she'd find herself with phone in hand calling him, and then she'd remember. Days after his death, she could still feel his presence as sure as if he were sitting beside her. A presence that didn't feel troubled, something it would have to be if Kenny had killed himself.

Darci grunted. If Steed McGraw could read her mind, he'd think her crazier than he already believed. If these weren't her thoughts, she'd think she was crazy, too. How could she prove Kenny didn't commit suicide? Would she really find the peace she sought if she did?

The chime of her cell phone interrupted the mounting number of questions Darci had no answers for.

Pulling her rental car to the grassy edge of the road, she answered the call. "Hello."

"Hello, Darci. It's Randall Clayton."

"Mr. Clayton." One of the blue bloods of Sterling, Randall Clayton was the most successful lawyer in town. A staunch defender of the downtrodden, he'd marched with Dr. King, and had given of his considerable wealth and time to many charities on the local, state, and national levels. If anyone was the pride of Sterling, it was Mr. Clayton. "What can I do . . ." Darci's cheery greeting drifted as she remembered Mr. Clayton was Kenny's attorney. "What can I do for you?"

"I'm calling about Kenneth Warwick's estate. Jackie gave me your number."

Darci lowered the radio volume. "I see."

"Kenny named you executor. Were you aware of that?"

She paused for a long moment before answering. "Yes, sir, I was." She just never imagined she'd be filling the post so soon.

"I detect hesitation. Would it be a problem for you to act in that capacity?"

"Mr. Clayton, I'm still grappling with the idea of Kenny being dead. To be talking about his will . . ." Darci groaned. Could she really say no?

"Darci?"

"I'm still here," she answered. "I'll do it, Mr. Clayton."

"Very good. The reading is scheduled for tomorrow morning at ten o'clock at his parents' home. I'll look forward to seeing you, Darci, but I'm sorry it's under these conditions."

"Me, too, Mr. Clayton. I'll see you tomorrow."

———————

Steed arrived at the station at seven-thirty the next morning. He'd barely gotten a wink of sleep and felt like crap. Thoughts of Darci Clarke, her beautiful face, gorgeous body, peach perfume, and unwavering belief Kenneth Warwick hadn't kill himself had haunted him all night long. How would he convince her to let him help? He couldn't lose that promotion.

The scent of fresh-brewed coffee enlivened his wired brain cells, giving him an immediate jolt. *Caffeine!* Making his way to the coffeepot, he poured himself a cup and inhaled the robust aroma before taking a big gulp.

The scalding liquid felt like a surge of electricity on his tongue. Steed spit it back into the cup. "Damn! Why is this coffee so hot?" he screamed at the handful of officers in the area. Rushing to the watercooler, Steed filled a cup and stuck his aching tongue into the cold liquid.

Chief Rogers approached, hands in his pockets and his eyebrows stitched in a curious line. "Bad night, McGraw?"

"No, sir," he lied, "just a run-in with an extremely hot cup of joe."

"Coffee is supposed to be hot, McGraw." Rogers loosened the buttons on his blue suit and leaned against the wall next to the coffee setup. "What happened with you and Darci?"

"Nothing."

"Doesn't look like nothing to me when you're taking your frustrations out on the poor officer who had the nerve to make coffee hot. What's going on?"

Steed swished the water around in his mouth and swallowed. "Sir, things aren't going well with convincing Darci that Warwick killed himself." Steed left the break room with a fresh cup of water and sat behind his desk. "She stormed off yesterday and explained she didn't want or need my help with this case because she didn't want to be humored."

Rogers stood before him, his arms folded and expression subdued. "In other words, you're not doing your job."

Steed groaned. His mouth felt like a grenade had exploded in it, and now Rogers was riding his back because he wasn't good at pacifying people. "Chief, I can't make Darci listen to reason."

"Don't try to."

"Huh?"

"You're going about this the wrong way." Rogers eased into the empty chair. "Stop telling her she's crazy, and start acting like you believe what she's saying. Darci's not going to be here very long, but she's got a lot of influence with a lot of important people."

"The mayor?" Steed grumbled.

"Yes, as a matter of fact. Why do you say it like that?"

"She mentioned he was a *friend*."

"He is that, and more importantly, he's our boss, so keep that in mind."

"What's the point, sir? She doesn't want my help. I can't make her let me help."

"You'll have to find a way. McGraw, your problem is your inability to bend. You are a wonderful investigator, but you're not very people friendly." Rogers stood and buttoned his coat. "If you want this promotion, you know what you have to do to get it." He rapped three times on the desk. "Keep me informed," he said, walking out the door.

Steed stared at the closed file. It seemed to mock him. Tease him. *Poor people skills.* He shoved the folder to the floor. "Damn!"

———∞∞∞———

Darci checked her reflection in the mirror, wondering if she looked the part of an executor. The navy blue pantsuit looked professional but not too official, and her shoulder-length dark hair, worn loose with full heat-generated curls, might hold out when the outside humidity did its worst. An extra shot or two of her super holding spray wouldn't hurt.

When the mist from the spray evaporated, she drew a breath to steel her nerves. She'd never gone to a will reading before and had never been an executor. Leave it to Kenny to give her both these experiences at once. He definitely had some big plans for her. The gnawing in the pit of her stomach said as much. She grabbed her purse and headed out.

The fifteen-minute drive to the Warwick house passed with concerns of what Kenny might have in store for her and memories of yesterday's run-ins with Steed. She'd taken more crap from that guy in one day than she'd ever taken from any other man. Plus, she'd almost kissed him. Not good. She needed to find answers regarding Kenny's death, but it would be a lot easier without a doubting detective and his hypnotic blue eyes making things more difficult.

She pulled into the driveway as Mr. Clayton got out of his car. His blonde hair was a lot whiter than she remembered and his beach ball belly had significantly deflated.

Mr. Clayton opened her door and greeted her with a big smile and warm embrace. "Darci, you look wonderful," he said, bussing her cheek.

She returned his smile. "So do you, Mr. Clayton."

"You ready to go inside?"

Darci shrugged. "I guess."

"You having second thoughts?"

"Second, third, and fourth thoughts," she confessed. "But Kenny is—" She closed her eyes for a moment and then continued. "Kenny was my best friend, and if this is one of his final wishes, I can't possibly say no."

Mr. Clayton rubbed her arm. "He had tremendous faith in you, and he was so very proud of your accomplishments. He always said if you weren't his best friend, you would be—"

"The perfect wife," she finished for him. "Yeah, I had the honor of being the lone woman in the world he thought matched his greatness. Kenny thought that was the highest compliment. He really loved himself."

"He did indeed. It's hard to believe he . . ."

"It's impossible, Mr. Clayton."

Three deep lines formed in the space between his eyebrows, marking his confusion. "What do you mean?"

"I don't—I'm having trouble believing Kenny could kill himself. He loved himself and life too much to do something like that."

"Darci, sweetie, I know how close you were to him and . . ."

"Yes, I was very close to him, but it's not just about that. It's knowing Kenny. He wouldn't kill himself."

"From what I heard, all the evidence says otherwise."

"That evidence is wrong, Mr. Clayton." She reached into her purse and handed him a dollar. "It's only a buck, but consider it a retainer for now. Just so what I tell you will stay between you and me."

He pocketed the dollar. "You have my full confidence. What's on your mind?"

"I'm going to work my own investigation. I need to find out what happened to Kenny."

"Darci, you know what happened to him. We all know."

"That's just it, Mr. Clayton, I don't know. What I know is Kenny wouldn't kill himself. All my questions about his death, this unlikely death, keep coming back to that."

"Do you know what you're saying?"

"Yes, somebody killed him, and his murderer is out free."

Mr. Clayton dragged his hand over his sun-kissed face. Normally, Darci would think he did it to wipe away perspiration from the morning heat, but that move appeared done out of sheer frustration. She'd seen a lot of that lately, especially after sharing her opinion on this matter.

"Darci," he began.

She shook her head. He had that "poor girl" look in his eyes. "Mr. Clayton, please. I don't need your pity or for you to tell me I'm nuts. I've gotten enough of that from Detective McGraw."

"Steed McGraw is a really good detective. I think what he says holds some merit."

"You think I'm crazy, too?"

"Not crazy, just emotionally invested. You don't want to believe your best friend killed himself, but that's what he did, Darci. Facts don't lie."

"What about my facts? Don't they count for something?"

"In this case, no, they don't."

She hung her head. Why couldn't somebody be on her side for a change?

Mr. Clayton raised her lowered chin. "I hope I didn't hurt your feelings, Darci. That's the last thing I want to do. However, I do want to spare you a painful, and what could prove humiliating, experience if you persist in finding some phantom killer. You need to accept what's true. Kenny is dead by his own hand."

"Fine," she said, now wishing she hadn't said anything at all. Mr. Clayton was the newest citizen of

Sterling to join her cousin and Steed McGraw as people who thought she was off her spool. She had a great deal of respect for the barrister, but like all the others, he was wrong, too.

"You sure you're up to this?" he asked.

Darci nodded. "Yes, sir, I am."

"All right." He placed his hand at the small of her back and directed her to the house. "Let's go inside."

Steed reviewed the contents of the Warwick file over and over. Everything was cut and dried. Why couldn't Darci accept that? Why did she insist on finding a conspiracy where none existed? He rubbed his forehead, hoping to ward off the blinding headache threatening to roadblock his thinking process. He needed to get his mind off this case, to have a moment of solace. To talk to someone who wouldn't give him grief. He pulled out his cell phone and placed a call to Fort Worth.

"Hello."

Tension fell from Steed's body like leaves from trees in autumn. Just the sound of that wonderful voice made everything okay. "Hello, Nana."

"Steed, sweetie, how are you?"

"Better now."

Seventy-three-year-old Jean Reynolds epitomized the term Southern belle. With strawberry blonde hair, freckled skin, and an accent so thick it made Scarlett O'Hara's sound like a Yankee, Nana was the balm that soothed his every emotional scrape. Steed had never known his mother's parents, and his father's folks had died when Steed was a young boy, so finding a grandparent in Jean was an unexpected and pleasant surprise.

"How are you, Mom, and everyone?" Steed asked.

"Everyone?"

He knew she meant Josh, her son and his stepfather. Steed didn't think much of Josh, but he loved the man's mother with all his heart. He'd felt an amazing kinship with Jean from the moment his mom, Beth, introduced them, but fought those feelings for a long time. It had been more than a year since his father's death, but the idea of his mother being interested in another man devastated Steed. It took nearly a year after their meeting for Nana to break down his defenses, but she'd succeeded, making the sting of his mother's marriage to Josh, when Steed was fourteen, a little easier to take. But just a little.

"Yeah, everyone," Steed said.

"Everybody's fine. Josh and Beth drove to Austin to look at a few horses. They should be back in a couple of days. Brett started at the newspaper last week, and Lori's little ones are keeping her busy. You should come down for a visit. You work too hard, and we haven't seen you since Christmas."

"I have to work hard, Nana. Right now I'm the only detective, so if I wanted to leave I couldn't. Plus, I'm up for a promotion and there's this case I'm working."

"That's good about the promotion, but this case must be a tough one. You sound tired, weighed down."

He couldn't keep much from his nana. "It's complicated."

"Does it involve a woman?"

"Nana," he dragged out like a whining four-year-old.

"Case or not, a man doesn't sound like you sound right now if there's not a woman involved."

"There's a woman involved, but not like you're thinking."

"What am I thinking, Steed?"

"You know what you're thinking, Nana."

"Is she nice?"

She was when she wasn't driving him crazy. "She's different," Steed said.

"I bet she's real pretty."

"She's gorgeous." *Too gorgeous.*

"What's the problem?"

Steed combed his fingers through his hair and groaned. He still needed a haircut. "Like I said, it's complicated."

"This girl doesn't like you?"

"No, I don't think she does, but I haven't given her much reason to. I've been a bit short with her."

"She's not a criminal, is she?"

He chuckled. "No, ma'am, she's not a criminal. She's a reporter."

"Is she on TV?"

"Yep, she's on TV."

"Why are you being rude to her?"

"I don't know. Well, I do know. She's making this case impossible. And if I don't satisfy her concerns, I probably won't get my promotion. She said I'm stubborn, Nana, and Chief Rogers thinks I'm not a people person. Can you believe that?"

Jean said nothing for several moments. "Are you still there?" Steed asked.

"Yes."

"Did you hear me?"

"I might be old, but I'm not dead or deaf. I was just considering what you said."

"Considering it?"

"Steed, do you want the truth?"

"Always," he answered.

"Your lady friend and Chief Rogers are both right."

Steed's jaw dropped. Had his nana implied he was a jerk?

"You're not a bad person, Steed . . ."

"Just a stubborn one who can't be nice to people."

"You can work on the stubbornness, but it'll take time."

"And my people skills?"

"How do you think they are?"

"I think I relate fine with people. I just don't coddle."

"Being pleasant isn't coddling. Can I say what I think?"

"Absolutely," he said, as if she wouldn't anyway.

"I think you keep people at a distance so as not to be hurt. When we met, you were a sad, lonely, and angry thirteen-year-old who was missing his father terribly. You wouldn't give poor Josh an inch."

"I know he loves my mother, Nana, but he's not my father. He'll never be my father."

"And that's the problem. Steed, you never got over your father's death, and because of that, you keep yourself closed off from people."

"I didn't do that with you."

"You tried, but I wouldn't let you succeed. You're good at shutting people out, but when somebody really cares, and you feel in spite of yourself, something wonderful can happen. Look at the two of us. I couldn't love you more if my blood was running through your veins," Jean said. "You're my grandson, and as your nana, I'm telling you this so you don't ruin what could be something good for you. I've waited a long time for you to call me about a girl."

"Nana, I didn't say I was calling about a girl."

"Sure you did." She laughed. "What's her name?"

"Darci." Steed flipped through the folder yet again.

"That's a nice name, for a nice girl."

A reluctant smile turned his lips. Darci was nice. Infuriating, but nice. And she was beautiful, and intelligent, and nerve-wracking. She drove him nuts.

"You be nice to her, Steed, and try to be nicer to people. I want you to get your promotion."

"I want me to get my promotion, too."

"Do what I say, and you'll get it. And if you mind yourself, you'll get the girl, too. You call me, Steed. I want to know what's going on."

"Yes, ma'am. Bye, Nana."

"Good-bye, Steed."

He hung up the phone, feeling better than he had this morning, but still at a loss as to how to deal with Darci.

If you mind yourself you'll get the girl, too. He couldn't allow himself to think that far ahead. First, he had to find a way to get Darci to give him a minute of her time, when it was clear she had no use for anything he had to say. What he couldn't do was give her false hope. Warwick's death was a suicide, and promotion or not, he couldn't pretend otherwise. Somehow or another, Darci would have to get that.

CHAPTER 7

Darci tried ignoring the hostile glare being shot her way from the glassy-eyed Eva, but after ten minutes of trying, she broke her idle conversation with the Warwicks and met the woman's glare with a harsh stare-down of her own. "Is there a problem, Eva?" she asked.

Eva shrugged. "I'm just wondering why you're here." She crossed her legs and tossed her dark hair over her shoulder. "Is that all right?"

"Darci's here because it's what Kenny wanted," Mr. Clayton explained. "I have the papers in order, so we can begin."

"Finally," Eva grumbled.

After reading the document naming Darci executor, Mr. Clayton divulged Kenny's bequest of his house to Darci, and his car, personal effects, plus $2.5 million dollars to his stunned parents.

"I know Kenny worked hard and invested, but where—where did he get so much money?" Suzette asked.

"The lotto," Darci explained. "He won it five years ago, but thought it best to keep it hush-hush."

"But he told you."

"Yeah. He said he had to tell somebody." Darci closed her hand over Suzette's. "I hope you're not upset."

"I'm not upset about not knowing about the money. I'm upset because he's not here. There're things about my son I never knew about. Things I'll never know." Suzette's voice wavered and tears streamed down her cheeks. "Never know," she repeated as she raced out of the room.

"Go on without us," Charles said as he went after his wife.

"There are a few more bequests to Sterling University, and some charities that . . ."

"Am I mentioned in the will?" Eva asked, cutting Mr. Clayton off and fidgeting nervously in the corner wing chair.

"Yes, you are, Eva," he answered.

"Then get to it."

"Very well. This section is a bit detailed and very involved. Kenny had very specific plans for you, Eva."

A big smile brightened Eva's face. Dollar signs danced in her glazed-over eyes. Darci felt sick to her stomach. Kenny was just buried yesterday and his sister, his only sibling, was practically chomping at the bit to get her hands on his money.

"What did he leave me?"

"Everything is detailed in this letter he left for Darci that he asked me to read aloud to you both," Mr. Clayton explained, pulling a business envelope from the folder he held. "Your parents have already left the room, which is good, because Kenny didn't want them here for this."

Darci groaned softly. Why wouldn't Kenny want his parents to hear the details of this letter? The more she wondered, the more uncomfortable she became. Whatever this was, she wasn't going to like it.

"Well, it's just us. Read the letter," Eva urged, her smile widening and her foot tapping anxiously on the floor.

Mr. Clayton opened the letter and began. *"If Mr. Clayton is reading this letter it means I'm dead, and that sucks. Nonetheless, with me gone, I still want to look out for my family . . . my sister. Darci, you are my dearest friend in the world, and besides myself, you are the most beautiful and together person I know. So, I want you—I need you to help my sister become the same way."*

"What does he mean 'become the same way'?" Eva sniped. "What is this about? How much money did Kenny leave me, and what the hell does Darci Clarke have to do with it?"

"I'm getting to all of that right now," Mr. Clayton answered. He continued reading. *"Eva, you're my big sister, and I love you, but I can't let you destroy yourself. I'm gone now, but Darci is the one person I trust to see this through. I left Mom and Dad most of my estate, but what remains of my finances is yours. Seven hundred and fifty thousand dollars."*

Eva's eyes bugged out. "Three quarters of a million dollars? When do I get it, huh? When do I get it?"

"There's a condition."

"A condition?" Eva's fixed her gaze on Darci. "This is about her, isn't it?"

Darci rolled her eyes. She definitely wouldn't like this.

"Yes," Mr. Clayton confirmed, "it is about Darci. Allow me to continue."

"Then continue!" Eva snapped.

Mr. Clayton read on. *"Eva, this money will be yours to do with as you please, after you fulfill one request. You are to check into Valley Creek Rehab and stay there until the staff deems you prepared to leave—for a time of up to six months. If you are released before the six months, you are to move into my house with Darci, where you will stay and be tested randomly for drugs for whatever time completes a year. One screw-up and you're done. If you complete this year without drugs or drinking, you will receive the bequest. Otherwise, you get nothing. And if you think you can get the money from Mom and Dad, think again. The money I left for them is in a special account that Darci will have to approve before any withdrawals may be made. If they need to pay a bill, she will see that it gets paid. If they want it for a trip, she will arrange the travel and lodging. In other words, she will know how every dime of my money is being spent. If you get even one red cent before this year is over and you've successfully completed rehab, it will be the only cent you get. In other words, you will be cut off completely, and the money will be disbursed as Darci sees fit."*

Eva's pale face reddened to a vibrant beet red. "He can't do that!" she railed.

"I'm afraid he can and has," said Mr. Clayton. "If you want to get this money, you'll have to follow his rules. There's a bit more to the letter. *'I imagine this makes you very angry, Eva, but I'm doing this for you because I love you. I love both of you. Darci, I know I'm asking an awful lot of you, but I need you to do this for me. It will mean you'll have to stay in Sterling for a while, but you should be very comfortable in my house, which is now your house, and doing this would mean more to me than you'll ever know. Thank you for being the best and hottest friend a guy could ever have. And, please, don't be sad about my death. I may be gone, but at least I made a gorgeous corpse. All my love, Kenny.'"* Mr. Clayton returned the letter to the envelope and handed it to Darci. "That's all."

"I'm supposed to check into rehab now? Just like that?"

"Yes, just like that. Kenneth did his best to keep your drug and alcohol addiction from your parents, but, lately, he'd noticed things were getting out of hand. With his upcoming trip to Rio, he wanted to make sure you'd be okay, in case the unthinkable happened during his jaunt. So, he added this letter to his will."

Eva stood and pointed at Darci. "She's supposed to see that I'm okay? This woman Kenny and my parents have always loved more than me? Forget it. I will not report to her!"

Fed up with Eva's griping, Darci leapt from her chair and advanced to within inches of the irate woman. "You know what, Eva, I don't care what you do! I'm here because it's what Kenny wanted. I swear, you are a sad woman. Your brother is dead and still looking out for you, and all you care about is getting your hands on his money! You don't have to like me, but you have to deal with me. If you want to walk away, feel free, but I won't allow you to put Kenny's money up your nose or down your throat. You know I can make it happen. And trust me, I will!"

Eva stepped around Darci and walked up to Mr. Clayton. "Kenny can't do this. He can't make me check into rehab. I don't have a drug problem! He can't keep this money from me."

Darci threw up her hands in frustration and returned to her chair.

"Eva, we've been through this," Mr. Clayton said. "The bequest is based on a condition, and if you want to receive the bequest, you have to satisfy the condition. It's that simple. If you're correct, and you don't have a drug problem, this year should be a breeze. There's no getting around this."

"We'll see!" Eva snatched her purse from the chair and stormed out. The chandelier rattled from the force of the door slamming behind her.

Mr. Clayton placed his glasses in his pocket and blew out a long breath. "That is one angry young woman," he said, sitting.

"Troubled is a better word," Darci remarked as she massaged her throbbing temples. "Did she look high to you?"

"I couldn't tell. I noticed the shine in her eyes, but maybe it was excitement or a lingering hangover symptom. I understand she was pretty hammered at Kenny's funeral."

"She was."

"She seemed to have her bearings today."

Darci nodded. "I guess so far, but it's still early."

"This is a lot more involved than you expected, yes?"

"Yes."

"I'll understand if you feel the need to decline the position of executor. Kenny did make provisions for me to assume the role if you declined for any reason. Eva is not going to make things easy for you, and with your questions surrounding Kenny's death . . ."

"I do have my problems with that, but I'm going to do what he asked of me. I need to do this for him." She turned to Mr. Clayton. "When did Kenny give you this letter?"

"About two weeks ago. Why?"

"Two weeks. I spoke to Kenny the day before he . . . the day before, and he was on Cloud Nine. Not at all a man who would shoot himself in the head less than twenty-four hours later. Even with this letter, he wasn't talking like a man who had thoughts of taking his life. Did he seem strange to you?"

"Not strange, but speaking of the prospect of death is never an easy situation. He said the letter was for in case something happened. And with his upcoming trip, I had no reason to question the validity of it."

Darci sighed. "Why is it I'm the only one who finds this suicide so inconceivable?" She opened the letter and scanned it for the telling line. "Here. '. . . *at least I made a gorgeous corpse.'* Does that sound like a man about to kill himself?"

"No, it doesn't, but . . ."

"No buts. Somebody killed him and made it look like a suicide."

"Made it look like a suicide? Darci?"

"I know I'm right, and I'll find a way to prove it. Kenny gave you this letter for just in case. I know he wasn't planning a sudden death." She stood. "Can I keep the letter?"

"It's yours." Mr. Clayton touched her hand. "Darci, sweetie, I think you should reconsider investigating. Nothing's going to bring Kenny back."

"But it will bring the people who loved him some peace." She gave Mr. Clayton's hand a firm shake. "Thank you for everything."

"I don't think I've helped you much, but you're welcome. If you need to talk to me, you know how to reach me."

"Yes, sir."

Darci left the house and pointed her car in the direction of the police department. The prospect of seeing Steed again brought an unsettling thrill in her stomach, like approaching the first dip on a roller coaster ride—exciting and scary. Her contradictory emotions about the detective aside, she had this letter, and that gave her purpose. Maybe once Steed saw the letter, he'd start seeing things her way, and begin using that detective mind to help her make some sense of all this.

Steed closed the Warwick file and rubbed his tired eyes. No matter how long he studied those documents, he would never find anything to suggest Warwick was murdered. How would he get Darci to see that? Steed dropped his forehead to the desk. Were a beautiful woman and promotion worth his sanity?

"Detective McGraw."

Steed looked up, pleasantly surprised to see Darci advancing to his desk. Maybe this beautiful woman was worth his sanity. The blue suit was a bit stuffy for his taste, but as always, she looked incredible. He couldn't decide if he preferred her hair pulled back to display her perfect bone structure, or down like it was now, with thick, bouncy curls framing her gorgeous face. One thing was certain, she had a hold on him he could neither understand nor explain.

"Ms. Clarke, I have to say this is unexpected. After yesterday, I thought we'd seen the last of each other."

"So did I, but something happened this morning to change my mind," she said, taking her usual spot in front of his desk.

Steed managed to keep his professional focus while fighting the trappings of her intoxicating perfume. Peaches never smelled so good. "And what was that?" he asked.

"Kenny's will was read."

"Okay."

"He left a letter. A letter he wrote two weeks ago. The specific details of the letter aren't important, but what is crystal clear is what I've been saying from the moment I came into this office yesterday. Kenny didn't kill himself."

"Did this letter say that?"

"No, but—"

Steed groaned. Maybe she wasn't worth his sanity. "Ms. Clarke . . ."

"Just wait! You're telling me Kenny took a gun and blew off half of his face—his gorgeous beloved face—there's no way. I might *possibly* find it easier to believe he had taken pills to kill himself, then he'd still be beautiful, but to take a gun to his head? No."

Amazing. Darci was even more dogged in her beliefs, and Steed hadn't thought that possible. "Darci, you're looking for anything that will give you an answer to why this happened, but you have to accept you may never get one."

"Not if you don't help me. Look, Steed, I'm a proud woman, I'll be the first to admit that, but I'm also willing to admit when I'm wrong."

Steed scoffed. "Is that right?"

"Yes, that's right. I'm not wrong about Kenny, and that's why I'm back here. I need your help to prove this."

"Darci, listen, I understand your—"

"Stop. I know what you're about to say, so don't say it." She pulled her pocketbook off her shoulder and dug inside, producing folded sheets. "I want you to listen to this. *'If Mr. Clayton is reading this letter it means I'm dead, and that sucks.'* Does that sound like a man about to kill himself?"

"That means nothing."

"No? How about this?" She turned to the next page. "*'And, please, don't be sad about my death. I may be gone, but at least I made a gorgeous corpse. All my love, Kenny.'* He made a gorgeous corpse? Nobody saw his corpse, save family, because half his head was blown off. The casket was closed."

"You've seen the pictures, you know why it was closed."

"All I'm saying is Kenny loved attention, and even dead, he would have enjoyed people taking one last look at his face. One final peek at the wonder that was Kenneth Warwick. He couldn't have shot himself."

Steed stroked his whiskered chin. "Can I speak now?"

"Not if you're going to tell me yet again how wrong I am." She shoved the letter back into her purse. "I'm sick of hearing that."

"Well, lady, I gotta tell you, I'm sick of you telling me you're right. Especially when this," he said, holding up the file, "tells me you're wrong."

"The letter doesn't change anything for you? I spoke to Kenny the day before everything went wrong. He was so excited about his trip to Rio, he got me a BlackBerry to ensure he would be able to reach me whenever something really exciting happened. I don't even know how to use a BlackBerry."

"And that means what? Somebody killed him? This file doesn't tell me that. As much as I want to say you're right, I can't, and telling you differently wouldn't help."

"You're saying every piece of paper in that file can prove, without a doubt, Kenny killed himself?"

Steed met her gaze head on. "Yes," he answered flatly.

"Okay." Darci dragged her chair behind his desk.

"What are you doing?"

"I want you to show me this irrefutable evidence. If you can do that, if you can show me that every sheet in this file proves Kenny killed himself, I'll back off. I'll drop this."

"You mean it?"

"Absolutely." She unbuttoned her jacket and hung it on the back of the chair. "My cousin Jackie thinks I'm too close to this to think rationally. Randall Clayton, a man I totally respect, is in agreement with Jackie. The way he looked at me at the reading with pity in his eyes . . ." Darci shook her head. "And then there's you. The detective who thinks I'm nuts."

"It's not that simple," Steed said, shifting his gaze from the V-cut of her sleeveless white blouse and the delightful view of her cleavage to her engaging dark eyes.

"No?"

"Uh-uh. Granted, I think you're a little blinded by your zeal, especially in regard to this case, but most of the time I guess that's one of your many positive attributes."

Darci peered at him over thick curled lashes. "You think I have positive attributes?"

"I do," Steed answered as the strange fluttering returned to his stomach. "Some of them are obvious. Your beauty, intelligence, and incredible laugh you don't use nearly enough. Then, there are the not-so-obvious things. Like your modesty when people recognize you. You don't like to draw attention to yourself, although you work in the public eye."

"You noticed all of that about me?"

Darci's lips seemed to move in slow motion, hypnotizing him, urging him to kiss them. Steed brushed his thumb against her chin. "I noticed a lot about you from the moment you walked into this office yesterday." He tugged gently on her bottom lip. "Lady, you bewitch me."

Longing and fear darkened her dark eyes all the more. Steed leaned closer. Darci held her hand to his chest. He could swear he heard her heart pounding, or maybe it was his.

"I don't want to be attracted to you," she confessed, her breathy tone barely above a whisper.

"Ditto," Steed murmured, before hungrily claiming her lips.

Whatever protest Darci dared to offer was lost in her sighs of pleasure as their tongues came together in a sensual duel. Steed feasted on her sweet mouth, wondering if he could ever get enough of her tantalizing kisses.

Darci's arms curled around him, clinging to him. The feel of her soft body, her scent, her taste, fueled Steed's need for her. He wanted more of her. He had to have more.

"Detective McGraw, I have that information you . . ."

The two pulled apart. Steed licked his lips, savoring the memory of Darci's kiss, while fuming at the interruption. "What is it, Jackson?"

"Sorry, sir." The red-faced officer approached with a file. "The information you wanted for the Warwick investigation." He dropped the file and left the office in double-quick time.

Steed leaned in for another kiss. "That kid has the worst timing."

Darci's pulled back. "Actually, I think his timing is perfect. That shouldn't have happened."

"No, it should have happened yesterday at Sophie's."

"This is not a good idea."

"Why not? We're attracted to each other." Darci shifted nervously in the chair. "Is there a guy in New York?" he asked.

"No."

"What about you and Warwick? How close were you two?"

Darci's movements ceased and anger returned to her eyes. He'd stuck his foot in his mouth again, but in this instance he didn't care. He wanted to know the answer to that question. "So?" Steed prodded.

"Why do you keep asking me that?"

Because you didn't want to kiss me again! "Because you keep insisting you two were very close," Steed said. "Maybe closer than you want to admit. You had a fight, he got upset and . . ."

"Stop!" She grunted. "I'm going to forget you said that, and I'm also going to forget what just happened here. Just show me your evidence."

"Darci, look, I'm—"

"Sorry?" She rolled her eyes. "Save it, Detective."

Steed shook his head. Detective again. Talk about taking two steps back. "I was trying to apologize."

"You're always apologizing. Saying you're sorry when you keep making the same mistake is a hollow apology, and I'm sick of hearing it. Let's just keep things all business between us. I think it would be for the best."

"I disagree."

"I don't care. I want to see your evidence."

Holding his tongue, Steed opened his file and dragged over Jackson's. "You've seen the autopsy report and you're heard Lorene's findings."

"I'll concede there was a gunshot wound to the head."

"Let's go from there. The gun was his, the only set of prints found on the weapon were his. This file Jackson brought in contains the prints from the gun, which we ran again." Steed plopped the unopened file to the center of his desk. "The burn marks, powder residue, and wound pattern are all consistent with the victim firing the gun on himself. It's open and shut."

She flicked one edge of his file. "That's it?"

"It's a damn sight better than the straws you're grasping at! My God, lady, what more do you need?" Steed grunted. He had to stop snapping. "I'm sorry."

"What else is new?"

"I'll tell you what's new. The maddening way you affect me. The way you make me feel like a pile of mush and an erupting volcano all at once. That's what's new!" Steed raked his fingers through his hair. "I don't like seeing you like this. Searching for something you'll never find."

"I won't find it if you don't help me."

"Help you? I'm trying to help you now, Darci. You need to deal with the fact Warwick killed himself and you'll never know why. You're going to keep finding things, anything that says you're right and there's some question, some doubt where none exists. That's your pain talking."

Darci shook her head. "No, it's more."

"No, it's not. I know it's hard to accept, but you have to do just that. I can help you with *this*, if you let me. I don't think Warwick would want you to do this to yourself."

"You have no idea what Kenny would want for me." Tears slid down her cheeks. "You don't give a damn about him. He's just another case to you."

"You're only partly right on that. I didn't know Warwick, but this is not just another case for me." He smoothed away the wisps of hair sticking to her tear-streaked face. "I can see how much you're hurting and how you desperately need some answers, but sometimes the answers you get aren't the ones you want. Deep down inside you know the truth. Your best friend is dead and your heart is broken. The only thing that makes sense is your grief. You have to deal with that first. Cry, and cry some more, and then you go on with your life. When the pain lessens, the truth becomes easier to take."

It amazed Steed how effortlessly he said those words. He meant them completely, but he'd experienced more than his share of trouble living them. *Do as I say, not as I do.* Darci had to follow this advice. He had to help save her from herself.

Steed cupped her face. His thumbs brushed away her streaming tears. "Darci, for your own good, you have to let this go." He brought her head to his shoulder, where she surrendered to anguished tears. "Just let it go."

CHAPTER 8

Darci peeled her face from Steed's tear-soaked shirt and smoothed the wetness from her eyes. How long had she been crying on his shoulder? "I'm sorry, I shouldn't have done that," she said, feeling more than a bit embarrassed for losing her composure in front of him.

"Hey, 'I'm sorry' is my line." Steed smiled. "Besides, I asked you to do it. Here," he said, offering her yet another perfectly pressed handkerchief.

She dabbed her blurry eyes. "I'll pay for your shirt being laundered."

"Don't worry about it. I have lots of shirts."

"And handkerchiefs, too."

He smiled. "You can thank my na—grandmother. Do you feel better?"

Darci shrugged. "I don't know," she answered. "I know what you said, and I know what I need to do, it's just . . ."

"It's going to take time, Darci. This is just the first step." He lifted a brow. "This is the first step, right? You're letting this go?"

"I have to, don't I? You won't give me any choice."

"There is no other choice."

"I don't think I'll ever believe Kenny could kill himself." The corners of Steed's mouth tightened. Irritation speckled his blue eyes. "That said," she continued, "I won't make your life miserable by insisting you help me prove it. I guess all I can do now is make sure Kenny's final wishes are fulfilled."

"His will?"

"Yes. I have the extreme pleasure of being his executor."

"You didn't know about this before?"

"I knew, but I didn't think I'd be doing it at thirty-two. Eva didn't know I'd be doing it at all."

"Warwick's sister?"

She nodded. "I'm not one of her favorite people."

Steed's mouth dropped in exaggerated outrage. "You mean somebody in this world doesn't like you?" Steed scoffed. "The nerve!"

"Ha-ha, McGraw. You seem to be warming up to me."

"That's because you're hot." His gaze raked over her body. Darci's pulse rate spiked. Steed could reduce her to ash if he took the notion. No man had ever made her feel like this. It scared her to death.

"So, what's the problem with this Eva?" he asked.

"It's involved." Darci walked over to the window. Two cardinals hopped about the sweltering pavement. Given the heat of the day, those birds could have been canaries suffering from the extreme temperatures. She chuckled at the silly thought.

"What are you laughing about?" Steed came over and closed his hand over her shoulder. "What do you see out there?"

It took all she had to keep her buckling knees from giving way. What was it about Steed McGraw? There were gorgeous men in New York. She'd even dated a few of them. But none of them made her feel so out of control. And she hated not being in control. She needed to get away from him, and quickly.

"It's nothing," she answered, returning to the desk. "Just a silly thought I got when I saw some birds." She grabbed her jacket. "I need to be going now."

"Don't rush off." He caught up to her. "I have a break coming up. I thought maybe we could grab some lunch at Miss Sophie's and actually get through a meal without growling at each other."

"I don't know," she hedged, inwardly jumping up and down at the idea of going out with him again, while simultaneously eyeing the door with thoughts of breaking out of this office and away from whatever this was he was making her feel.

"Why don't you know? You said you weren't seeing anyone."

"I'm not."

"Neither am I."

"We don't even know each other."

"You kissed me."

"No, you kissed me," she readily clarified.

"We kissed each other. That hardly makes us strangers. Yeah, we started off on the wrong foot, but I have faith we can continue on this positive course." He brushed a stray hair from her cheek. "I think we've made amazing progress today."

Darci couldn't argue with that. He'd made a lot more progress than she'd ever wanted him, or any other man, to make, and that was the problem. There was a reason she'd never been seriously involved with anyone in New York. Relationships were troublesome, and she just didn't want trouble. Life was so much easier when you didn't have those ties and the expectations that came with them, plus her career left little time for it.

"You gonna have lunch with me?" Steed asked again.

"I don't think it's a good idea."

"I think it's a great idea. We tried to start over yesterday at Miss Sophie's, and things went pretty well until we got on the Warwick case again. With that hurdle crossed, we can get to know each other better. I do believe we're off to a pretty good start."

"One kiss is not a start."

"Of course it is. It's a beginning. We're attracted to each other, and we're both single." He paused for a long moment. "You can't tell me it's a racial thing because I'd never believe it."

"It's not that, either."

"Then what?"

If she told him, he'd probably think she was lying, and she didn't feel like explaining herself. "I have a lot to deal with right now," Darci answered, which wasn't a lie. "You said it yourself, I need to grieve for Kenny. And I need to start accepting this . . . the way you said he died."

"His suicide."

She sighed loudly. *Steed and that word!*

"You can't even say it, can you?"

"I'm trying, it's just not that easy. I need . . ."

"Time, I know. What happens for you next?"

"I settle Kenny's estate."

"Then you're going to be in town for a while?"

"As long as it takes."

"And your job in New York?"

"I was in contract negotiations before I arrived. I need to call my agent and let her know what's going on."

"Think I can call you sometime?"

No! No! No! "Sure," she answered, wondering where that quick response came from as she walked to the door. *What happened to not wanting trouble?*

"Darci, wait. I don't know your number."

"You're a detective. If you really want to reach me, you'll find a way. Besides, I can't make this too easy for you."

"Too easy?" He laughed. "Okay, I'm game. You'll be hearing from me tonight. In the meantime, you try and have a good afternoon."

"Given the fact I might have to deal with Eva, I won't hold my breath on that one."

———∽∾∽———

"What the hell do you think you're doing?"

Kenneth Warwick glared at his irate sister through steel bars and closed his eyes again. "I think I'm stuck inside a cinder block prison, trying desperately to pretend I'm on a tropical beach and not being held captive by my drugged-out sister and her crazy boyfriend in some dingy cabin."

"You shut that fresh mouth or I will shut it up for you."

Kenny's eyes flew open. "You mean for real this time? I can't believe you, Eva. How could you do this to me?"

"How could I do this to you? What about what you've done to me!"

"What I've done to you?" Kenny leapt from his cot and wrapped his hands around the bars that blocked his path to freedom. "All I've ever done is try to help you. Mom and Dad never knew about your substance abuse problems because I kept it from them. When you needed money, I gave it to you. I helped you in every way I could, and this is how you repay me? Make our parents and the world think I killed myself. This is beyond cruel!"

"I didn't make this situation. I just used it to my advantage."

This situation. Kenny sighed. It would be laughable if it weren't so sad and impossible to believe. A few short days ago he was walking on air, preparing for a hot date with a buxom blonde from the station. Eva coming up behind him when he'd arrived home hadn't surprised him, but it had ticked him off. Pleading for money, and edgy from coming off another high, probably the prescription drugs she was partial to, Eva and her sorry state were the last things he had wanted to deal with.

After her usual "I need" speech, Kenny had offered her food, but not another dime. They had stepped inside his house, and that was when everything changed. He had found some stranger on his couch, wearing his favorite suit, and looking more like his clone than he wanted to admit. That stranger, who introduced himself as Jason Hyde, became an integral part in the deception his sister and her demented beau had perpetrated on Kenny and the rest of the world.

The door slammed, jostling Kenny from the memory of his not-so-distant past. Eva's partner in crime, a dark-haired, beady-eyed guy named Fritz, walked in.

"How much you get?" Fritz asked.

"Seven hundred and fifty thousand," Eva said.

"Yes! I told you he had big money." Fritz rubbed his hands together like an evil cartoon madman.

A few inches taller and a couple of pounds heavier than Fritz, Kenny knew he could take the man if those bars weren't between them. How Fritz found information about his financial status baffled Kenny, but since he was sitting in a block prison cell inside a cabin, Fritz had to have pull somewhere.

"I can't get the money until I finish rehab," Eva explained, her angry eyes burning holes through Kenny. "I want my money. I'm not going to be at the mercy of Darci Clarke."

"It's *my* money and you don't have a choice. I'm dead, remember?" Kenny returned to his cot. "Guess your little plan's not working like you hoped, huh? Only a drug fiend would think something so foolish would pan out." So far, it was working, but with his sister's addiction and a fervent hope that sibling compassion still resided somewhere inside her heart, he figured he could find his way through a crack, work on some doubt, and get the hell out of this. He glanced at the metal toilet/sink in one corner of his prison. He had to get out of here, and get some fresh clothes. He'd been in his beige suit for days.

Eva stomped over to Fritz. "This was your idea!"

"And you went with it!" Fritz held up his hands and took a breath. "Don't let him shake you. We can get this money."

"How?"

"Yeah, Fritz, how?" Kenny echoed. "My wishes are written out clearly, and there's no way Darci won't follow through. As a matter of fact, she's gonna realize something's wrong. She, if no one else in this world, knows I wouldn't kill myself."

"Darci's in her *'I can't believe Kenny would do this'* phase, but to the world you're dead. And she can't deny that."

"Nobody can deny it, because I made it so," Fritz added. "I'm well aware of police procedure, and that poor slob who decided to blow his brains out on your couch is you. It's like Jason Hyde was never there. His clothing, his wallet, his mere existence. *Poof.* I covered all the bases."

Kenny squeezed his eyes shut. How he wished he could turn back time. Jason explained he had sent many letters, which was probably true, but Kenny never answered letters that didn't come from women. The man wanted Kenny to be his friend, to have people see them out together so he'd be accepted by association. Eva and Jason. Two people who wanted something from Kenny, and then went too far when they didn't get it.

Had he kept Eva out of his house or sent that pathetic man an autographed picture or something, this turn of events wouldn't have happened. He knew he had a way with women, but Jason Hyde's devotion to him had gone far beyond the usual fan appreciation. The fact the man looked so much like him freaked him out even more. Being friends? Hanging out? Breaking into his house and wearing his clothes? That was a little too much.

When Kenny had attempted to call the police, Jason pulled out a gun. A Desert Eagle Mark XIX semi-automatic pistol, one of a half-dozen firearms Kenny's deceased uncle had left him. Kenny wasn't much of a gun fan, but he'd loved his uncle, and felt obliged to keep the collection. Considering at least one of the guns was loaded, that decision had bitten him big time.

Kenny kept the Mark XIX and the other guns in a locked display case in the living room. A display case Jason managed to have a key for, along with a key to Kenny's front door. Jason had apologized profusely for letting himself in and trying on the suit, but swore he couldn't go back to jail. Feeling sorry for Jason, Kenny had assured him he wouldn't call the cops and told him he could go, but Jason turned the gun on himself anyway. Moments later Fritz rushed in and Kenny's life changed.

Kenny opened his eyes, staring at his captors. "Darci is going to realize something's wrong."

"Not gonna happen." Fritz swaggered over and held onto the bars. "You're stuck with us," he said. "If you want things to get better, you'll find a way to undo what you did."

Eva approached and touched Fritz's arm. "Don't taunt him, Fritz." She flashed Kenny a smile. He wanted to kick her. It was too late for his sister to play sweetness and light. "We need money, Kenny. I'm sure you can think of something to change this will."

"What?" Kenny snapped. "Dead men can't talk, and they sure as hell can't change wills." He expelled a quick breath. "You made this mess, Eva. So you either wait out the year, or you let me go. I don't owe you a damn thing."

"What do you owe your dear friend Darci?"

There was no mistaking the threat in her tone. His sister was off her spool, but he couldn't show his alarm. "You can't do anything to Darci," Kenny said.

"No?" Eva clicked her tongue. "You willing to risk that? The world thinks you're dead. How hard do you think it will be for us to make it look like grief overcame poor Darci?" She stared at him. "I want her hands out of my pockets, Kenny. You better see that it happens."

CHAPTER 9

"You'll have to excuse the lived-in conditions," Steed said, grabbing a shirt from the back of his couch and tossing it into the closet. "I don't have many visitors."

Darci chuckled. "Why am I not surprised?"

The plush upholstered sofa and loveseat done in a creamy beige color complemented the glossy hardwood floor, but the strewn clothes and countless mugs stained with remnants of black coffee weren't exactly the ideal accessories. This was definitely a bachelor pad. It even smelled like his cologne.

"I'm usually a bit tidier than this," Steed said, gathering more shirts and tossing them in a laundry basket in the corner of his living room. "I had a little trouble finding a clean shirt for our date." He kicked a white sock under the couch and sighed. "I should have cleaned. I didn't think we'd end up here, and . . . I'm really much neater than this. There's just been so much going at the station, and—"

"It's okay. We usually go back to Jackie's after our dates, but after two weeks, I figured I'd spare you another inquisition from my family," Darci said with a laugh, moving to the couch.

"That's fine. I like your family." Steed joined her. "Jackie and Carl are great people, and Ronnie and Craig's interest in law enforcement is very exciting. They have great questions. They remind me of myself at that age, always asking Uncle Pete a million things about cases and procedures. I couldn't get enough of that. Sorta like you are with anything peach related." He laughed.

"Ha-ha. I like what I like. I'm consistent," she said. "Now, Uncle Pete. He was your father's partner, right?"

"Yeah. He's great. Even after Mom left New York and remarried, Uncle Pete would call me and come down to Texas to visit Lori and me. He was even kind to Brett."

"He shouldn't have been kind to Brett?"

"He didn't have to be. Brett is Mom and her husband's son. Lori and I are Dad's. Uncle Pete was good to all of us."

"Your stepfather wasn't good to you and your sister?"

The pained look on Steed's face made Darci wish she hadn't asked the question. Steed had talked about his family, not nonstop by any means, but he'd mentioned them. Mostly his Nana Jean, the mother of his stepfather he barely mentioned.

"He was fine. It was just different. Josh is a wealthy rancher and he seemed to always be throwing money around."

"Seemed to? You didn't like him because he was wealthy?"

"I didn't say I didn't like him."

"You didn't have to. You change when you talk about him. I hear resentment in your voice."

"It's not resentment, it's just . . ." Steed expelled a breath and the tension she saw on his face melted away with a smile. "You never stop being a reporter," he said with a kiss to her cheek. "It's a good thing I like you."

"Imagine that," she said with a laugh. It didn't surprise her he'd changed the subject, he often did, but he felt what he felt for a reason, and she'd wait until he was ready to share why. Darci took in her surroundings. "This is a great house. A bit big for a single guy."

"Three bedrooms and a couple of baths. I like my space, and my privacy, and this house gives me that."

Darci walked over to the fireplace and picked up a frame. The smiling face of the older red-haired woman left no doubt of her identity. "Nana Jean, right?"

Steed smiled. "Yeah, that's Nana. And the two munchkins in the other frames are Krista and Cody, Lori's daughter and son."

"Where are photos of the rest of your family?"

"In an album. These are the people who don't hassle me. So, they get places of honor."

"Krista is what, two?"

"Three. Cody is almost one. I saw them at Christmas." Steed's eyes brightened. "They're wonderful."

"Steed McGraw has a soft spot for children. You are full of surprises."

"That surprises you?"

"Frankly, yes. The guy I met at the police station two weeks ago seemed more like a coal in the treat sack at Halloween type. The more time I spend with you, the more . . ."

"What?" Steed said, wrapping his arms around her waist.

"The more I like you," she said, closing her arms around his neck and melting into his kiss.

——∿∿——

Steed knocked on Chief Rogers's door and waited for an answer. Maybe, after two months, he was finally getting word on his promotion. He had kept his end of the deal, and in the process got a lot closer to Darci. He couldn't believe how important she'd become to him in such a short amount of time. In a matter of days, they'd gone from biting each other's heads off to barely being able to keep their hands off each other.

Darci had decided against re-signing with *Heart of the Matter,* and to Steed's delight, permanently moved back to Sterling. All of the TV stations in Crider, the nearest big city located thirty miles north of Sterling, approached Darci with job offers. The most lucrative coming from WCR with a proposal of Kenny's vacant spot, monthly features on the morning show, and outs for special projects. The notion of stealing Kenny's job bothered her, but with help from Jackie, Steed had twisted Darci's arm into accepting the position. However, nothing could convince her to move into Warwick's house. She insisted she would move in if Eva decided to follow the wishes of Kenny's will, but she refused to live there alone or permanently, so last week she'd sealed the purchase of her parents' old house, where she'd already started moving in.

The only downside in all of this was her weeklong trip to New York to tie up loose ends and retrieve the rest of her things. She'd be back in town today, and Steed hoped to have good news with word of his promotion.

Darci had become his biggest cheerleader, insisting he had his promotion in the bag. Steed smiled. She wasn't like any other woman he'd dated, specifically with her peach fascination. She wore peach-scented perfume, she loved peach cobbler and peach ice cream, and she even had peach-colored furniture. He was surprised when she bought a black Lexus.

He was falling in love with her. He'd never loved any woman that wasn't related to him. Oh, he'd said it a time or two in his younger days to get a score, but it had just been words. Thinking about those words with Darci in mind made him happy. He wanted to take care of her, talk to her, hold her and kiss her. He wanted to find a way to take away the pain she still carried over Warwick's death.

Although Darci had dropped her need to find Kenny's "alleged" killer, she still hadn't accepted Warwick's suicide. She tried to pretend otherwise, but Steed knew better. Darci needed time, and he understood that more than anyone. He would give her the time she needed, and all the support she could handle. And maybe some good news would help that along.

Steed gave three more hard raps to Rogers's door.

"Come in," said Chief Rogers.

Steed entered to find Mayor Benjamin with Rogers. Steed's heart pounded. Was he finally getting his promotion? He'd dressed in a suit and shaved in anticipation of Darci's arrival, but maybe these things would be to his benefit in regard to this meeting. "You wanted to see me, sir?" he said.

Rogers motioned to the empty chair next to the mayor. "Yes, McGraw, sit down. We need to discuss some things."

Steed sat and took a cursory glance at the mayor. "What is it?" he asked.

Mayor Benjamin turned sideways in the chair. "You were the lead investigator in the Warwick case, correct?"

"Yes, sir, I was," Steed replied, hating that stupid question. He had been the only detective back then. Malena Holston, a sorority sister of Jackie's, had been hired as the newest detective a month earlier. Steed liked her. It was different sharing office space with a woman who loved plants and goldfish, but Malena was hard-core. A wife, mother, and great detective, Malena handled her business. "The Warwick case has been closed for two months. Is there a problem?"

"I would say there is," Rogers answered. "I want you to take a look at this and tell me what you make of it." He tossed a file to the edge of the desk.

Steed picked up the manila folder and scanned the four pages within. "It's fingerprints, sir," he said, not quite understanding the point of all this.

"You notice anything about these particular prints?"

"There are at least two different sets. A couple of the pages have the different prints together."

"That's right, Detective," said the mayor. "Can you guess why that is?"

Steed rubbed his clean-shaven chin, getting a strong suspicion this meeting wasn't about his promotion. "I can't begin to guess, Mayor. What's the problem?"

"The problem is those are two different sets of fingerprints. One set belongs to Kenneth Warwick, and the other to a man named Jason Hyde."

"Jason Hyde? Should that name mean something to me?"

"Yes, I think it should," Rogers answered. "Seems his fingerprints were on the gun that killed Kenneth Warwick." Rogers clasped his hands and leaned over the desk. "Think you can explain that to me?"

———

Darci placed the last of her knick-knacks on the fireplace mantle, kicked the box labeled "Living Room" to the flattened stack in the corner, and scanned the room. As she'd expected, her overstuffed peach-colored living room group complemented the crème-colored carpeting and walls perfectly. With her paintings, her photos, and her crystal figurines all around, Darci's old home was officially her new home, and it felt strange and exciting.

Up-and-coming professionals of every race and nationality had transformed the working middle class neighborhood to an upwardly mobile suburbia. Laughing children played at the corner park constructed five years earlier, while their sitters read romance novels or gabbed about the latest gossip while managing to keep a watchful eye. Things were different, but one thing remained the same, the neighborhood was about family. And even with Jackie, Carl, and their brood a few houses away, Darci didn't have one. At least not like the ones surrounding her on every side.

Darci walked over to Jackie and her doctor husband, Carl, who were sprawled on the couch taking a much-deserved breather. "Okay, I think we're done," she said, plopping next to Jackie.

"I can't speak for my wife, but I've been done since I pulled this couch in here." Carl grunted as he rotated his shoulder. "My young brothers-in-law didn't waste any time leaving once that U-Haul hit the driveway," he said.

"In their defense, Tommy and Jay did fly to New York, load the truck, drive it here, and help take most of the items out when we arrived."

"Yeah, well, they could have helped take them all out. They're younger than me. What about Steed? Did the card accompanying that large bouquet of peach roses he sent over explain his absence?"

Darci smiled. Just the mention of Steed's name made her feel like some silly schoolgirl, and gave her more than a passing thought of achieving the family her home was missing.

She leaned forward, inhaling the fragrant display on her coffee table. "Steed had to work, but I'll see him later."

"From the glow on your face, I can tell you're counting the minutes until he's here," Jackie teased.

Darci's face grew warm. "I'm not glowing."

"No, you're blushing," Jackie corrected with a laugh. "You really missed him, huh?"

"Yeah, I did. I can't believe how much I did."

"Okay," Carl said, standing. "It sounds like girl talk is coming on, and I'm not in the mood to listen. So, I'm gonna let you girls have your talk. I'll drive home and take a nap before my shift at the hospital."

"I didn't mean to run you off, Carl. Actually, I was about to order up some lunch. I wouldn't have been able to get this place settled without you two."

"We didn't mind helping, and I don't mind leaving. I have the E.R. tonight, so a nice nap will do me a whole lot of good."

"Are you sure?"

"Positive. You ladies enjoy your talk."

"Thanks again, Carl."

"You're welcome." Carl gave Jackie a kiss and whispered something in her ear that evoked a giddy laugh.

Darci grinned. She loved watching them. After eighteen years of marriage, Jackie and Carl still acted like newlyweds. "I see the magic is still alive," she said as Carl walked out the front door.

"When you have the right man, it's very easy to keep the fire burning. His long hours at the hospital and my late classes at the university sometimes make finding time a challenge, but we love each other, so we make it work." Jackie clutched Darci's hand. "Now, about you and Steed?"

"What about us?"

"You tell me. You've been seeing quite a bit of him."

"I haven't seen him in a week."

"Only because you were out of town. "I bet you talked to him every night."

The warmth in Darci's cheeks returned.

Jackie laughed. "I got my answer." She kicked off her sneakers and pulled her feet up under her bottom. "This is great, Darci. Steed's a good man."

"He is a good man. He certainly keeps me guessing." Darci laughed. "My first impression of Steed was that he was a gorgeous jerk, but there's so much more to him than a hot body and bad attitude. He's sweet, very polite and well-mannered, and he has a crazy sense of humor. He's not the most talkative guy in the world by any stretch, but you mention police work and he's off. Then, there's another part of him. Steed's had a lot of pain in his life."

"In regard to his father?"

"Yeah. Sometimes, I think he's about to tell me more about it, but then he stops. He'll change the subject, or divert my attention with um—" She cleared her throat. "Other things."

"Other things?" Jackie said, bobbing her head.

"Not that other thing," Darci readily answered, feeling where her cousin was headed. "Not quite."

"Does Steed know about . . ."

"It hasn't come up."

Jackie laughed. "I won't touch that one, Darci, it's too easy. But seriously, you'll have to address this soon."

"Maybe not."

"How do you figure?"

"Because I think I'm in love. That changes things."

"You think you love Steed?"

"Yeah, I really think I do, but I don't know." Darci sighed. "I came home for my best friend's funeral, and even after two months, I haven't accepted he could have killed himself. But somehow, because of Steed, I've been able to make a grudging peace with what the facts show."

Jackie shook her head. "I don't understand."

"Neither do I. Like I said, I think I love Steed, but I still don't think Kenny could commit suicide. And I'll admit it's crazy to think that, but I do. Which is why I'm confused about my feelings for Steed. Do I know I love him, if I can't know Kenny killed himself, even when everything says he did? How can I be sure of one when I can't be sure of the other, and they both feel so absolutely right?"

"I'm good at solving problems, so long as they are of the math variety. I can't help you with this one, but you know who can. Talk to Steed when he comes over tonight."

"And tell him what? I think I love you, but I think Kenny didn't kill himself, too?"

"You don't think he already knows that last part?"

"I don't think he does, and why should he? It's what we butted heads over from the very beginning. My disagreeing with him put a question on his ability to do his job. Who wouldn't be angry about that? Steed's a great cop, he's up for a promotion, and I'm not going to upset him with my feelings, especially when it won't change anything." Darci hugged a pillow to her chest and sighed. "This worries me," she said. "As a reporter, I'm trained to keep my personal opinions out of my stories, and I do that, but Kenny committing suicide is so wrong. And granted, this is emotional for me, but I'm keeping my reporter's mind here. And my facts tell me Kenny wouldn't do this. To accept he did will destroy everything."

"Come again?"

"My instinct. As a reporter, it's easy to get things to click because facts make it easy. But this doesn't click. These facts are off. How can I continue to do my job well and trust my feelings for Steed when I have questions about facts I shouldn't have? I don't doubt Steed's ability for one second, but I know Kenny. What am I supposed to do with this?"

"Talk to Steed." Darci's cell phone rang. "Maybe that's him now," Jackie said.

Darci checked the caller ID and rolled her eyes. "No such luck." She placed the phone to her ear. "Yes, Eva."

Jackie stood and pointed toward the hall. "I'll be in your bedroom," she mouthed.

Darci nodded as Jackie disappeared into the bedroom.

"Where have you been?" Eva asked, her tone sharp.

"Away," Darci answered. "Are you ready for rehab?"

"I'm not going to any damn rehab. I don't need it."

"Then I don't think we have anything to discuss."

"I need to get into Kenny's house."

"No, you don't."

"I think I left something when I stayed there. The key I have doesn't work anymore."

"Because I had the locks changed. Tell me what you left and I'll get it for you." Darci grimaced. Why did she said that? She hadn't been near Kenny's house since the shooting, and she was in no rush to go. She'd allowed Mr.

Clayton access to have the place cleaned, the wall repaired, and the locks changed, but going in herself . . .

"I can get it myself," Eva said.

"Feel free, if you can find your way in without breaking any windows or locks."

"It's my brother's house."

"That he left to me, and I won't let you in there to find things to pawn to support your habit."

"Fine! It's a ring. A diamond and emerald ring. I must have dropped it when I used the shower in Kenny's master bath. I took it off in the bedroom and it's probably somewhere around there. Just find it and let me know when you do."

Abrupt silence followed Eva's words. Darci tossed the phone on the table and cursed herself. Why did she let herself get caught up in Eva's crap?

———◆———

Kenny watched as Eva paced the room. He'd seen less anxious lions in cages at the zoo. She clearly needed a hit, and her constant motion was making him dizzy. He rubbed his face, feeling the wiry whiskers that had grown. He glanced at his reflection in the toilet/sink. With the beard and his hair growing out, he looked like caveman. He'd been here way too long. "Stop the pacing, Eva. It's not helping," he said.

"The only thing that will help is for me to get my money. Are you sure this is going to work?"

"Did Fritz put the letter in the house?"

"Would he have gone through so much trouble to get a key to those new locks if he hadn't?"

"Then Darci will find it." Kenny drew a breath. "She'll find the letter, read that I reconsidered forcing you into rehab, and then you'll get your money."

Eva's glazed eyes brightened. "I'll get my money?"

"Yes."

Her squeals of delight filled the room. "Seven hundred and fifty thousand dollars." She clasped her hands together. "What I can do with that."

"I can only imagine."

Kenny closed his eyes. This letter, the bridge that would lead Eva to his money, was also his only hope for salvation. *Please, God, let Darci remember the code.* She had to find him and get him out of this mess.

—◆◇◆—

"There's been a mistake." Steed closed the file and dropped it on Rogers' desk. "Those prints belonged to Kenneth Warwick."

Jacob crossed his arms. "And how do you know that?"

Steed frowned. The mayor's tone was a lot harsher and a whole lot more accusing than he liked. Jacob Benjamin could be upset about losing Darci, whom he never had in the first place, but intimating Steed didn't perform his job correctly was another thing.

Struggling to keep his growing anger in check, Steed met Jacob's gaze and addressed his question. "I know because I saw the gun by Warwick's hand. CSU tested the prints and they came back as Kenneth Warwick's. I studied the scene inside and out. It was suicide."

"How do you explain Jason Hyde's fingerprints?"

"I can't explain them. Who is Jason Hyde?"

"That's what you need to find out, McGraw." Rogers handed over the file. "Holston can help you with the details."

Steed dropped the folder to his lap. "How did this come about anyway? The case was closed. What made you look again?"

"You were up for a promotion, Detective. A promotion that hinged upon how you handled this case," the mayor answered. "I wanted to ensure all T's were crossed and I's dotted. I guess it's a good thing I checked."

Steed rolled his eyes. *Yeah, just great.* "Actually, Mayor, this promotion hinged upon how I handled Darci and her thoughts on this case. She didn't want to believe her friend killed himself, and it was put upon me to convince her of the truth."

Mayor Benjamin sat up in his chair. "Is she convinced?"

Instead of answering with the true response of 'No,' Steed said, "The case was closed, wasn't it?"

"Yes, it *was.*"

Steed gritted his teeth as he glared at the mayor. It took all he had not to flatten him.

Rogers cleared his throat, pulling Steed's attention from the mayor. "McGraw, just get with Holston and look into this," he said. "The last thing we need is for word to get out that something has gone awry with this case."

"Yes, sir, I'll get right on it."

"You do that," Benjamin added in his authoritarian way. "I understand Darci will be anchoring the local news in Warwick's place. It will not bode well for any of us if this case is not as cut and dried as you've always said."

"I'm well aware of what Darci does for a living, and I wouldn't worry about her painting the department in a bad light." Steed gave Benjamin's shoulder a pat as he made his way to the door. "She has a soft spot for me."

The mayor's disgusted grunt gave Steed the slightest bit of satisfaction, but it was the only bright spot in the whole meeting. No promotion and lots of flack. He slammed the folder against his thigh as he walked to his office.

"Detective?" called Jackson.

Steed didn't miss a step as he continued to his destination. "What is it?" he asked, loosening his tie.

"You have a few messages," the young officer answered, getting in step behind Steed. "One is from Ms. Clarke."

Steed turned around and snatched the pink slips from the smiling officer. "Thanks." He got to his desk and searched for Darci's message. A smile touched his lips as he read. She had gotten in a few hours earlier, and wanted him to call when he had a moment. Feeling better than he had since he stepped into Rogers's office, Steed grabbed the phone and dialed her number.

"Hello, you," Darci greeted. "Thanks for the beautiful roses."

"You're welcome." Steed sighed, her happy voice just the lift what he needed. "You sound wonderful," he said. "Did you have a good trip?"

"It was productive, a little sad saying good-bye to everyone, but Sterling is where I want to be. Jackie is helping me get squared away. How has your day been?"

He flicked the edge of the file and sighed. "That's a story for another time. I can't wait to see you."

"How long do you plan to wait?"

Steed smiled. "Not too long. There's something on my desk that needs my attention, but I have every intention of leaving this place at five. So, I guess I'll see you at five after."

She laughed. "Just get here in one piece."

"I will. I really missed you, Darci."

"I missed you, too. See you soon."

Steed hung up the phone, and with a renewed sense of purpose, opened the Warwick file. *What's with these fingerprints, and who the hell is Jason Hyde?*

CHAPTER 10

The grandfather clock in the living room chimed five times. Darci smiled. Steed would arrive soon. She dashed over to the hall mirror. The floral print baby doll dress made her look cute and the updo hairstyle sexy. And after ten glorious minutes in the shower, she felt refreshed after a long day of unpacking boxes, dusting, stocking the house with groceries, and cooking dinner.

Umph. When had she turned domestic? Add to that anticipating the arrival of her man from a long day at work—she had a flash of a brown June Cleaver flitting around the kitchen, baking cookies, and humming a happy tune. Why did that picture seem so appealing? Was her new old neighborhood rubbing off on her?

The ringing doorbell gave her little time to consider the question. She dashed to the door. Steed was nothing if not punctual.

Bright blue eyes and a dazzling smile warmed her from the sudden blast of the brisk November air. "Darci." Steed gathered her in his arms and seized her mouth in a kiss.

Darci's lips parted, granting Steed's seeking tongue the access it demanded. Moans of pleasure rumbled in her throat. Steed's skillful hands explored her body, along the curves of her hips and roundness of her backside.

Steed buried his face in the crook of her neck. His arms tightened around her. "I've missed you so much."

"I missed you, too, but if you hold me any tighter I might be spending more time away from you." She squirmed against him, barely able to move. "I'll be at the hospital in traction."

His grip loosened. "I'm sorry. I've really missed you."

She dragged the back of her hand against his cheek. She didn't mind Steed's whiskers, but she loved when he shaved. Add the treat of seeing him in a suit . . . He looked downright edible. "I'm glad you missed me." She pecked his lips and escorted him into the living room. "So, do you want the revamped grand tour? Things have changed a bit since your last visit."

"Not yet. The only thing I'm interested in looking at right now is you." He took her hand and slowly twirled her around. "You are so beautiful."

Steed smiled, but Darci detected distraction in his eyes. "What happened today?" she asked.

"My girlfriend came back from a trip to New York," he said, caressing her cheek.

"You know what I mean. What's going on? You're in a suit, and you seem a little down. Bad news about the promotion?"

"No news yet, and if I seem down it's because it's been a crazy day. But seeing you makes everything okay." He kissed her hands. "How about that tour." He drew a deep breath and smiled. "My keen sense of smell detects the aroma of green peppers."

"They don't call you 'Detective' for nothing." Darci laughed. "They're stuffed. My mother's recipe."

"Smells delicious."

Darci walked to the kitchen. Steed followed. "I hope they taste as good," she said.

"I'm sure they will."

"Even if they didn't, I bet you wouldn't say so." Darci checked the peppers and then shut off the oven, deciding to let them stand for a while.

"Me?" He pressed his hand to his chest. "Am I one to hold back on my feelings?"

"Honestly?"

"Absolutely."

"I don't know," Darci said.

Steed followed her into the living room and to the couch. "You think I hold back on my feelings?" he asked, cozying next to her.

"It depends. You totally evaded my question about what's bothering you, but that aside, most things you put out there without hesitation. That's you being tactless."

Steed frowned. "I'm not—"

"Yes, you are. But that's not even the point. There are times when I think you want to tell me things, but you stop just short. You allow me a little peek inside of you, and then you close the curtain. Sort of like an emotional flasher. You open up yourself and show me everything and then," she snapped her fingers, "just like that, you close up."

"Sometimes it's better not knowing things."

"You can't say that to a reporter. It makes us all the more anxious to know what's going on."

"Ignorance is bliss, Darci."

"And knowledge is power. I won't force you to talk, but know when and if you're ready to unload, I'm here for you."

"You're here for me." Steed shook his head. "Considering the way we started, it's amazing we're together. What's even more amazing is I can't—I don't want to imagine my life without you in it. Darci, I—"

Darci closed her hand around his. Her heart rate increased tenfold. Was Steed about to say the words? The words she felt resided in her heart and grew bigger and stronger with every passing second. "You what?" she prompted.

His ringing cell phone broke the moment. He looked down at the glowing blue display. "It's the station. I need to get this." He excused himself to the back hallway.

Darci fell against the couch, feeling certain when Steed got back, his near confession would be a thing of the past.

"Yes, just put a copy on my desk and Malena's. Thanks, Jackson." Steed placed the phone in his pocket and checked his watch. Ten minutes. No more interruptions tonight and absolutely no thoughts of work—as hard as that might be. On his way to the living room, he spotted Darci in the kitchen.

He slipped his arms around her waist and settled his chin on her shoulder as she added chopped tomatoes and cucumbers to a wooden bowl of salad greens.

"Is everything okay at work?" she asked.

"Ground rules for tonight: let's not talk about work, unless it's yours." He smacked a kiss to her cheek and stole a cucumber slice from the bowl. "I saw your promo today. You looked incredible."

"I forgot they were scheduled to air today. It was weird shooting those spots." She continued to chop cucumbers. "It's been weeks since I accepted the job, but I'm still uncomfortable with this."

"You shouldn't be," he said, swiping another cucumber and popping it in his mouth.

"I can't help it. I stole Kenny's job."

"Warwick is dead, Darci. You didn't steal anything from him."

"It's not that simple for me."

"I know. I'm not making light of your feelings, it's just . . . I don't want you to beat yourself up. Warwick's death wasn't your fault."

She wiped her hands with a dry dishtowel. "Can we make an adjustment in your rules for tonight?"

"Sure."

"Let's not talk about work or Kenny, okay?"

Steed nodded. "Agreed."

Darci swatted his hand as he went for another cucumber. "The garlic bread is almost ready, so if you don't fill yourself stealing from my salad bowl, we'll eat in about five minutes." She placed the bowl in the refrigerator and removed a bottle of red wine. "I thought we could eat in here. Is that okay?"

She led them to the breakfast nook on the far side of the kitchen. A beautiful view of the starry night sky presented a perfect backdrop to the candlelit round table for two.

"This is really nice, Darci." Steed picked up the corkscrew and opened the wine. The setting was perfect—romantic and comfortable. As romantic and comfortable as the words about to fall from his lips before he got the call from Jackson. *I love you.* Smiling, Steed poured them both some wine. "A toast," he said, handing her a glass. "To us."

Darci clinked her glass to his. "To us."

—⁓—

Following the delicious dinner and two servings of Miss Sophie's peach cobbler, Steed shooed Darci to the living room to relax while he cleaned up the kitchen. Twenty minutes later he returned to the living room. Darci sat curled on her couch reading a booklet of some kind.

"What's got you so absorbed?" he asked.

"This," she said, picking up a square box from the floor. "Do you know anything about BlackBerries?"

"You're not talking about the fruit, are you?"

She laughed. "No."

"I know a little about a lot." He sat beside her and took possession of the do-it-all cell phone. "Warwick gave you this?"

"Yeah. He wanted to make sure he could reach me at all times to brag about his wonderful trip to Rio. He was going to stop in New York on his way to Brazil to teach me how to use it."

"Yes, my sweet Darci is electronically challenged." Steed pressed a few buttons on the keypad. "This is top of the line."

"That was Kenny. Nothing but the best for him. He had to make sure pictures of the country and details of his conquests could come through from thousands of miles away."

"He bragged about his women to you?"

"I was his best friend. To Kenny, I was like one of the guys, except I'm a girl. He told me everything." Sadness darkened her once-happy face. "He would have told me if . . . Nothing."

Steed set the BlackBerry on the table and brushed his finger against her cheek. His heart went out to her. She was trying so hard, but she was far from accepting Warwick's suicide. He feared she never would. And if she knew about this fingerprint thing . . . Living with unanswered questions had dogged him since his father's death. But he'd dealt with his pain alone, shutting out his mother and sister and being stoic, until Nana broke down his defenses.

Even after that, he kept people at a distance, never wanting to get too close. Feelings hurt, and he didn't want to hurt anymore. Grieving for his father had consumed most of the room in his heart, and he didn't want to make room for anything else. But Darci had found her way in. His wildest dream and worst nightmare rolled up into one beautiful, infuriating package. A package he loved with all his heart and wanted to take care of, to help with her pain—this seemingly unending pain.

Just how close was she to this guy?

The green-eyed monster that lived in him and twisted in his gut almost every time she mentioned Kenny's name demanded he get an answer to that question. "You two were just friends? Nothing more?"

Darci expelled a sharp breath and pulled back. Annoyance and glee prominent in her dark eyes. "No, we weren't *just* friends. We were *best* friends. We had a closeness that's rare between a man and a woman. And no, Steed, it did not include sex." She nudged her elbow in his side. "Happy now?"

Steed smiled. "Actually, yes, I am." He kissed her cheek. "I'll be honest with you, Darci, I was jealous."

"No!" she said in feigned, overly dramatic surprise.

"C'mon, Darci, you're so passionate when you talk about him, it's no question you love him. I couldn't help wondering how much you loved him."

"I loved him a lot, and I always will. And although I find it endearing, you have absolutely no reason to be jealous."

"That's nice of you to say, but I love you, Darci. And a guy can only take so much of his woman going on about another man, even if that man is dead, before he gets . . ."

Her midnight eyes lit up. A big smile turned her lips. "What did you say?"

Steed grunted. *What indeed?* He hadn't planned to say the words cloaked in a fit of jealousy, but they'd been said, and he couldn't say he was sorry she finally knew. "I said I love you. And I do. I love you very much." He brushed his finger against her nose. "Is that being wide-open enough for you?"

"Steed." Darci scooted onto his lap, eliciting an immediate flow of blood to that part of his body. "I love you, too." Her arms slinked around his neck and her soft lips settled on his and parted.

Steed's hands trailed the curves of her body and up to her breasts, filling his open palms with the warmth of her firm, full mounds. His thumbs flicked her hardened peeks through the thin material of her dress and bra. She moaned softly, shifting against his growing arousal. It was all he could do to keep from crying out loud. Steed tore his lips from hers. Passion and longing filled Darci's eyes as he unbuttoned his shirt and she lowered the straps to her dress and pushed it halfway down her body.

The contrast of her lacy white bra against her supple bronze flesh turned him on even more. His lips grazed the swell of her breasts as he loosened the hooks of her bra and dropped it to the floor. He pulled back, marveling at the cone-shaped mounds of flesh. "So beautiful," he murmured, leaning forward to tease and taste the distended dark tips. Darci's arms curled around his neck as she writhed against him, inciting his need for her all the more. Desperate to be one with her, Steed lowered her to the couch and reached for the button of his slacks.

"Steed, stop!" Darci shot up, placing her hands on his chest. "I'm sorry. I can't do this."

Steed glanced down at the intense knot in his pants. She couldn't be serious. "Why?" He pressed her shaky hand against him. Her breasts rose and fell from the pounding of her heart. Taut nipples puckered under his gaze, silently screaming for the attention of his lips. She wanted him. He could tell in her kiss and her every touch on his skin. Even her beautiful eyes said so. Her words said "I can't," but her eyes and actions said "I want to."

"Can't you feel how much I want you? How much I love you?"

Darci jerked her hand away and pulled up the straps of her dress. "I do, but I can't. I'm sorry." She scurried to the far end of the couch and tucked her feet under her bottom.

"What is it, Darci, is it not a . . . a good time?"

"No, it's not a good time, but it's not the reason you're thinking. It's not that time of the month."

Steed pulled on his shirt. "Then what is it?"

Darci wrapped her arms around her shoulders. "I, uh . . . I . . ."

Steed edged toward her, feeling her tense up the closer he got. Since they started seeing each other, things had never progressed beyond some hot kisses on the couch. He figured her grief played a part, but tonight was different. Things had progressed to more intimate touching and exposure of flesh from other than a few of his loosened shirt buttons. "Darci, what's wrong? You can tell me anything."

"I don't know about that."

"Try."

"Steed, I . . ." She released a breath.

"Just tell me. It can't be as bad as you think. I mean, what are you gonna say, you're really a man or you're a virgin or something?" He laughed.

She didn't laugh back. Steed's heart dropped. "My God, Darci, you're not a man, are you?"

"No, but I am a virgin," she confessed. "And I want to stay one until I'm married."

CHAPTER 11

I'm a virgin. Hearing that blew Steed away, but that other part. *I want to stay one until I'm married.* Sterling High wasn't a Catholic school, was it?

"Are you going to say something, Steed?"

"What do you want me to say?"

"Whatever you're feeling," she said.

Steed walked over to the fireplace. He fingered the pictures on the mantle. Darci and her parents. They would definitely be proud, if not shocked, to learn she hadn't . . . He turned to her. "You're a virgin?"

"Yes, I'm a virgin."

"Darci, you're gorgeous."

"What are you saying? Only ugly women can be virgins?"

"No, it's just . . . You're thirty-two."

"Only preteens can be virgins?"

"But you're on television."

"Oh, so only nuns can be virgins? We've covered looks, age, and career, is there anything left?"

"I'm just surprised. I would have never guessed in a million years you would say what you said." He raked his fingers through his hair, exhaling deeply. "You're a virgin."

"How many times are you going to say that?"

"I don't know. Until it sinks in."

"Does it change things?"

He nodded. "Yeah, Darci, it does."

"I thought so." She left the couch and pulled open the front door. "There are no hard feelings."

"Darci, close the door."

"You just said . . ."

"I know what I said, just let me finish saying it."

She closed the door and returned to the couch. Steed drank in her beauty as the soft lamplight bathed her face in a halo-like glow. She was more of an angel than he'd known.

"Steed, you're staring."

"Yes, I am." He smiled. "I didn't think you could dazzle me any more than you already had, but, lady, you are full of surprises. You're already an impressive woman, but to hear you're saving yourself—that's incredible. There aren't a lot of women like you in the world."

"You make me sound like I'm perfect or something."

He grunted. "Let's not get carried away. I think an awful lot of you, Darci, but you're not close to perfect. Even though I think you're pretty perfect for me."

"Then you're okay with this?"

He clicked his tongue. "How can I answer that?"

"I don't know. Yes or no?"

"It's not a yes or no answer."

"Sure it is."

"Maybe for you, but not for me. Your mind is made up on this situation, and you've been living with it for thirty-two years. You might waver a bit, like you did tonight, but in the end you're going to stick to your guns. As okay as I am with this tonight, I can't say how okay I'll be if it got this intense again. Do you get my drift?"

"You're not okay with this, are you?"

"Darci, I'm totally okay with you being a virgin. I'm shocked, but I'm okay with it. It's getting used to what it means for me that's the tricky part."

"Are you sorry I told you?"

"I don't know." Steed drew a deep breath. He'd never had any significant relationships, just sexual ones. Sex defined the interest he'd had in the women he dated. But Darci wasn't like the other women he'd dated. He loved her, and she was the only virgin he'd ever encountered. This made things very different. "I don't know where we go from here," he said.

"I don't understand what you mean."

"Before, I didn't know about your—your status, but now that I do, I don't want you to be uncomfortable. I can't lie, Darci, I want you, but wanting you is like wanting a key to Fort Knox. I can't have it."

"Steed, it doesn't have to be like that. I do love you, and things—things could change."

"I would never want to put you in the position of going against yourself."

"You wouldn't, and you haven't. I've never gone as far we had tonight, but I've never felt the desire to before now. I thought you should know about me, but I don't want it to change anything between us. In New York, I didn't get to church as often as I do now that I'm back home, but growing up it was a Sunday ritual. The concept of waiting became ingrained in me. Back in high school, I saw how lightly most of the girls and guys, especially Kenny, took sex. But I didn't. I couldn't. I have one virginity to lose. It's a precious gift. And the only way I could ensure I would have no regrets would be to wait. So I've waited."

"I think it's admirable."

"Admirable?" Her face scrunched. "Look, I don't have any preconceived notions, Steed. I didn't tell you this to pressure you. I—"

He pressed his finger to her lips. "Shhh. I don't feel pressure, and you shouldn't feel any, either. We're adults and we love each other. Neither one of us is going to do anything we don't want to do, okay?"

Darci kissed his lips and snuggled into his arms. "Okay."

The ringing telephone roused Darci from her sound sleep. Her eyes still closed, she fumbled for the annoying contraption. "Hello," she grumbled, her voice weighted with sleep.

"Have you been to the house yet?"

Eva's voice woke her completely. Darci shot up and looked at her alarm clock. Eight-twenty. The alarm wouldn't go off for ten minutes. The fact she'd lost valuable sleep time to this nuisance of a woman made her crabbier than she already felt. "What do you want, Eva?"

"My ring. I told you about this a week ago. What's the holdup?"

"I have things to do, and your problems aren't foremost on my list."

"Look, you said you'd get the ring. Get it." The sound of a dial tone ended the conversation. Darci replaced the phone and leaned against the headboard. She didn't have a lot planned for today, so going to Kenny's and searching his bedroom for this mysterious ring could be done. But going to Kenny's . . .

Darci switched off the alarm before it sounded and reclined against the headboard. She hadn't been in Kenny's house since before he—before he died. *Died.* Over two months later and she still grappled with that. Steed didn't talk about it, but she knew he worried about her. Maybe going to the house would help. Kenny was gone, and even with her doubts of how he died, he wasn't coming back. That was the hardest thing of all to accept. How in the world would she be able to go into his house? Her house.

The phone rang again. Darci checked the caller ID and smiled as she answered. "Hello, Detective."

"Good morning, Peaches." Steed laughed.

"Hey!" she playfully chided.

"Just kidding, Darci. I didn't wake you, did I?"

"No, Eva beat you by about five minutes."

"Eva?"

"Yes. She thinks she left something at Kenny's, so it looks like I'll be taking a trip there today. I don't trust her going in alone." Darci sighed. She didn't trust Eva at all. Funny how she'd never mentioned this ring until the call last week. If Eva had anything of value in Kenny's house, she would have demanded access to it long before now. What did that woman have up her sleeve?

"You okay going there by yourself?" Steed asked.

"Honestly, no, I'm not. I feel strange just thinking about it, when I know Kenny won't be there."

"Want me to come with you?"

"Would you?"

"Sure. When do you want to go?"

"When are you free?"

Darci heard paper rattling as Steed groaned. "The way my desk looks it may be never, but how about lunchtime? Noon?"

"That's fine for me, but only if you're sure."

"I'm sure."

"Okay, I'll see you at noon. And I'll grab you a sandwich on the way."

"You don't have to do that."

"I want to. This really means a lot to me, and since I'm taking your lunch break, the least I can do is bring you some lunch. I'll see you later. And no more of that Peaches thing."

"Yes, ma'am." He chucked. "Bye."

———❧———

Steed hung up the phone. Hearing Darci's voice was the lift he needed, and now it was back to work. He returned his full attention to the Warwick file and those Hyde fingerprints.

"Have any news for me, McGraw?" Rogers said, entering the office and settling into the empty chair at the desk.

"I'm still looking into it, sir."

"How is it Hyde's prints weren't discovered before?"

"I don't have a clue." Steed held up his finger and beeped Jackson at the front desk. "Get in here," he said.

"Why are you calling in Jackson?" Rogers asked.

"Retracing steps."

Moments later the young officer stepped in. "What can I do for you, Detective?"

"A while back, I asked you to take the gun from the Warwick case to the lab for retesting. Do you remember that?"

"Yes, sir. I gave you the results back in September. I actually remember the day because it was . . ." The young man paused. His cheeks reddened.

Rogers sat up. "It was what, Jackson?" he asked.

The officer cleared his throat. He glanced at Steed before turning his gaze to his feet. "It was the day I came in and Ms. Clarke was with the detective," he explained.

Steed pressed his fingers to his lips, remembering the day in question. He never did look at that file, as he'd managed to convince Darci of the facts without having to do so. How could fingerprints change? "Thank you, Jackson, that'll be all."

Rogers's eyes stayed on Jackson until he left the office. He slowly turned around. Steed swallowed audibly, feeling a cross-examination coming. "You want to explain that?"

"Nothing to explain, sir. I remember the file."

"So, you knew there were other fingerprints on the gun."

"I didn't say that."

"You're not saying much of anything, McGraw, and it's been a week." Rogers leaned forward. Irritation darkened his eyes, and his lips thinned with annoyance. "I want to know what the hell that was about just now, and I want to know now!"

"I had the prints checked during the course of my investigation, and when Darci showed up making a big stink, I had new prints pulled and run as an appeasement measure." Steed drew a breath. "Hyde's prints showed up the second time."

"How is that possible?"

"I don't know. A lab screwup I suspect."

"And since we returned the gun to Warwick's family, we can't pull new prints to check which were right."

"We know which ones were right. Warwick's death was a suicide. That is a fact."

"No, McGraw, it's a mess!" Rogers slammed his open palm onto the desk. "You clean it up. The mayor is breathing down my neck over this!"

Steed grunted. "Benjamin is ticked because I'm involved with Darci."

"What was that?"

"The mayor is angry because I'm seeing Darci. He can't stand it. He saw us out to dinner a few days ago, and if looks could kill, Malena would not only be your newest detective, she'd be your only one."

Rogers sat back in his chair. "That's ridiculous. Jacob Benjamin is a happily married man."

"He may be happily married, but he's not happy with the fact Darci and I are a couple."

"Is that what you and Darci are? A couple?"

"Yes."

"You haven't mentioned this new set of prints to her?"

"What would mentioning this to her accomplish? It won't bring Warwick back to life. She has enough to deal with finalizing his estate." Steed opened the file and pushed it to Rogers. "You see these pictures? With a little time I can explain away those fingerprints, but these pictures, powder residue, and wound patterns can't be explained away. That is Kenneth Warwick, and he's dead via a self-inflicted gunshot wound. That's what I know. And I'm not going to tell Darci about some prints that will further incite the feelings of foul play she already has. I'm not doing it."

Rogers stood. "I won't tell you how to handle your relationship, just handle this case, and do it soon."

―⤳⤳―

Kenny watched Eva as he finished the last of a hundred sit-ups. She seemed engrossed in the goings-on of some ridiculous talk show where the guests were fighting like a bunch of crazed gamecocks. From what he'd gathered, the topic was sibling betrayal. Humph! Eva didn't have to watch a program to get that. Thanks to her, they were living that particular subject, and it felt like he'd been living it forever.

The block prison he spent his every hour was so tiny, he had to fold the cot to have room enough on the floor to work out. If he didn't work out, fat Kenny from grade school would make an adult appearance due to the greasy takeout Fritz brought him every day. Had that man never heard of Subway?

Kenny grabbed a hand towel off the toilet/sink combo and dried the sweat trailing down his chest. Damn that Eva. He had to get out of here. He needed a hot shower, a manicure and massage, and he needed to get laid. He had so much stress. Kenny leapt off the bare floor and wrapped his hands around the bars, tugging on the door. It didn't budge. It never did.

Eva turned away from the television. "You really should stop trying to escape. You are not Harry Houdini. Besides, if Fritz thought for one second you could get free, he wouldn't leave me alone with you."

"How could you go along with this?"

"It's not personal, Kenny. I needed money."

"Do you know how foolish this is? Keeping me here and having Mom and Dad think I'm dead. My God! How can you even look at them after what you've done to me?"

A glimmer of guilt flickered in Eva's eyes. She dropped her head for a moment, and when she looked up the glimmer was nowhere to be found. "This isn't my fault, Kenny. I asked you for money, but you wouldn't give it to me. I didn't make that guy shoot himself, and I didn't come up with this plan, but I think it's a good plan."

"How can you say that with a straight face?"

"Because I believe it."

Eva turned back to the television. Kenny continued to watch her. Something was different. She wasn't fidgety, and though her thinking was muddled, she spoke clearly and rationally in a warped sorta way. She didn't seem high, at least not in her usual way. "What did you take?" he asked.

"Take?" She looked over her shoulder at him, laughing. "I didn't take anything. Fritz made me his special breakfast drink. It calms me down and keeps me sharp and focused."

"Sharp and focused?" Sounded like a downer to him. But she seemed jittery sometimes, too. Not her usual high. "Where did you meet Fritz?"

"On the highway." Eva turned to Kenny. "I was driving after a couple of drinks and he pulled me over. I didn't want trouble, and he didn't want to make any for me, so we worked out a deal." She smacked her lips and smiled. "We've been inseparable since."

Kenny's stomach turned. "I suspect his appeal lies in those power drinks he gives you," he said. "Don't you want better? This man is killing you."

"Fritz isn't killing anyone. He cares about me. He doesn't judge me."

"No, Eva, he uses you." Kenny's gaze darted about the tiny room. "Look around. You spend hours in this dump every day. We must be in the middle of nowhere, because that damn generator outside could wake the dead, yet not a soul has come around."

"That's the plan, Kenny. No electricity, no meter reading, no guests. Just lots of privacy."

"Don't you want more? Don't you think you deserve more?"

"I have more now, and I'll have even more when I get my money. Besides, Fritz takes great care of me. I don't live here, I come to visit you. You're my brother, Kenny. I'm not heartless."

"What?" Kenny shrieked.

"I'm not. I do care about you. You eat three times a day. I brought you clothes, and toiletries. You have a TV."

Kenny glanced at his gray sweatpants, one of five colors with T-shirts and socks Eva had purchased for him. "Gee, thanks," he quipped.

Eva frowned. "Don't get fresh. None of this would have happened if you had given me the money when I'd asked for it. I only wanted a couple of thousand. You have millions."

"You're not my responsibility, Eva."

"You're my brother."

"The brother you have locked away! I don't owe you anything. You're a grown woman who needs to take care of herself. But what do you do? Latch on to someone, anyone, who can make you believe he's the answer to your prayers."

"This is different. Fritz loves me."

"How can he love you when you don't love yourself? You're in a world of trouble and it's going to get worse if you don't stop this now. Let me go, Eva. I can protect you. I won't mention you to the authorities. All you have to do is let me go and get some help."

"Shut up!" Eva clicked off the television and tossed the remote to the wobbly table in the center of the room. "I don't need any help, I need money. And as soon as Darci goes to the house and finds the letter, I'll get it."

"And then you'll live happily ever after? Have the drugs destroyed your conscience, too? You won't be able to sleep nights knowing what you're doing to me and our parents."

"I sleep like a baby every night. I can keep doing it."

"With the help of Fritz and his power drinks," he said. "Tell me, Eva, what are you going to do when the money dries up and Fritz's eyes starts roving?"

"Fritz isn't going to leave me. He loves me."

"Just like your two ex-husbands and the other string of losers you've been involved with? C'mon, he's no different. In fact, he's worse. You're up to your neck in legal problems."

"Shut up!" Eva's face reddened. She stalked menacingly to the barred door. "I'm sick of hearing you talk. If you say another word, your good friend Darci is going to pay the price. You understand me?"

The unfeeling stare in Eva's eyes scared him. She was capable of anything, and he couldn't risk Darci's life. Shaking his head in dismay, Kenny continued his workout in total silence.

CHAPTER 12

"Hiya, Malena," Darci said as she passed the detective leaving the station.

"Hey, Darci," Malena said with a smile. "What's going on?"

She lifted the plastic bag she carried. "Lunch with Steed."

"I was just on my way to Sophie's to meet my honey, too."

"Tell Trey I said hello. You two will have to join Steed and me for dinner sometime. I'll invite Jackie and Carl, too. We'll make it a party."

"Sounds good. Trey and I have been meaning to catch up with Jackie and Carl again, and although I'm with Steed a lot, I never get to be with the both of you. Being back in Sterling is a great change of pace from Chicago, but I've been so busy, I've hardly had time for fun. So, I'll be in touch."

"Great. I'll look forward to hearing from you." Darci waved good-bye and made her way inside.

"Hello, Ms. Clarke," Jackson said with a smile.

Darci returned his smile. "Hello, Lucas. How are you?"

"I'm good, ma'am, thank you. You can go right on in, the detective is expecting you."

Darci gave his hand a cordial pat. A warm pink colored his cheeks. She bit back a chuckle. This young man was way too polite and gentle to be a big, bad cop. She loved Steed to pieces, but the more time Jackson spent around him, the more Steed's tough-as-nails traits would rub off. That poor kid would never be the same. Maybe with Malena on board things would even out for him.

Darci reached into the plastic bag and handed Jackson one of the three subs. "This is for you. Turkey breast and ham. In case he keeps you too busy to take a break," she said, nudging her head to Steed's door.

"Thank you, ma'am. I really appreciate this."

"You're welcome, and, please, stop with this ma'am thing. You can call me Darci," she said, handing over condiment packets.

He shook his head. "Oh, no, ma'am, I couldn't do that."

She tapped her hand on the desk and made a half-hearted attempt at being stern. "I insist, Lucas."

"Yes, ma' . . . Ms. Darci."

Darci laughed. "I guess that's close enough. I'll let you get back to work." She knocked on Steed's door and stuck her head in.

Steed's eyes lit up. He waved her in as he held the phone to his ear. "Almost done," he mouthed, motioning for her to take a seat. "Yes, that's Hyde. H-Y-D-E. Send me whatever you have. You have my fax number." He nodded. "Thank you. Yes, I'll be in touch if I need anything else." He hung up and gave her a big smile. "Hi."

She leaned over the desk and gave him a little kiss. "Back at you." The folders and papers littering his desk rattled under the weight of her hand. She backed up to the chair and sat. "You know, if you're busy, we can do this another time."

"I'm never too busy for you," he said, gathering up the files.

A loose page slid to the floor.

"I'll get it," she said, reaching for the facedown sheet.

"It's okay, Darci, I can . . ." He took the page from her hand. "I have it, thanks."

"Sure," she said, a bit perplexed by his odd reaction. Her reporter's mind made her curious to know what was on that paper. "This must be a big case?"

Steed shoved the page into the folder and shut it in his top desk drawer. "Yeah, it's keeping me on my toes." He pointed at the plastic bag. "Is that lunch?"

"Uh-huh," she answered, taking the hint. "Ham and cheese just the way you like it."

"Extra pickles?"

"Of course." She extended his sandwich and a bottle of water. "We can eat first. There's no rush."

"Are you sure there's no rush or is it just you putting off going over there?"

"Maybe a little of both." She shared the napkins and packets of mayonnaise, mustard, and vinegar left in the bag. "It's going to be strange walking into Kenny's house after everything and knowing he won't be there." Darci unwrapped her turkey sandwich and started eating.

"You still do it," Steed said, tearing off a corner of the mayonnaise packet with his teeth, adding a thick line of the condiment to the six-inch sandwich, and taking a big bite.

"Do what?"

Steed finished chewing and said, "Avoid saying how Warwick died. You at least manage to say death, died, or dying when you mention him, but you won't say suicide or killed himself." He continued eating.

"What does it matter?"

"It matters because you're going into his house today. It's where your best friend took his life."

"You don't have to keep saying that," she said between bites of sandwich.

"I think I do. It's been months, Darci, but you still don't believe he killed himself, do you?"

Darci stopped eating. She drank some water and wiped her mouth. Steed wouldn't like her answer, but she knew it wouldn't come as too much of a surprise. "No," she said. "This is not about you or how you handled the case. It's me. This is my problem."

"Your problems are my problems. Have you thought about counseling?"

"Counseling? You back to thinking I'm crazy?"

"You know better than that." Steed closed his hands around hers. "I don't think you're crazy at all, just grief-stricken. You're functioning in your daily life, but you won't put this in its proper place, and you need to do that."

"I know you're worried about me, but there's no need. Yes, I'm having a little trouble getting this to sink in. In my head, I accept what you said about Kenny as true, but my heart is still playing catch-up. In time, my head and heart will find a happy medium."

"I didn't mean to sound pushy." Steed opened his bottle of water and downed half. "I know it takes a while to deal with losing someone you love." He pulled a cluster of pickle chips from the sandwich and popped one in his mouth.

"Your father?"

He nodded.

"Tell me more about him," she said.

"What do you want to know?" Steed ate more of the pickles.

"I don't know. Was he a pickle and cucumber fiend, too?"

Steed laughed. "Yes," he answered with a nod. "Dad was my hero. A good man, and a great cop. I still miss him."

"You said he was killed in the line of duty."

"A domestic call gone wrong. He was my age when he died." He grunted. "I actually thought thirty-six was old back then."

Sadness crept into Steed's eyes, glazing his blue orbs with unshed tears. Darci's heart broke for him. After almost twenty-five years, it was still hard for him to talk about his father and how his father died. She took Steed's hand. "Let's talk about something else," she said. "What are your Thanksgiving plans?"

"I was planning to spend it with you," he said, polishing up the last of his sandwich, and wiping his mouth.

"You were?"

"Why do you sound surprised?"

"Because you didn't say anything."

"You don't want to share Thanksgiving with me?"

"Steed, I want to share everything with you."

A wolfish grin brightened his face. *"Everything?"* he said, rising from his chair.

"Everything." She leaned over the desk, meeting his lips in a deep, full kiss.

Steed's tongue invaded her mouth, taking possession of hers. She leaned further over the desk as he clasped one side of her face, keeping their mouths together. Deep moans rumbled in her throat as Steed's drugging cologne and sensual kiss transported her to a fog-filled land of need, want, and longing.

Just as she felt herself succumbing to the aura of this new and enjoyable place, Steed broke away. "I'm sorry," he said, licking his slightly swollen, red-stained lips.

"For kissing me?" Darci moved around the desk and curled her arms around his neck. "I like when you kiss me. I especially liked that one." She brushed her lips against his.

He groaned softly and backed away. "Darci . . ."

"What's wrong?"

"I shouldn't be kissing you like that."

"Why not?"

"You know why not."

Darci frowned. This was what she got for telling him she was a virgin. "Steed, you never have to apologize for kissing me. We're in a relationship and already agreed that nothing will happen we both don't want to happen.

I don't want you handling me with kid gloves because you know I'm a virgin. I'm the same woman I was before you found that out last week."

"Not exactly." Steed smiled. "But I understand," he said with a kiss. "I promise to never apologize for kissing you, but I do think now is a good time to leave. We need to get to Warwick's, and there are a few things I need to take care of when I get back here." He grabbed his jacket from the back of his chair and held out his hand. "Let's go."

Darci returned to her chair. Second thoughts made her feet feel like cement blocks. "Maybe we should do this another time," she said, cleaning up from their lunch.

"You can't keep running from this."

"I'm not running."

"No?" He sat on the edge the desk and took her hand. "What are you doing?"

"I'm giving you time to work on this case that's got you so tied up." She dropped the gathered items in the nearby waste can. "You said you have things to take care of, and I can see you're pretty busy. Going to Kenny's can wait."

"You sure you want to do that? Weren't you going to find something for his sister?"

"A ring."

"If you don't get this ring for her soon, she's going to be calling you and riding you until you do. I know she's not one of your favorite people."

Darci groaned. "That woman makes me crazy."

"You said she has a history of substance abuse. And if she's using again and needs this ring to get a fix, she won't leave you alone. It might be in your best interest to do this now. And not just to get Eva off your back. I think you need to do this for you." He squeezed her hand. "I'll be with you the whole time."

"Thank you, Steed." She kissed his hand. "I wouldn't be able to do this without you."

"Yeah, you would, but you won't have to. And that goes for everything you do." He helped her out of the chair and handed over her purse. "Let's go."

CHAPTER 13

Steed blew against his clasped hands and shifted from one foot to the next in the fifty-degree weather, waiting for Darci to get the nerve to leave Warwick's porch and walk into the house. She pressed her hand against the door. Unshed tears pooled her eyes. Steed wrapped his arm around her shoulders. "Are you all right?"

"I don't know," Darci answered. "Inside is . . ." She stepped away from the door. "I don't think I can do this."

"Hey." Following behind, Steed squeezed her shoulders and kissed the back of her head. Her tense muscles relaxed. "Listen to me. I know this is hard, but you need to do this. You need to face your demons."

Darci turned around. Her frown surprised him. "Face my demons?" She pushed away the wisps of dark hair the wind thrashed against her face. "That's coming from you? Steed, your father has been dead over two decades and you still have a hard time talking about him."

"That's different."

"Yes, it's different, because it's you. It's your pain. This is my pain," she said, patting her hand to her chest.

"And you'll always have your pain if you keep avoiding this." He held out his hand, refusing to turn the conversation on to his shortcomings. "Let me have the key."

Darci slid her hand into the pocket of her mini leather jacket and pressed a single key into his open palm.

"It's going to be okay." Steed opened the door and stepped aside. "Come on in."

Darci released a breath and stepped over the threshold. Her gaze darted about the room. "Oh, my." Smiling, she approached the fireplace mantle and pressed a silver-framed picture to her chest.

Steed joined her. "What is that?" he asked.

She showed him the picture. "Kenny's twenty-fifth birthday. He did everything big, and this party was no exception."

Steed couldn't argue with those words. He looked about the expansive house. Cathedral ceilings and hardwood floors ensconced in two stories of a 3,000-square-foot house. It was impressive. Like a weekend cabin compared to the mansion his mother and stepfather lived in, but very nice all the same.

"It seems Warwick liked to go all-out. I guess when you win millions in the lotto you can do that."

"Kenny could be a bit frivolous at times, but he was generous with his money, and he was extremely smart when it came to investing. As charitable as he was, he wasn't foolish, which is why he only told me about winning the lottery. He wasn't about to paint a target on . . . a target on his back."

Sensing Darci steps away from slipping into "Kenny was murdered" mode, Steed redirected the tone of the conversation. "So, Warwick kept working after winning millions?"

She nodded. "After taxes, he had about half the winnings, but Kenny loved his work, and more money meant more investing. Besides, he enjoyed the adulation of the scores of women who threw themselves at him for being the hot guy on the news."

Steed listened to her talk and wondered how she and Warwick could have been so close. A womanizer and a virgin. "I can't believe you and he were best friends. Two people couldn't be more different."

"Kenny and I weren't that different, at least not fundamentally. We both loved our families, reporting the news, and each other. We understood each other and didn't judge. I guess on the outside looking in, the two of us would make an unlikely pair of best friends, but it worked. I was the yin to his yang. There was nothing I couldn't tell him, and he me. That's why this . . . I'm sorry, Steed, but this just doesn't make sense. He wouldn't have killed himself."

Steed pinched the bridge of his nose and groaned. How much longer would this go on? "Darci, you said you were going to let this go."

"I tried. I am trying, but I'm not there yet." She walked over to the couch. "This is where it happened?"

Steed nodded. The overstuffed leather couch looked as good as new. "Yes, right here," he said, touching the center of the sofa.

"Kenny's couch. You should have heard how he talked about this couch. Handcrafted with the finest Italian leather." She shook her head. "There's so much wrong with this."

"You're doing it again."

"And what is that?"

"You're looking for any and everything you can to make this suicide some murder conspiracy."

Darci shook her head. Defiance burned in her eyes like an eternal flame, strong, intense, and unwavering, but he was feeling just as strong. "No," she said defensively.

"Yes." Steed cupped her face, forcing their eyes to meet. "Darci, you have to listen to me. There is no conspiracy. You can cook up as many theories as you want, but it won't change the facts. Warwick killed himself, and you may never know why." Steed sighed. "Darci, you always ask about my father."

She folded her arms across her chest and met him with a pointed stare. "Yes, and you never say much."

"Well, I want to say more now." Steed drew a deep breath and sat. He'd never talked openly to anyone about his father's death. It was too painful for him. But his love for Darci and his need to help demanded he talk to her. "Dad had what he called intuition, his gut feeling about people. In the months before he was killed, he'd mentioned this couple who owned a little store that were always at each other's throats about their son. Dad often talked about going in to buy a pop and having to break up a verbal battle. Even with the arguing he saw, Dad had insisted the pair loved each other and they weren't the least bit violent, just a little excitable."

"Excitable?" Darci joined him and took his hand in hers. The warmth of her touch had the most amazing effect on him, and for the first time while thinking of his dad's death, Steed didn't feel like he was about to cry.

Steed chuckled. "Yeah, that was Dad."

"What happened with your father and the couple?"

"On a particularly hot afternoon, with Uncle Pete waiting out in the cruiser, Dad walked into the store to buy some ice cream. The couple was arguing again, but this time the man had a gun. Dad ended the argument, but he also ended up dead."

"What happened to the man?"

"He died from a brain aneurism about a year into his prison sentence. He was charged with involuntary manslaughter. It was called an accidental shooting, but it didn't change anything for me. My last memory of my father is of his perfect instinct getting him killed. I never thought that could happen. My Dad couldn't be that wrong about someone. But he was. And it left me without him. I still miss him." He grunted. "Mom moved on."

"Uh-huh. That explains your resentment of your stepfather."

"I'm not . . ."

"Yes, Steed, you are. You rarely say his name. You mostly call him your mother's husband."

"That's what he is."

"You're too hard on him. You admit he's a good man."

"His being a good man is one thing, his trying to be my father is something altogether different."

"But you were close to your father's partner, Pete Mulhaney, a man you call uncle. You still swear by the man."

"Pete was a cop, and he was there for me. He didn't try to take Dad's place. He helped me grow up to be a good man and a good cop." Steed expelled a sharp breath. "Wait a second, this is not about me."

"Okay, okay. I just find it puzzling you could love Josh's mother so much but barely be civil to him. That said, I'm glad you talked about what happened with your father, Steed. It explains a lot. But when all is said and done, it has nothing to do with my situation with Kenny."

"Ugh!" Steed shot up, pacing. "It has everything to do with it, Darci."

"No."

"Yes!" He stopped moving and turned to her. "I wish your gut feelings could make this a lie, but it can't. That's what I want you to see." He resumed pacing. "Sometimes the people we love do things we don't understand. Warwick is dead because he killed himself, just like my father is dead because he followed some instinct that was wrong. My father trusted a damn instinct and it got him killed." Steed's face grew hot. His heart raced and steps quickened. "Gut feelings, instincts, they don't mean a damn thing! A wrong instinct killed my father, and I'm angry about it. I'm angry at him for dying. I am so angry at him." Hot tears slid down Steed's cheeks. He swiped them away, sniffling, but never missed a step. "Instincts don't mean a thing. Not a damn thing."

Darci caught his arm when he passed, ending his pacing. She pulled him down beside her. Her fingers twined with his. "Feels good to get things off your chest, huh?" she said.

"I hope I didn't scare you. I don't know where that came from."

"I suspect it came from a twelve-year-old boy you locked away when you lost your father. And you didn't scare me." She kissed the back of his hand. "You've been carrying this anger around for a lot of years. It was time to let it go."

"I knew I was angry about Dad dying, the whole situation of why. But, I loved him. I didn't know I was angry at him."

"I think maybe subconsciously you did. If your father hadn't gone into the store, he wouldn't have met the people. If he hadn't met them and deduced they were good, he wouldn't have come back. If he hadn't come back, he wouldn't be dead. Is that about right?"

Steed stared at her in amazement. "Pretty close," he said. "How did you know all that?"

"I heard what you said today and what you hadn't said before. I'm a reporter and an interviewer. It's my job to listen, especially when I care so much about the person doing the talking." Darci's fingertips combed through the hair at his temple, her touch calming him all the more. "How do you feel?"

"Lighter." Steed exhaled a deep breath. "I feel lighter."

"Unloading a lot of anger will do that."

"I want you to unload your burdens, too, Darci."

She rolled her eyes. "You just couldn't have your moment."

"I'm okay, Darci. I'm more okay than I've been in a long time, but I'm worried about you. You need to get away from this 'Kenny wouldn't kill himself' thing. It's unreasonable."

Darci's loud, drawn-out sigh broke the lingering silence that followed his words. "I'm going to Kenny's room to look for this ring." She left the couch and walked toward the staircase. "Are you coming?"

Steed stood. Maybe he could give talking some sense to her another try upstairs. "Yeah, I'm coming."

"I think Eva must have been high when she called me. There's no ring here." Darci closed the last of the drawers of Kenny's cherry wood armoire. "You have any luck?"

"Nope," Steed answered. "I have one drawer left to check." He rummaged inside. "Socks, handkerchiefs, a box of cufflinks." He pulled out an envelope. "This has your name on it."

"What?" Darci made her way over.

Steed passed her the envelope. "It was tucked in a corner."

Darci sat at the foot of the bed and examined the front and back of the envelope. "It's Kenny's handwriting." She ripped open the envelope and found a two-page letter. She silently read the words. After reading it once, she read it again.

"What does it say?"

"In a nutshell, it's negating everything Kenny said in the letter he left with his will." She dropped the letter on Steed's lap and walked to the window overlooking the fishpond in back of the manicured grounds. "Something's not right about it."

"Seems legit to me."

"I don't know." She returned to the bed and took the letter. "Why is it here?"

"This is where he wrote it."

"That's fine, but why didn't Mr. Clayton have it? C'mon, Steed, you're the detective here. Help me out."

"What do you want me to say?"

Darci rolled her eyes. Times like this she really wanted to shake him. "I think Eva planted this letter."

"You said it's Warwick's handwriting."

"Yes, but she could have forged it. This is about his money. A letter reversing another letter that essentially cut Eva out of his will if she didn't go to rehab. Way too convenient I'd find it now, don't you think?"

"I guess it's rather fortuitous for Eva, but there's nothing you can do. You have to give this letter to Mr. Clayton."

"No, I don't. I have to think about this."

"Darci?"

"I'm serious. Eva planted that letter. If Kenny was going to give it to Mr. Clayton to pass on to me, it would be on his dresser or coffee table so he wouldn't forget it. Not inside a drawer."

"It's his sock drawer. He would find the letter in there."

"Ugh! Stop being a cop for a minute and be my boyfriend. See things my way for a change!"

"I see a lot of things your way, you're just wrong when it comes to Warwick. You don't like his sister, so you're going to think the worst of her regardless."

"With good reason. Eva is bad news, and Kenny was too good to her."

"She's his sister."

"Sometimes tough love is the best love."

"That's what I'm trying to give you, but you get angry and accuse me of not being on your side." He draped his arm around her shoulders, and brought her close to him. As much as she enjoyed Steed's affection, she was in no mood to receive it right now. She wriggled from his arms. Steed sighed. "I love you, Darci. I want you to move on from this."

"This letter is different."

"It's not different."

"Yes, it . . ." She released a drawn out breath. "Steed, let's drop this. I'm taking this letter with me, and I'll *consider* giving it to Mr. Clayton. That's the best I can do."

"It's your decision," he said, the unmistakable edge to his voice saying "suit yourself." "Are you ready to go?"

"More than." She stuffed the letter in her purse and walked out the door.

———∽∾∽———

Silence hung between them on the drive back to the station. Steed pulled into his parking spot and kept his gaze straight ahead. "I don't like this," he said.

"What?" Darci replied tersely.

Steed turned to her. "You know very well what. You're right next to me and you feel a million miles away."

"I have a lot on my mind. Things you don't want to hear about." She cut her eyes.

"I honestly thought going to Warwick's would help you."

"It did help me, but not the way you wanted. Talking about Kenny is something we can't do, because, inevitably, it leads us to this place. I don't want tension between us."

"Neither do I, but how can we not talk about your best friend? What kind of relationship can we have if we put limits on ourselves? Don't mention this, don't do that. That's not what I want."

"Is that a virgin dig?"

Steed closed his eyes for a long moment. *Don't get angry, Steed. Don't get angry.* "No, it's not," he said, "but if you thought so, you have more issues than I imagined."

159

Steed regretted those words the moment they passed his lips. He blew out a long breath. "I'm sorry. I shouldn't have said that."

Darci sighed. "No, I'm sorry. I shouldn't have implied it." She took his hand. "I know where you stand on that. It's just . . . I'm a little overwhelmed about this situation with Kenny, and I don't want to fight with you."

"And not agreeing with you will cause us to fight? Being an only child has spoiled you. Having your way is not a rule."

Darci dropped his hand. "I'm apologizing, and you call me a spoiled brat."

"I didn't."

"You may have the gold shield, but I'm not stupid!"

"No, just single-minded and hardheaded!"

Huffing, Darci crossed her arms and looked straight ahead.

Steed turned her chin, forcing their eyes to meet. "When it comes to Warwick, you're like a dog with a bone, Darci. You know what's right, but you just won't let this go. Do you know how hard it is for me to see you like this? Do you care?"

"Of course I care. I'm trying, Steed. I know what the facts say, I get that, but I can't dismiss what I feel is right in my heart to appease you."

"You're not appeasing me, Darci. The evidence tells me Warwick killed himself, not my personal opinion."

"That's just it! You see everything through the glare of that damn shield of yours. It becomes personal."

"It's personal because I love you. I want you to move on from this notion you can never prove."

"Let's not do this again. I have to deal with this my way."

"Fine, Darci. Whatever." He reached for the door handle.

Darci touched his shoulder. "Don't leave angry, okay? This doesn't have to come between us, and it won't if we don't let it."

"I want to believe that, Darci, but for you to believe what you do means . . ."

"Means things are the way they've always been. Steed, you're the best thing to happen to me since I came back to Sterling. Maybe since ever. And as much as you drive me crazy, and you do, I love you, and I don't want to lose you."

"I don't want to lose you, either." Steed reached over the gearshift and gathered her in his arms, inhaling her sweet scent, enjoying the warmth of her body. "I love you so much." His mouth found her, seizing it in a slow, deep, and thorough kiss that Darci returned with equal fervor. They were definitely in this thing together, even if it didn't always seem that way.

Darci brushed her finger against his lips. "Are we okay?"

"We're fine." Steed didn't know how fine she was, but he wouldn't push the Warwick issue, just as he wouldn't mention the print mix-up which would only feed her irrational thoughts. He escorted Darci to her car. "We still on for dinner?"

"Uh-huh. Your place at six."

"See you then." He kissed her good-bye and walked into the station.

"Detective." Jackson removed the phone from his ear and approached Steed. "I've been trying to reach you."

"My cell died. What's going on?"

"The chief wants you in his office. There's a woman waiting to talk to you in regard to Jason Hyde."

CHAPTER 14

Steed walked toward the chief's office. "Who is this woman, Jackson?" he asked.

"She's Hyde's mother."

"How long has she been here?"

"About fifteen minutes," Jackson answered.

Steed knocked on Rogers's door and walked in without being invited. A mixture of foul body odor and arthritis rub hit him full force. His gaze shot to the sixtyish platinum blonde who looked to be in need of a couple of hot meals. "Chief, you wanted to see me?"

Rogers stood and waved him over. "McGraw, I'm glad you're here. This is—"

The woman extended her hand to Steed. Her redder-than-red lips spread into a wide smile. Leather pants matched her lip color, and a dingy white sweater hung over her knobby shoulders and slight build. "Genrose Allen," she said.

"Nice to meet you, ma'am. I'm Detective Steed McGraw," he said, giving the woman's crooked hand a quick squeeze before taking the empty seat next to her. Her smile grew wider. Steed cringed. That old woman was checking him out.

"Ms. Allen here wants to file a missing person report," explained Rogers. "Seems her son hasn't been seen or heard from in over two months."

"My Jason has been known to disappear for days at a time," Genrose elaborated, "but he usually calls or comes home when he gets tired of rambling." A hacking cough shook her skeletal frame, her pale face reddened.

Chief Rogers handed her a bottle of water from his small fridge. "Have some of this," he said.

"Thank you," Genrose managed between her violent coughs. She took several swallows and soon her red face returned to its pale tone.

"Are you all right?" Steed asked.

"Much better, thank you." She placed the bottle near the edge of the desk. "My Jason is always looking for acceptance. Friends. He was an awkward kid. Never really fit in. A little slow."

Steed pulled his notepad and pen from his jacket pocket and flipped to the first clean sheet. "When did you last see him?"

"He came by the house the day after I met with my new doctor. My arthritis is so . . ."

Steed rolled his eyes. He did not want to hear the rundown of this woman's medical problems. "Ms. Allen, you were saying."

"Oh, yes. I haven't seen Jason since September fifth."

"Why did you wait so long to file a report?"

"I thought he'd come back." Genrose reached into her purse and pulled out a flattened pack of cigarettes.

Steed wondered how a scratchy throat could produce a coughing fit like the one Ms. Allen had. Now he knew her body odor probably masked the stench of stale tobacco. He hated cigarette smoke, but compared to her scent, he couldn't imagine which was worse.

"Do you mind?" she asked.

"Not inside the building, ma'am," Rogers kindly explained, before Steed could offer his "Hell, yeah, we mind!" response.

"Oh. Oh, well." She returned the pack to her purse.

"About your son," Rogers continued. "You said the last time you saw him was early September?"

"Uh-huh. Like I said, he goes off for days at a time before I hear from him. It's not unusual."

Steed met the chief's gaze. His superior clearly shared his concern. He turned to Ms. Allen.

"Days aren't two months, ma'am," Rogers replied.

"That's why I'm here now."

"Have you talked to any of his friends?"

"Jason didn't have many friends. He—he got into a little trouble a while back. Did a few months in the Crider jail." The woman scratched her neck, leaving scarlet trails behind. "The element in lockup ain't what I had in mind for my boy."

The chief sat back in his chair. The springs squeaked under the pressure of his weight. "What's a little trouble, Ms. Allen?" he asked.

"Breaking and entering."

"Humph!" Steed grunted.

Genrose's glazed gray eyes flashed. "Don't be judging my boy, Detective. It was a misdemeanor. Jason made some mistakes, but he has a good heart. People take advantage of him because he's so nice. All he ever wanted was for people to like him." Her voice wavered and tears slid down her wrinkled cheeks. "I'm worried about him. I'm scared something's done happened to him."

Rogers handed Steed a box of tissues and nodded toward Ms. Allen. The frown on his superior's face spoke volumes. *Work on your people skills, McGraw!*

Steed handed Genrose a tissue. "I'm sorry if I came off as judgmental, ma'am. It's just more often than not criminal offenders become repeat offenders. Maybe your son fell in with that bad element again."

"Could be, but he would still call after a while, and he hasn't. He moved here from Crider a few years back, and the two boys he hung with there haven't heard from him, either. I don't like making a fuss, but I think I have to make a fuss now." She sniffled. "Something's wrong."

"Do you have a recent picture?"

"Yes." She fumbled around in her purse and pulled out a snapshot. "Here you go. He's a handsome boy, ain't he?"

Steed took the picture and gave the woman a faint smile. All mothers thought their sons were handsome. The phrase "A face only a mother could love" wasn't around for nothing. Steed gave the photo a sideways glance to find Hyde wasn't the dog he'd expected him to be. In fact, behind the scraggly beard overshadowing his dark hair and light eyes, Hyde wasn't bad looking at all.

"Was Jason involved with anyone?"

"No," Genrose answered, mopping her tears with the tissue. "He liked a lot of girls, but nothing happened with them. From time to time, Jason helped at a locksmith's down here at the strip mall. He mentioned there were a lot of pretty girls working in the clothing stores, but I can't think of any names."

"Did he live with you?"

"No. He stayed in a boarding house just inside town. He liked that it was close to the Milford Mall. He would walk to the movies. He liked to walk."

"How could he afford his own place? You said he worked occasionally at the locksmith's."

"Jason got disability for his challenges."

"Did he get his last two checks?"

Genrose nibbled on her bottom lip and shrugged. "His checks came to my house. He didn't have a bank account, and he can't drive, so I would take him to the places too far to walk, cash his checks, and bring him the money when he asked for it."

"You didn't get suspicious when he didn't ask for it the last couple of months?"

"He owed me money. I figured he wanted me to keep it. Are you gonna try to find my boy or not?"

"Yes, we're going to get right on it, Ms. Allen," Chief Rogers assured her, sitting forward. "We'll just need the address of this boarding house, the name of the lock-smith shop, and your information."

Steed jotted the details Genrose shared and stood. "I'll talk to the locksmith and try to look around his room. Maybe I can get some information for you, ma'am." He reached into his back pocket and pulled a business card from his leather carrier. "If you think of anything, regardless of how insignificant you feel it might be, give me a call. If I don't answer, please leave a message and I will get back with you. We'll have to keep the picture for a while, okay?"

"Okay." Genrose took the card and dropped it in her purse. "Please find my boy." She looked from the chief to Steed. "Please."

"We'll do all we can, ma'am," Steed answered with a reassuring pat to her spindly arm. After showing her out, he returned to his chair. Rogers pulled out a can of air freshener and filled the room with a hazy, floral-scented cloud.

"What do you think, McGraw?" he asked, walking about the room as he continued to spray.

Steed waved his hand before his face. He couldn't decide which was worse, Ms. Allen's body odor or the smell of blooming spring flowers mixed with it.

"I think if Jason Hyde is anything like his mother, he is a pathetic human being. What mother who really cared would wait over two months to file a missing person report?" Steed coughed. "Chief, please," he begged, staring at the man and his hissing spray can.

"Sorry." Rogers returned to his chair and dropped the can in his desk drawer. "She thought he was coming back. What's strange, he's been gone for as long as Warwick's been dead, and his fingerprints were on the gun. You were with Darci earlier. You still haven't mentioned this to her?"

"No, I haven't. This is the last thing she needs to hear."

"Maybe she knows this Hyde."

"I doubt Darci knows this guy."

"You're not going to bother to ask?"

Steed shook his head. He wasn't about to play the Warwick card after what had happened today. "If I can help it, I won't mention Warwick's case to Darci again. She needs to deal with her feelings on this, and adding suspicions won't help."

"With Hyde's fingerprints on the gun, wouldn't it stand to reason that Warwick knew the guy?"

"If we went with the notion the fingerprints weren't a mix-up, sure. But Warwick committed suicide. That's a fact."

"Then explain away Hyde's prints, because right now they are also a fact."

"I will do just that." Steed dropped his notepad and the photo in his pocket and walked to the door. "I'm off to the boarding house."

<hr />

Darci studied the words on Kenny's letter as she made her way to Jackie's office at Sterling University. She'd agreed to disagree with Steed, but she needed someone else's opinion. And though Jackie, like Steed, thought she was nuts when it came to her belief about how Kenny died, Darci hoped this letter would at least change her opinion a little bit. There was something more to this letter, something that gnawed away at her. She only wished she could figure out what. Darci looked up from the letter just in time to butt heads with her cousin.

"Ow!" Jackie rubbed the grape-size knot swelling on her forehead. "Didn't anyone ever tell you not to read and walk at the same time?"

"I'm sorry, Jackie, it's just this letter." She walked around her cousin and entered the office, not the least bit fazed by the collision. "You're not busy, are you?"

"I was just about to grab a soda from the vending machine, but I guess I need the can as a cold compress now." Jackie winced as she touched the red knot on her forehead. "Girl, you have a head like a brick."

"I'm sorry. Look, you sit down, I'll grab you a drink." She handed over the letter. "Read this while I'm gone. We need to talk."

Ten minutes later Darci returned to the office. After nearly taking her cousin out, she felt the least she could do was get some ice for Jackie's injury and buy her a cheeseburger. If anything could put her cousin in a forgiving mood, it was a cheeseburger. Luckily, Jackie's building was right across from the student union.

"You made it back?" Jackie said, her chin propped in her open palm. She sniffed and lowered her arm. "Is that a cheeseburger I smell?"

Darci laid out the purchased items. "Yes, with everything on it." She dug in her purse at the sight of Jackie's bright smile. "And look." She produced a red rectangular pack. "Cinnamon gum to fight the onions."

Jackie eyed Darci curiously as she placed the plastic bag of ice to her forehead. "You must really want something bad. Why are you bribing me?" she asked.

"It's not a bribe," Darci said with a straight face.

"Uh-huh."

"Mostly not." Darci pulled a chair closer to the desk and sat. "I feel awful about running into you, so I went to the union to get you some ice, and ended up buying a burger, too. That and I wanted to give you time to read the letter. I know I should have called first, but I started driving and ended up here. I thought you might be able to shed some light on this."

"I don't know how much light I can shed," said Jackie, unwrapping the burger and taking a bite. She closed her eyes and chewed, her face the picture of bliss. "Forget the national fast-food chains. This school makes the best burgers in the world."

Darci smiled. "I guess your head is feeling better."

"About as well as my stomach right now," Jackie answered with a smile. After another bite of the burger and a couple of swallows from the can of diet cola, Jackie wiped her mouth with a paper napkin and put on her serious face. "What do you expect me to say about this letter?"

"What do I expect? You read it, right?"

"Yes, a couple of times."

"And?"

"And what? Kenny wrote a letter changing his mind about the other letter. There's nothing strange about that."

"The letter is strange, Jackie. Why would he write a letter for me when all he had to do was call Mr. Clayton?"

"Darci, you have to remember Kenny wasn't thinking clearly. He killed himself. Maybe he thought Mr. Clayton would detect some distance in his voice."

"Argh!" Darci waved off her cousin's words. She didn't want to hear that.

"Did you think you'd come racing in here and have me agree with that warped thinking of yours because of this letter?" Jackie's eyes widened when Darci didn't reply. "You did. Sweetie, neither this letter nor anything else will change what is. You have got to get over this. It's not good for you."

"What's not good for me is my loved ones not believing me."

"That's not fair." Jackie took another bite of her burger and put the rest aside. After a few more sips of cola, she popped a stick of gum in her mouth. "We do believe in you, but when it comes to this issue, you won't see reason."

"I see reason, Jackie. I know how things look. I just can't push aside what my instincts are telling me."

Darci's thoughts raced back to Steed's words prior to his epiphany. *Warwick is dead because he killed himself, just like my father is dead because he followed some instinct that was wrong!* She shook her head. Steed was wrong. Her situation with Kenny was different.

"Let's say you're right and Kenny didn't kill himself. How will that truth make you feel better?" Jackie asked.

"It will give his parents and me some closure," Darci answered without hesitation. "It will confirm I was right to trust my instincts, and most importantly it will put the person who did this behind bars."

"That's just it, Darci, there's no person. An autopsy was performed. The authorities did their jobs. A self-inflicted gunshot wound killed your best friend. Hoping for some miracle evidence, some proof you'll never get, won't change that."

Darci shook her head. "I've heard this speech from you and Steed too many times, and I can't listen to it anymore. There's something missing. Something is not right about this."

"Darci?"

The pity in Jackie's voice and the look in her eyes as she shook her head in that "poor thing" way was all Darci could stand. She grabbed the letter from the desk and stood. "I need to go now."

"Don't rush off," Jackie said.

"There's no reason for me to stay."

"We can talk."

Darci looked at her cousin. What could they possibly talk about now?

"Sit down," Jackie directed, as Darci remained firmly planted. "Please."

Darci flopped back into the chair and folded her arms. "I don't know why I'm staying."

Jackie returned to her chair. "You know."

"I'm not crazy. I'm just trying to understand."

"Sometimes we never understand things. Everything doesn't have a solution, but this is one instance where the answer you have is not the one you want. You can't change this, Darci. Kenny is gone, and it's because he made the choice."

Darci shook her head. "No."

"Yes." Jackie sighed. "Do you think he'd want you going on like this?"

"Absolutely. I think it's the main reason I still have these doubts. I can't explain it. I know my thinking is irrational. Trust me, I know. But I can't shake this. Sometimes, I swear I can hear Kenny calling out to me."

Jackie groaned. "Oh, boy."

"See, that's why I hadn't said anything to you about this before now. I imagine Steed's reaction would be identical."

"Is there any wonder why? You know what's true, but you don't want to accept it, and now you're telling me Kenny's talking to you?"

"I didn't say he was talking to me. He's calling to me. Just saying my name over and over, like he needs me to hear him. To hear his cry. I hear it, Jackie. I can't ignore it."

"Do you care what I hear? You talking like you don't have a rational brain cell in your head."

Darci frowned. She'd just had this talk with Steed. Had he called Jackie? Was she in the middle of part two of some one-on-one intervention? "Did Steed call you?"

"No, I haven't spoken to Steed since we all had dinner the other night. Why?"

"Nothing," she said. "I know how it sounds, Jackie, but there's something about this." Darci clutched the letter in her hand. "I'm going to figure out what."

"And if you don't?"

"I will. I have to." Darci returned the letter to her purse and stood. She wouldn't give her cousin another opportunity to display her "poor Darci" look. "I'm going to leave now. Enjoy the rest of your burger."

"I'm sorry I couldn't help you."

Arguing that point occurred to Darci. Jackie could've helped, but she wasn't keen on sugarcoating, so she didn't bother. It was her way. "Me, too," Darci said. "See ya."

Darci bundled her jacket tighter around her as the frosty fall air chilled her to the bone. Hyped when she left for the food, she hadn't felt the near-freezing temperatures. Now she felt every bit of it—cold, harsh, unrelenting, much like the opinions of her loved ones in regard to Kenny's death. An opinion she would probably share if the shoe were on the other foot. Unfortunately, the shoe was on her foot.

She activated the keyless entry and ignition starter for her car. The horn beeped and headlights flashed as she thanked whoever had invented heated seats. She would go home, make some cocoa, run a hot bath, and soak her tensions away. Then, she would read this letter again and again until she figured out what nagged her about it, because Jackie and Steed were of no help.

"Darci!"

She turned to find Jacob Benjamin approaching. Jacob had a face that belonged on the big screen, but a body that belonged on a treadmill. A fact that made seeing him run up to her like an out-of-control bull a bit disconcerting. Moments later he reached her, gasping for breath.

"Hey, I thought that was you." Even with the chilly temperatures, sweat glistened his forehead. "Whoo!" He fanned his face. "What are you doing here?"

"I was visiting my cousin."

"That's right, she's a professor."

"Mathematics."

"So, what do you think about the turn in the case?"

Darci squinted. That little jog must have gone to his head. "What are you talking about? What case?" she asked.

"Kenneth Warwick's."

"Kenny?"

Jacob pulled a handkerchief from the pocket of his heavy dark coat and mopped his shiny forehead. Darci detected an almost gleeful glow in his eyes. She couldn't decide if that was a good or bad thing, just as she couldn't decide if the uneasy fluttering in her stomach meant whatever he had to say was something she wanted to hear.

"Detective McGraw didn't tell you?"

"Steed and I don't talk much about Kenny's case."

Jacob grunted. "I can understand why," he muttered.

Darci jammed her hands in her pockets and balled them into tight fists. "What is it, Jacob?" she asked, in no mood to witness this one-sided pissing contest he seemed intent on having with her absent boyfriend.

"You might have been right."

"Right about what? Just spit it out already!"

"There was another set of fingerprints found on the gun used to kill Kenny. The case has been reopened."

CHAPTER 15

Ten minutes after leaving the station, Steed reached Hyde's boarding house. The owner, Flora Dupree, a sassy, white-haired, brown-eyed grandmother showed him to Jason's room. Her pink house shoes brushed softly against the spiraling hardwood staircase as she ambled up the steps and shuffled down the hall to the third door on the left. She pulled a ring of keys from the pocket of her lime green housedress and unlocked the door.

"He paid up the rent until the end of the year, so I couldn't show the room to anyone else," she said with the faintest hint of a Creole accent. Curious eyes turned to him. Her tiny frame blocked the path to the door. "Jason's not in any trouble, is he? I know he had a bit of a checkered past, but he's a good boy. He wouldn't hurt a fly."

"I can't say that he is, ma'am. I'm just wondering if there's something in his room that can tell me where he went."

"Do you have a warrant? I watch *Law & Order*. I know you need a warrant to search his room."

Steed chuckled. This old lady reminded him of Nana Jean. She watched *Law & Order*, too.

"I do need a warrant to search his place, but I'm not looking for anything that would get him into trouble, and his mother wanted me to come. I'm trying to help him. You wouldn't want anything to happen to him, would you?"

"No, I wouldn't, but I do think I should go in with you."

Steed opened the door and extended his hand through the walkway. He would show Rogers and everyone else how much of a people person he could be. "Feel free," he said.

"This isn't going to take long, is it?" She checked the slim gold watch on her left wrist. "My show comes on in ten minutes."

"I'll try to be brief, ma'am, but if you need to leave, I won't hold you. I like my shows, too," he added with a wink.

Her brown eyes widened. "You watch the shows?"

Steed nodded. "Sure do. I like the one on Channel Two at three," he confessed with a laugh. The officers at the precinct would flip with the knowledge of his guilty pleasure and the fact he recorded it religiously every day.

"That's my show, too. Such nice-looking young men on there." A deep rouge colored her caramel cheeks. She bowed her head slightly. "Just like you."

"Why, thank you. I'll take that as a high compliment."

Her wrinkled old hand covered his. "You're a nice young man. I like you." She raised an eyebrow and smiled broadly. "Are you married? I don't see a ring."

"No, ma'am, I'm not married, but I am spoken for."

"Too bad. There's a young lady next door that— Oh, what does it matter now? Let's go on in."

Steed stepped inside the room and looked around. A bed, mirrored dresser, and chest of drawers. Nothing struck him as unusual. "Are his things still here?"

"Yes. I haven't touched anything." The shrill ringing of a telephone turned Mrs. Dupree's attention to the door. "That's down the hall," she said. "You go on and look around. I think I'll go downstairs when I'm done and get ready for the show."

"You go ahead. I'll be fine."

She nodded and hurried out as fast as her old legs could carry her. Steed did another scan of the room. He had a hard time buying into Jason Hyde being connected in any way to Kenneth Warwick's death. There had to have been a mix-up in the lab when he ran those prints the second time. Warwick committed suicide with his own gun, so there'd be no fingerprints other than his. But for Darci's sake, and that of his job, he would continue to look around.

Finding nothing under the bed, Steed tried the drawers, and except for some jeans, shirts, underwear, and girlie magazines that were at least fifteen years old, got zip there, too. He eyed the door straight ahead. Probably his closet. He'd check there and be on his way.

The powerful scent of mothballs nearly knocked him out when he opened the door. He shook his head. An old lady definitely owned this house. He flipped the light switch and performed his final search. There wasn't much there—a few shirts and suits hanging perfectly centered, and a couple of pairs of shoes. He checked the pockets of the suits and found a ticket stub from a movie seen on September second and seventy-three cents.

Steed sighed. Well, he'd tried. Stepping back to close the door, he spotted a piece of paper on the floor next to some scuffed white sneakers. He picked up the small sheet and turned it over. Kenny's name and the call letters and address to the television station were scribbled in red ink. He pocketed the paper and checked the closet again. Wire hangers scraped the metal rod as he pushed through the clothing. There had to be something else here.

He shoved the clothes to the left side of the closet and stuck his head inside. An expletive fell from his lips from the sight on the right side wall—a veritable shrine dedicated to none other than Kenneth Warwick.

<hr>

Darci sat at a booth at Sophie's, staring blindly at the letter she'd gotten from Kenny's. She couldn't believe the turn this day had taken, and more than that, she couldn't believe Steed could have shared this information about Kenny's case and chose not to. Why didn't he tell her?

Jacob returned to the table with two large cups of coffee. "Are you all right, Darci?".

"No," she answered flatly, pushing the cup aside. "Why did you tell me this?"

"Are you upset because you didn't want to know, or because you wanted to know from your boyfriend and he didn't tell you?"

"What do you have against Steed?"

"I don't have anything against McGraw. I just want him to do the job the city is paying him to do. This is a big deal."

Darci agreed, but she refused to let Jacob know that. He seemed to be getting some perverse pleasure at the idea of her being angry with Steed, and she wouldn't give him the satisfaction of knowing she was. "If Steed thought this was a big deal, he would have told me," she said.

"But he didn't."

"Exactly. Steed is a wonderful investigator, and neither of us have reason to question his abilities in regard to this case."

"But you have questioned it, Darci. I didn't tell you to come to me and ask that I light a fire under the Sterling Police Department; you did that. You wanted answers to what happened with Kenny, and now that you're getting them, you're angry."

"Darci?"

Miss Sophie's warm voice rescued Darci from the abyss of anger she found herself falling deeper into. She turned to the old lady with a smile. "How are you, Miss Sophie?"

"I'm fine. Real fine." She checked around the small room. "Steed's not with you?"

"No, ma'am, he's working."

"Ahem! She's here with me, Miss Sophie," Jacob said.

"Where is that sweet wife of yours, Jacob Benjamin?"

"Home."

Miss Sophie's hands found her hips at Jacob's curt response. Annoyance turned her full, smiling lips into an unhappy scowl. "Who put a bee in yo britches?"

"You'll have to excuse him, Miss Sophie," Darci spoke up. "The mayor has a lot on his mind."

"It seems so." Miss Sophie grunted and turned back to Darci with a smile. "You having some lunch?"

"No, ma'am, just the coffee," Darci answered, fiddling with the corners of the letter.

Miss Sophie motioned to the pages. "What you got there?"

"A letter from Kenny."

"Really?" She wiped her hands on a dishtowel tucked inside the pocket of her apron. "I remember how Kenny would sit right over there," she jutted to the row of stools at the counter, "coding those letters you would write to each other." Miss Sophie laughed her bubbly laugh that warmed Darci from the inside out. "After a couple of minutes, he would smile and tell me just what you wanted for dessert, and when you'd be here to eat it. And you would do the same thing with him. Y'all two would come up with some things."

Jacob cleared his throat, tapping the sugar dispenser against the table. "Thanks for sharing the memories, Miss Sophie, but Darci and I need to discuss some things in private. If you don't mind," he said pointedly.

"I'll talk to you later, Darci." Miss Sophie gave her a kind smile. "You tell Steed I said hello when you see him."

Darci nodded. "I will."

Miss Sophie shot Jacob a hard glare and then took off to exchange warm greetings with her other patrons.

Darci scowled at Jacob. "That was uncalled for."

"Forget Miss Sophie for a minute. What are you going to do about what I told you?"

"What am I going to do?"

"Yes. McGraw kept something from you. If this is such a strong relationship, it should be based on trust."

"You're not giving me relationship advice, are you?"

"I'm making a point. Did he tell you about the promotion?"

"Yes. Did he get it?"

"With your reaction to the case reopening, why would you think he would?"

"What does my reaction have to do with his promotion?"

"Everything. You don't know the details?"

Darci closed her eyes, groaning. "Just spill it, Jacob."

"His job was to keep you quiet. To prevent you from making a big deal out of Kenny's case. If he did that, proved he could handle the case and you, he would get his promotion. The case isn't handled, and I'm not so sure you're going to keep quiet about this. Why do you think he didn't tell you the case was reopened? Think about it, Darci. It's all about him and his promotion."

Darci's face grew hot, violently hot, as her body trembled from memories of Steed's declarations of love and his insistence she get past her feelings about Kenny for her own good. Mocking laughter echoed in her head. *Her own good.* It was never about her, but about his promotion. She was just a means to an end.

"Darci, I . . ."

"Stop it, Jacob. Just stop!" Ignoring the curious glances of other diners, Darci grabbed the letter and slid out the booth. "I don't want to hear another word from you!"

Racing from the restaurant, she climbed behind the wheel of her car and drove until the tears burning her eyes made it impossible. Loose gravel pummeled against her car as she pulled onto the dying, cold-beaten grass lining the roadside. Dropping her head to the steering wheel, she surrendered to the tears, while a torrent of unanswered questions rained down on her.

Jackson stood from his desk as Steed came barreling through the door of the station with a head of steam.

"Get in here!" Steed slammed his open palm against the door and stormed over to his desk. Somebody was gonna explain what the hell was going on around here and make some sense of what he found at Hyde's room.

Jackson rushed inside. "Yes, sir?"

"I'm going to ask you again about the gun from the Warwick house. Did you run it directly to the lab for retesting?"

"Yes, sir. I rushed it right over, just like you said."

"Who was there?"

"I'm sorry?"

The man's confusion only added to Steed's anger. "Who the hell was at the lab when you dropped off the weapon?"

"The lab tech Liz Carwin. Is everything okay, Detective?"

"I don't know yet." Steed dropped into his chair and flipped open the Hyde file. Feeling the officer's gaze on him, Steed asked, "Is there something else, Jackson?"

"Not really. Ms. Clarke called."

"Did she leave a message?"

"Uh, yes, sir, she did."

"What is it? I don't have all day."

"She sounded a little upset."

"Upset?" Steed closed the folder and gave Jackson his undivided attention. "Sad upset or angry upset?"

"Both, I think. Sounded like she was crying."

"What was the message?"

"Uh . . ."

Steed rubbed his temples, trying desperately to stave off the headache he felt coming. "Just spit it out already!"

"She said to tell you to go to hell, sir."

Steed dropped his hands and looked up at Jackson. "What?"

"That was the message."

"Did she say anything else?"

The young man shook his head and Steed sent him on his way.

Go to hell? Was that some sort of delayed reaction from their earlier disagreement? Grabbing the files on Warwick and Hyde, Steed headed for Darci's. After she explained what had her upset, maybe she could tell him if the name Jason Hyde meant anything to her.

CHAPTER 16

Fools rush in.

That phrase replayed in Darci's head as she soaked in her lilac-scented bath. She shouldn't have left that angry message for Steed. She should have waited until dinner so she'd be able to look in his eyes and watch for his reaction to her questions. To listen to his explanation for keeping the information about Kenny's case being reopened away from her. To hear him say he wasn't with her just to get a promotion. He had to say that.

Darci rose from the tepid water. Fifteen minutes in this tub and she'd never gotten swept away to that land of no worries. She rolled her eyes. Advertisers and their lies. She should have stuck with her peach bubble bath.

Thick drops of lather fell from her body as she stood and reached for the sheet towel. After drying off, she wrapped the cottony softness around her body and padded into the bedroom.

"So, you were in there?"

Darci froze. Steed sat on the edge of her bed, with an open file on his lap, and a bright smile on his face. He was too sexy for his own good, but between her anger and unanswered questions, she doubted his gorgeous face and hot body could deter her from her quest for knowledge.

What was he doing in her bedroom anyway? "How did you get in here?"

"I rang the doorbell, but you didn't answer." He closed the folder and tossed it to the other side of the bed. "You told me where you keep the spare key, so I let myself in."

Steed's eyes engaged in a slow, blatant journey of her towel-clad body. His lips curled into an appreciative smile as he made his way to her. The tips of breasts hardened under his perusal and her skin tingled as though zapped by an errant bolt of electricity. She silently cursed him for making her feel like this, and her body for being so completely receptive.

"Mmm. You smell so good, and you look even better," Steed said in that deep, gravely voice that made her body shiver.

The giant peach towel suddenly seemed too small. Darci hugged her arms about her shoulders and met Steed's approach with a hard glare. "Don't take another step," she warned, certain she would lose what little resistance she had if he did.

Steed stopped and lowered his foot to the floor. "What's bothering you? What was with the phone message?"

Returning anger halted the sensual stirrings Steed had aroused. Darci met his gaze head on. "You couldn't decipher that? Maybe you're not as good a detective as you think. 'Go to hell' seems pretty straightforward to me."

"Did I do something?"

"It's what you didn't do."

"I don't understand."

"Apparently, you never did."

Steed dragged his hand over his face. "Darci, I'm not in the mood for riddles. I don't know why you're upset, but I'll make it up to you, whatever it is." He rubbed his chin. "Tell me something. Does the name Jason Hyde mean anything to you?"

Darci stared at him in disbelief. He did not just end what she knew would be the fight of the century to question her about some guy, when he—*Hyde?* That was the name he was talking about when she arrived at his office. No wonder he almost broke his neck getting that loose sheet from her hand. That paper involved Kenny's case.

She closed her eyes. *One. Two. Three.* After reaching five she stopped. She could count to a million and it wouldn't help. Darci opened her eyes and pointed to the door. "I want you out of here."

"What's wrong with you, Darci?" Steed took a step forward, his hand extended. "What did I do?"

She slapped his hand away. "Don't even think about touching me! It's not what you did, Steed, it's what you didn't do!"

"What didn't I do? Things were fine when I left you this afternoon. We had our disagreement, but we made up. Where is this hostility coming from?"

Darci held his gaze, forcing herself not to cry. Even with her anger, she loved Steed so much. She had to give him the benefit of the doubt. One more chance to make this right. To prove her feelings for him and his for her were more important than a promotion. "Is there anything you need to tell me?"

"No. I told you about my father, Darci. What else would you think I have to tell you?"

Darci's heart shattered. "The truth." Hot tears slid down her cheeks. "I guess that was too much to hope for." She sniffled. "I'm not saying this again. I want you out."

Steed made yet another approach. "Darci, what . . ."

She stepped back. "Don't come any closer."

"Why are you angry with me? What have I done?"

"You did nothing! That's the problem. For months, I've been struggling with uncertainty. Feeling like I'm losing my mind. And instead of helping me, you kept quiet and allowed my suffering to continue. How can you say you love me and hurt me like this?"

"Darci, sweetheart, I do love you, but I don't know what you're talking about. I've been honest about everything."

"Everything except Kenny and how his case ties into your promotion! Why didn't you tell me his case was reopened?"

Steed's face blanched. "Who told you?" His eyes narrowed. "Benjamin?"

"It doesn't matter."

"The hell it doesn't!"

"What matters is you didn't tell me."

"Darci, there was nothing to tell."

"Did you or did you not reopen this case?"

"I didn't reopen it, but it has been reopened."

"And you didn't think I needed to know that?"

"No, I didn't. Darci, nothing's changed. Warwick committed suicide. If I'd thought telling you would help, I would have. It's not going to help."

"Because you say so? The case got reopened for a reason." *These fingerprints you haven't mentioned.* "What was it?"

Sighing, Steed smoothed his hand over his cheeks and along the hint of the five o'clock shadow dusting his strong jaw. Darci hated when he hedged. It meant he was trying to think of the right thing to say. She just wanted the truth.

"Well?" she prompted.

"There's been a mix-up."

Darci adjusted her towel. "What kind of mix-up?"

Steed eyes wandered again. "It's very hard for me to concentrate with you standing there like that."

"Fine. I'll change." She pointed to the door. "You wait in the living room. When I come out, be ready to talk."

———

Steed paced the length of the floor in front of the fireplace. He took the liberty of building a fire, hoping the crackling wood and vibrant flames would somehow calm Darci. She didn't smell like peaches. Maybe that explained her tension.

Trying to understand her anger and how she found out about the case drove him crazy. It had to be Benjamin. That guy had it in for him, and wanted nothing more than to see him and Darci apart. Steed's chest tightened. The butterflies in his stomach were not the kind he liked. From the way Darci had looked at him, Benjamin might finally get his wish. Steed shook away the thought. He couldn't lose her. Not over this.

"All right, I'm ready to listen."

Steed stopped pacing and looked up. Darci had loosened the hair piled atop her head and replaced the towel with an oversized white T-shirt and faded blue jeans. He preferred her in the towel, but she looked comfortable, and the slightest bit soothed. That gave him hope. "You look nice."

She frowned. "Save the compliments. Why didn't you tell me about the case?"

Darci's testiness stung him like a hungry fire ant. She wasn't at all soothed. "Why are you so hostile?"

"Why am I—Why am I hostile? I'm hostile because my best friend is dead, and I just learned the man I love kept the reopening of my friend's case from me. I can't understand that. Because I can't understand, I'm hostile! Why didn't you tell me about those fingerprints?"

"How did you . . . How much did Benjamin tell you?"

"I don't want to talk about Jacob! I want to know why you didn't tell me about all this."

"There was nothing to tell. I don't understand why the case is even reopened, because it won't change what is. Warwick killed himself."

"There's more to it. How did these fingerprints happen?"

"I had the gun retested when you demanded more action. The new prints belonged to some guy named Jason Hyde."

"Hyde? That's who you asked me about before."

"Does the name mean anything to you?"

"Why should I answer that?" She folded her arms. "You don't think it makes a difference!"

"Darci, would you stop this?"

"No, I will not! How dare you ask me a question about this case when you didn't even tell me it was reopened!"

"You know why I didn't tell you. I have to follow this up because it's my job, but it doesn't change the facts."

"Your job and the facts!" Darci blasted. "Like the fact you're with me to get your promotion."

"No. Darci, I'm not with you because of a promotion. That promotion is not more important to me than you, and not mentioning Warwick's case had nothing to do with it. I'm with you because I love you." He closed his hands over her shoulders. "I don't know who this Jason Hyde is, but I know your friend committed suicide, and I know I want you to accept that. Telling you about those prints wouldn't have helped."

She shrugged his hands away. "I don't need you to think for me, Steed. I tried doing things your way, and it didn't work. I need to do what I need to do for me now."

"Even if it hurts you?"

Tears spilled from Darci's eyes. "I'm hurting now."

"Baby, please, don't cry." Steed reached out to smooth away her tears, but, again, she shrank from his touch. "Darci."

She held up a quaking finger. "Don't touch me!"

"I'm sorry."

"Stop apologizing. Just go."

"Would you at least tell me if the name Jason Hyde means anything to you. Do you know him?"

"No, I don't. Are you done?"

"Not quite." He expelled a breath and continued with his toughest questions. "Was Warwick seeing anyone special? Someone he didn't want the world to know about?"

Darci glared at him. "What are you getting at?"

"Was Warwick gay?"

"Ugh!" Darci shook her head. "You never give up."

"It's just a question."

"Where did it come from?" she fired back. "This Jason Hyde? You'll reach for anything, Steed. Kenny was a lover, but only of women. He was as straight as an arrow."

Somehow, Darci saying that didn't surprise him.

"It's time for you to leave," she said.

Steed decided not to argue. Time alone would do her good, and give him a chance to connect the dots of this case. "Try to calm down and think while I'm gone. I'll call you later."

"No, you won't. We have nothing more to discuss. And, FYI, I'm going forward with the story I told you about when I first came to town."

"The story?"

"Yes," she answered. "The many, and there are *many*, problems with the Sterling Police Department. I'm going to make sure the public knows all about them. I start at the station at the beginning of January, and I'm going to begin the new year at my new job with a bang."

"To what end?" He took a few tentative steps forward, not wanting to antagonize her more, but desperate to be close to her, to somehow reach her and reason with her.

"What do you think will happen if you do this story? It won't bring Warwick back to life, and it won't change the fact he killed himself. Darci, nothing is going to change that."

She folded her arms across her chest, the act one of defiance and a clear sign his touch was not welcome. "I don't want to hear any more of this."

"You have to." Disregarding her stance, he closed his hands over her shoulders. She recoiled at his touch. Steed dropped his hands, hurt by her dismissal, but just as angry with her behavior. He hated when she cried, but hated when she acted like an insolent five-year-old even more. "Darci, I'm sorry. I'm sorry about all of this, but I know my being sorry means nothing to you. You won't be satisfied until I say you're right, that there's some phantom killer of Kenneth Warwick. But you know what—I'm never going to say that. Not ever."

"Because it would mean you're wrong, and you can never be wrong."

"Not about this. Facts don't lie."

The sound of her mocking laughter rang in his ears. "Is that so? Tell me, Detective, what about those fingerprints? Facts aren't always factual." Darci pointed to the door. "Now get the hell out of my house!" New tears filled her eyes. "I never want to see you again."

"You don't mean that," Steed said with a confidence he didn't feel. "You're angry, but we love each other. We can't let this case come between us. Just today you said we didn't have to."

"*We* didn't let it. *You* let it! *You* did this. Being a cop keeps you constantly in protect mode, but I don't need you to protect me. I begged you to help me with this case, to help me find out what happened with Kenny, and you didn't! I do love you, Steed, but loving you hurts too much, and I've had enough."

Enough? No. He had to reason with her.

Darci stepped away, as if sensing his approach. She shook her head. "No more." Tears rolled down her cheeks. "It's over, Steed." She walked to the door and pulled it open. "Go."

Over? Go? Hot tears slid down Steed's cheeks. "Darci?"

She lowered her head, sniffling.

Steed picked up the files from the table and made his way over. The brisk autumn air raced in from the open door. Dry leaves skittered about the cement porch. He'd imagined he and Darci stargazing on this very porch later this evening as they had the night before, but there would be no more of that. There would be no more anything.

Steed's body burned with want as he brushed against her on his way out. Her breath caught and their eyes met as the familiar spark passed between them. What they had was so good, but this Warwick hurdle appeared bigger than their love, and no matter how hard they tried, they couldn't seem to cross it.

"I'm not going to apologize for doing what I think is best for you, even if you think I should, and even when I know it will go a long way in easing the anger you're feeling toward me. I love you, Darci. I love you too much to lie to you. Warwick committed suicide. You might not want to hear it or accept it, but that's the way it is." He expelled a breath. "Good-bye."

CHAPTER 17

Darci peeled her face from the tearstained pillow and looked over her shoulder to the glowing red digits on the clock radio. Six fifteen. She'd spent the last two hours since Steed left in a surreal state of heartbreak and exhaustion. Longing for his presence and the warmth of his voice and touch, while cursing herself for wanting a man who could do what he'd done to her. And then say he did it *for* her. Humph!

She reached for a tissue. No more tears and no more thoughts of Steed. Twisting on the bedside lamp, Darci picked up Kenny's letter and rested against the headboard. This letter made as much sense as Kenny dying from suicide. Why write a letter to her when all he had to do was call Mr. Clayton and tell him to destroy the original letter?

The rumble in Darci's belly interrupted her train of thought. She rubbed her stomach, remembering she hadn't eaten since the sandwich with Steed over six hours ago. If Jacob hadn't done everything he could to fuel her anger with Steed, she would have a nice plate of leftovers from Miss Sophie's to . . . *The code!* Could that be it?

Darci sifted through the pages of the letter. "How did it go? How did it go?" She closed her eyes and squeezed them tight, urging the childhood ritual to return.

"Numbers. A sequence of numbers." She looked at the note. The word 'change' was underlined. *Underlined meant what?* "Change. Six letters." She snapped her fingers. "Got it!"

Twenty minutes later, the jumbled words and letters Darci scribbled onto a notepad came together to answer her every question. She grabbed the phone and dialed the station.

"McGraw."

Darci noted tension and sadness in his tone, but he only had himself to blame for that. "Steed, it's me. I . . ."

"Darci, I'm so glad you called. Look, I—"

"Steed, stop. I didn't call to talk about us. This is about Kenny."

He grunted. "Isn't it always?"

Darci ignored his snipe. "I was right," she said.

"Right?"

"The letter. Kenny. He didn't kill himself."

Steed groaned. "Damn it, Darci, why do you . . ."

"I have proof. It's not what you think. Everybody was wrong. Kenny didn't die. He didn't die."

"Darci . . ."

"Stay there. I'll be right over."

Ripping the coded message from the notepad, Darci stuffed it and the letter in her purse and raced out of the house. The security light illuminated the dark driveway, bringing Darci's attention to a very flat front left tire. "Damn!" She knew how to change a tire, but she'd never done it, and she had no time to waste. She would just have to borrow Jackie's car.

Darci raced down the street, focused on getting to her cousin's and driving to the station. When she turned the corner, bright headlights appeared behind her out of nowhere. She moved to the sidewalk and looked over the shoulder, just in time to see the car coming straight for her.

—◇◇◇—

After straightening the folders and papers on his desk for the umpteenth time, Steed glanced at his watch. Half an hour. She should've been here twenty minutes ago.

What did she mean Warwick didn't die? If she believed that to be true, she was too wound up to drive. Why didn't he go to her? If something had happened to her, he'd never be able to . . .

The ringing phone startled Steed from his fearful thoughts. He jammed the handset to his ear. "Darci?"

"No, no, Steed, it's . . . it's Jackie," she said, sniffling.

The alarm in Jackie's usually calm voice shook Steed to his core. For her to be so upset . . . Tears filled his eyes. "What happened?"

—◇◇◇—

Steed steadied his nerves as he did every time before entering Darci's room. After seven days, the heartbreaking sight of her lying so still, recovering from a closed-head injury, bruised ribs, and a severely sprained ankle, never got any easier for him to take.

The clack of his boots against the shiny linoleum floor broke the monotony of electronic tones from machines monitoring Darci's stats. Steed took a seat at her bedside, being mindful of the IV as he pressed her warm hand against his cheek.

"It's a beautiful day," he said, stroking her hair. "It's mild, the sky is blue, and there's no chilling breeze. You'll have to wake up soon so you can enjoy this. Winter is around the corner, Darci. There won't be many more days like this."

Steed sighed. Not so much as a flutter of her eyelids, yet the doctors remained optimistic. They'd given Darci medication to alleviate brain swelling and help her pain. With the numerous bruises and contusions her body withstood, they thought the rest would do her good and were hopeful she would soon awaken from her coma. But after a week, fear she would never wake up kept a constant knot in Steed's throat. He didn't doubt the doctors, but he needed to see her awake.

Tears filled his eyes. "Darci, please, wake up. Just open your eyes for a little while, please." He lowered his head to her shoulder. "I miss you so much. All I can think about is the way we left things. The way I let you down. Darci, I promise, if you just open your eyes, let me look at those beautiful dark eyes, I'll help you. I'll do anything you want to prove this theory you have about Warwick. Just wake up."

"You'll do anything?"

Steed lifted his head from Darci's shoulder. Her onyx eyes looked back at him. "Darci."

"You'll help me?" she said, her voice low, raspy. "Did you mean that?"

He smoothed the tears from his eyes, smiling. "Is that all I had to say to get you to wake up?"

"Yeah. Did you mean it?"

"Yes, Darci, I meant it. I can't tell you how scared I've been. Your parents are here. Jackie and I just got them to go to her place and get some rest. How do you feel?"

"Sore. What happened?"

"You don't remember?"

"I remember leaving Kenny's and being very angry with you, but we worked past it and were going to have dinner later."

"That's all?"

"Is there more?"

Steed considered the question before answering. If she didn't remember their fight, it might be best not to tell her, at least not until he talked to her doctors. From the shows he'd seen on television, soaps mostly, it wasn't a good idea to inform people of things they didn't remember, especially if it would come as a shock. Having a fight with him was one thing, but not remembering she broke things off and why was something altogether different. "You got hit by a car," he said. "You were unconscious for a week."

"A week?"

"Yeah. Thanksgiving is a few days away, but it's today for me. I'm so glad you're back."

"How did I get hit by a car?"

"You were in your neighborhood, a few feet from Jackie's house. You were thrown about ten feet. The doctors said you were lucky to land on the lawn of Jackie's neighbor and not the pavement. That thick grass probably saved your life. We're still investigating, but we don't have any solid leads. The car never stopped and no one saw anything." Darci would live in a neighborhood with no nosy neighbors. She was on the lawn twenty minutes before being found.

"I got hit by a car." She rubbed her forehead. "That might explain this monster headache." She grimaced. "And everything else that aches. Ow! What happened to my foot?"

"It's sprained. You got pretty banged up." He patted her shoulder. "Don't try to move too much. I'll get your doctor."

Darci took his arm before he left her bedside. "You'll help me with Kenny? You didn't just say that to get my attention, did you?"

"I would have said anything to get you to wake up, but I meant it. I hadn't felt this alone or scared since right after my father died. From now on, I want you to know you can count on me. Even if I don't agree with you, I'll accept that's a part of our dynamic, and still do everything I can for you." He kissed her hand. "I love you."

"I love you, too." She brushed her fingertips through his hair and smiled. "I'll have to get hit by a car more often."

Steed frowned. "Don't even joke about that."

"Sorry. Are you sure there's nothing more to tell about my health? You paused for a moment before answering me."

"No, there's nothing more. I'm just glad you're awake."

While the doctors and nurses looked Darci over, Steed whispered a prayer of thanks and then called her family.

Jackie answered on the first ring.

"Hi, Jackie, it's Steed," he said.

"Is everything okay?"

"Everything is great." Steed smiled. "Darci woke up."

"She did!"

"Yeah. Just now."

"Uncle Chuck, Aunt Darlene, Darci's awake," Jackie announced.

"Thank the Lord," Steed heard Mrs. Clarke say in the background.

"How is she?" Jackie asked.

"Sore. But she's alert and talking. She's back."

"That's so good. We'll be right there, Steed."

"Okay. I'll see you soon."

Steed stuck his phone in his pocket and leaned against the wall. *Kenny didn't die.* Darci's words were back, haunting him. Steed brushed his fingers against the stubbly week-old whiskers covering his face. Darci couldn't explain how she came to that unlikely conclusion, so he'd have to find out for himself.

After much arm-twisting, Steed had convinced Chief Rogers to agree to the next step he wanted to take in the investigation. With that hurdle crossed, Steed pulled out his address book and made another call.

"Hello."

"Hello, Mrs. Warwick. This is Steed McGraw."

"Detective, how is Darci?" she asked.

"Much better. She woke up a bit ago."

"Oh, that's so wonderful. Is that why you called? To tell us the good news?"

"Yes and no."

"What is it?"

"If it's okay, I need to come over and talk to you and your husband about your son. I need to make one stop first, but I can be there in an hour."

CHAPTER 18

"You want to what?"

"Shhh." Steed placed his finger to his lips. "Mr. Clayton, lower your voice."

"Lower my voice?" The lawyer walked to his door, looked outside, and then locked the door behind him. The older man rubbed his face as he made his way back to his chair. "Let me get this straight. You want me to file a court order to have Kenneth Warwick's body exhumed?"

"That's right."

"And why would I do that?"

"His case has been reopened."

"What does that have to do with me having his body exhumed?"

"You're a lawyer with lots of influence, especially with judges. I think if you talk with the Warwicks, they'll agree to the exhumation, and we can get this done."

"Steed, you're not answering my question. You have insisted from the beginning Kenny killed himself. Why would you want to exhume his body?"

"Because of Darci. The idea she could have died thinking the man who claims to love her didn't do all he could to help with something that meant so much to her haunts me. I want Darci to get over this. I want her every question, her every doubt, satisfied. Darci is going to see what I've known from the beginning. Warwick killed himself."

Mr. Clayton rubbed the back of his neck. "This seems a bit drastic to show a woman you love her."

"It's not just about that."

"What else is it about?"

Steed stuck his thumbs in the back pocket of his jeans, not at all excited about disclosing more information. Much like he felt when he'd called Benjamin earlier. The mayor was none too happy to hear Darci had no recollection of their conversation, but for her health, promised not to remind her of it. Steed released a deep breath.

Mr. Clayton shook his head. "Look, I'm a busy man, Detective. Tell Darci I'm glad she's feeling better, and I'll try to get by the hospital to visit her later," he said, gathering some papers strewn about his desk.

"Can I invoke privilege?"

"I'm not your attorney."

Steed tossed a quarter on the desk.

Mr. Clayton grunted.

"Don't be insulted," Steed said, "I just don't have time to pull a bill out of my wallet."

"I'm listening."

"Before her accident, Darci called and told me—she told me Warwick wasn't dead."

"She what?"

"She said Warwick wasn't dead. She doesn't remember any of this, and I'm in no rush to tell her, but because of that, and some other inconsistencies, I feel compelled to look into it. Since the identity wasn't in question during the first autopsy, the collected prints weren't checked, so it's being done now."

"Wouldn't that be enough?"

"It would be if I could trust those findings to be accurate, but I can't. Hell, I can't be sure anything's been accurate with this investigation. I want this case settled. The body seems the best place to start. So, will you help me?"

———⁂———

Kenny shifted on the tiny cot, searching for the foreign concept of comfort. His body was used to down feathers and silk sheets, not this hideous green refuse Fritz must have snatched from the back lot of a military store. For all the time he'd been captive, the things that kept him sane were his constant prayers and hope that somehow, someway, Darci would find him.

The door slamming against the wall startled him. Kenny looked up to see Fritz, red-faced and agitated, storm into the room, with Eva following closely behind.

"Fritz, you have to calm down. It might not be . . ."

The loud smack to Eva's face roused a dormant instinct in Kenny he didn't realize he had. He leapt from the cot and made a feverish attempt to break free from his prison and run to his sister's aid.

A deadly burning gaze froze Kenny's movements. Stomping over, Fritz pulled a revolver from the waistband of his slacks and pointed it between the bars and directly at Kenny's head.

"Fritz, don't!" Eva shouted.

Kenny's heart pounded as the angry gunman turned blazing eyes on his sister. Fear infiltrated every pore of his body, but he refused to show any emotion. He would never give Fritz the satisfaction, and to show fear at this moment would be of little good to Eva. If she saw he was afraid, there was no telling what she would do. And what was she doing? She'd been anything but sisterly since he'd become her captive, yet now she was coming to his defense.

Eva sniffled as she wrapped her arms around Fritz's. "You should calm down."

"Calm down! That bitch woke up!"

Kenny studied the irate man. What was Fritz talking about? He looked over at his sister, hoping she'd press the matter.

"Darci?" said Eva.

"Who else?" Fritz barked. "If she's said anything . . ."

"Darci?" Kenny repeated. He looked from Eva to Fritz. "What are you talking about? What happened to Darci?"

"Shut the hell up!"

"I will not!"

Fritz pointed the gun, but Kenny refused to back down. If Fritz didn't have a pistol, and this was a movie and not real life, he would reach through the bars and try to strangle the man. He held Fritz's furious glare. "You're not going to shoot me," Kenny said. "You need me, whether you choose to believe it or not. And if I die, you'll never get my money. And if anything happens to Darci, and you're responsible, the cops won't stop looking until they find the guilty party, and you'll spend the rest of your miserable life behind bars."

"No one can touch me."

"No? Then why are you so worried, huh? Now, answer me! What happened to Darci?"

While Fritz stared at him tight-lipped, Kenny heard what he needed on the television his sister left playing when she raced out to welcome Fritz. A breaking news report, following the conclusion of the soap Eva watched faithfully, stated Darci had regained consciousness after being struck by a car.

Whatever else the reporter said got lost in the roar of blood in Kenny's ears. His eyes cut to Fritz. "You son of a bitch! You ran over her." Kenny struggled to free himself, pulling on the bars, desperate to break free and somehow get his hands around Fritz's neck. "What the hell is wrong with you?" He looked to his sister. "Damn it, Eva, how could you let him do this?"

"I didn't let him," she said. "I didn't know about it. Besides, if Darci had just given me my money, Fritz wouldn't have been in her neighborhood to try to talk to her."

"Talk to her? He ran her down like she was a stray dog! Darci is following my wishes. Do you not know a will is a legal document? She can't do what she wants. She did what I asked of her. And you tried to kill her, just to get to *my* money!"

"It's my money, Kenny. You left it to me."

"For when I was dead and if you followed conditions." He grunted. "Why am I explaining this again? Is being high that important to you?"

"You two shut up!" Fritz shouted.

"We should have waited until his trip to Rio and kidnapped him like we first planned. You decided to fake his death, Fritz. That wasn't my idea."

"It's too late for second thoughts now. What's done is done." Fritz moved toward Eva and dragged his forefinger against her cheek. Eva recoiled and stepped back. Fritz grabbed her arm. She tried to pull away but the man's hold wouldn't loosen. "We're in this together, Eva."

Kenny watched the unlikely exchange. If he could help his sister, right now he wasn't sure he would. It was amazing how fast things happened. He'd gone from despising his sister, to wanting to help her, to despising her again in two minutes flat. Faking his death was bad, but to learn they'd planned to kidnap him . . . Was there no end to what she'd do to get his money?

Eva persisted in her struggle for freedom. "Let go of me."

"Never." Fritz's eyes narrowed. "I'll always have a hold on you, whether I'm touching you or not. If I go down, you are going down with me. It took using my considerable connections and cashing in some big favors to set this whole thing up, and those same connections can make it look like you did it all." Fritz pushed Eva away and turned his gaze to Kenny. "And you'd better watch that eyeballing, because if anything does happen to me, you're dead." He pointed the gun at Kenny's head. "And this time it will be for real."

—◦∾◦—

"I don't understand."

Steed gazed over at Mr. Clayton as the Warwicks processed all they had just said. Suzette had seemed to age twenty years in the past ten minutes, but the confusion in her eyes remained the same.

"You want to unearth my boy?" said Thomas, who didn't look any more stable than his wife. "The medical examiner said . . ."

"I know, I know," Steed answered with a nod, "but there are some questions. The second examination will more than likely back the first, but I think if there's any chance foul play could have been involved, we have to look into it."

"Foul play?" Suzette's troubled gaze met the lawyer's. "Randall, you think we should do this?"

Mr. Clayton glanced at Steed and said, "I think you should follow your instincts."

"If you were me, would you allow this?"

After several quiet moments, Mr. Clayton nodded. "Yes, I believe I would."

Suzette held her hand out to her husband, who took it in a comforting grip. Steed found the couple's closeness in the wake of their personal tragedy awe-inspiring. He and Darci squabbled all the time, but he loved her with a passion as strong as their varying opinions, and he wanted a long and happy life with her. If Darci didn't remember everything before he could prove or disprove her theory, he felt they could have that; but if she did remember . . . Thinking the worst wasn't an option. "Mr. and Mrs. Warwick?" Steed prompted.

"All right, you can do this," Thomas said. "Can you tell me what you're looking for, Detective?"

"I can't say that I'm looking for anything specific, I'm just checking out a few things."

"Darci trusts you," said Mrs. Warwick. "She's like another daughter to us, so we're going to trust you, too. Does she know what you want to do?"

"Not yet." He intended to forever prove Kenny had killed himself and that those Hyde fingerprints were a crazy mix-up before telling Darci. Hopefully, this would occur long before she got her memory back. "It would be best if you didn't mention this to anyone, either. Not until it's over."

"Besides Darci, the only person we'd want to tell is Eva, and we haven't seen her since Kenny's will reading. She'll call now and again, but . . . We won't say anything, Detective. What happens next?" asked Thomas.

"Well?" Steed turned to Mr. Clayton.

Mr. Clayton pulled a document from his briefcase and handed Thomas the paper. "I'll need your signature to give permission for the authorities to exhume Kenneth's body. If you have any questions, just ask."

"I think it's safe to say we have questions about all of this." Thomas shook his head. Steed could feel the man's doubt stirring all the more. "It just doesn't seem right to exhume Kenny. Whatever went on with him, he's at peace now. To disturb that . . ."

Steed closed his eyes. Just when he thought he had them convinced, he got pulled back five steps. "I do understand your concerns, but if I didn't feel this was absolutely necessary, I wouldn't be here. We'll be respectful, sir."

Suzette shrugged when her husband's gaze met hers. "Whatever you think is right, I'll stand by you."

The sound of scribbling filled the quiet room. Thomas handed Steed the signed document. "There you go," he said. "I hope I haven't made a mistake."

Steed said nothing as he nodded. *Kenny didn't die.* Darci's words were never far from his mind. He, too, hoped he hadn't made a mistake.

CHAPTER 19

Darci opened her eyes to find Steed at her bedside. "Hey." She pulled the bed up to a reclining position, stifling a yawn. "How long have you been here?"

"About half an hour," he answered.

She gazed about the room. "Have I been relocated to a flower shop? Where did all these blooms come from?"

"Your adoring fans, friends, family, and me. Lots of people love you, Darci. How do you feel?"

"A little woozy. The pain medication," she explained.

"You need it. You got pretty banged up."

Steed closed his hands around hers. The warmth and strength of his touch was like a tonic for her whole body. It made her feel safe and so womanly. Darci smiled. How she'd missed simple things like holding his hand.

"Why are you smiling?" Steed asked.

"Because I love you. My parents do, too."

Steed grinned that cute, slightly coy, very sexy grin of his. Even with her body bruised and battered, it wasn't so broken it couldn't feel all the wanton emotions Steed stirred in her.

"Your parents love me?" he said.

"Well, they like you. At least they haven't said anything mean about you. I think they need a little more time." She laughed.

"I see that sense of humor is about the same."

"I think it's the drugs."

"Me, too. It's even worse than usual." He kissed her hands and held them close to his chest. "I'm so glad to see you like this. Just earlier today, you were . . ."

"Shhh. I'm awake now, and I don't plan to do my imitation of Rip Van Winkle anymore."

"I'm very glad to hear it." He smiled. "So, uh, what exactly did your parents say about me?"

"That you were quiet. 'The strong, silent type' is what Mama said. They both noted how much you seemed to care about me."

"I appreciate their sentiment, but I care about the environment. I love you, Darci." Steed drew a deep breath. His easy expression became more serious. "I'm not a perfect man. God knows I have my shortcomings. But, Darci, my love for you is the purest, most honest thing in my life. I have made some mistakes in this relationship, but this being in love thing is new for me. I'll probably make more mistakes, but it's never to intentionally hurt you. Watching you lie here so still for so many days . . ."

Darci pressed her fingers to his lips. "Steed, I'm not used to you talking this much and in such a deeply emotional way. It's making me a little uneasy." She gave him a smile. "I'm okay now. You don't have to do this."

"Yes, I do. While you were unconscious, all I could think about was how we always butted heads about Warwick. We lost time we'll never get back, and until you get closure, it will be more of the same."

"You said you would help me prove my theory about Kenny. Is that why you're talking like this?"

"More or less."

"So, what's the plan?" Steed walked to the window, gazing out into the dark fall night. Darci wondered what, if anything, held his attention so rapt. "Steed?" she said.

He turned around. "Yes?"

"I asked how you're going to find out what happened with Kenny. Are you going to have the case reopened?"

"I can't really discuss any specifics." Steed returned to the chair at her bedside. "I'm going to help you, Darci, but all I want is for you to get well. You have to take care of yourself."

"What is it?"

"What?" he said.

Darci watched Steed closely. "You're distracted. What aren't you telling me? Have you found something already?"

Steed made a funny face. He did that often when he wanted to change the subject and make her laugh. Usually it worked, but not this time. "Don't even try it, McGraw," Darci said. "We're going to talk about this."

He sighed. "Let's talk about it later, Darci."

"Later is now."

"No, later is later. You need your rest."

The emphatic tone in his voice angered Darci all the more. She hated when he played cop twenty-four/seven. She didn't need protecting, she needed answers. A frown tightened her face.

Steed took her hand and grazed her cheek with a feather-soft kiss. Just like that, her anger vanished. She would never understand how one man could anger her, calm her, and make her feel like the most beautiful woman in the world all without breaking a sweat.

"Darci, I promised I would help you with Warwick, and I will."

"You still think I'm nuts, don't you?"

"It doesn't matter. You feel the way you feel, and I'm going to help you get peace of mind. When there's something to tell, you'll be the first to know."

"I want to believe that, Steed, but I already feel like I'm in the dark. I can't remember hours of my life. That's scary."

"I know. Has the doctor said anything?"

"That I have to give it time, and when I need to remember something I will."

"Sounds like good advice. I know he also said you should get your rest, so I'm going to go." Steed stood and leaned over the bed. "I came back to say good night." That devilish grin returned to his lips. His eyes sparkled. "Think I can have a kiss? My mom used to always kiss my boo-boos and make them better. I have no problem kissing every inch of you, but I think your lips would be the more ideal place . . . at least for now."

Darci tried not to smile, but failed miserably. "Why do you make it so hard for me to stay angry with you?"

"Is that what I do? When did I start doing that?" Steed snapped his finger. "Oh, I know, you're still foggy from that head injury, right?" He laughed.

"Are you going to stand there cracking on me or are you going to kiss me?"

"I like option two." After a tender kiss, he caressed her cheek and said good night.

Darci settled into bed, but worry kept sleep elusive. Steed wasn't leveling with her. He felt loving her meant keeping her in the dark, and right now she didn't need that. Somehow, someway, she had to get her memory back. If he wouldn't give her the answers she needed, she'd have to find them for herself.

———

"Knock, knock!" Darci smiled as Jackie stuck her head inside the door. "Is somebody ready to go home?"

"Somebody has been ready for a long time," Darci answered, placing the remainder of the clothes and toiletries her parents had brought into her overnight bag, a feat that was a lot harder while dependent on crutches. "I can't believe I've been here for thirteen days."

"Since you were only awake for six, I can believe it." Jackie joined Darci at the small dresser. "You hobble over to the bed and let me finish this for you."

Grateful for the assistance, she did as Jackie instructed.

"I thought Steed would be here," Jackie said.

"Me, too, but I got a call from him earlier saying he got caught up in a case." She suspected it was Kenny's case, but Steed would never tell her that. "I'll see him later."

"Are you sure you don't want to come home with me? Carl and I would love to have you, and I don't feel comfortable with you being alone with your sprained ankle. Plus, you have bruised ribs, and bruised everything else. My God, you were hit by a car and were in a coma. You shouldn't be alone."

"You sound like Mama and Daddy, and I practically had to beg them to go back to Florida."

"But you want Uncle Chuck and Aunt Darlene in Sterling."

"I do, but not to hover. I'm home now. I guess I kinda want my parents home, too, just not as nursemaids. Besides, I won't really be alone, you're just down the street, and Steed will be around a lot of the time."

"Things are going well for you two?"

Darci nodded. "For the most part, yes."

Jackie zipped the bag and sat in the empty chair next to the bed. "I don't think I like the way that sounds."

"Steed is being very protective of me, and I appreciate that, but he does it too much. It's like he's trying to think for me, and I don't like that."

"Why do I get the feeling this is about Kenny?"

"Steed told me he'd help me."

"Help you?"

"I've had a problem with the way Kenny died for a long time, and right before I regained consciousness, I heard Steed say he'd help me find out what happened with Kenny."

Jackie groaned. "Darci, that man was so beside himself when you were comatose, he would have said anything to get you to wake up. I know you're not going to hold him to that."

"Yes, I am."

"He did his job. What more do you expect him to do?"

"I don't know, but I can tell you this, something is going on. Jackie, I can't remember anything from several hours before that car hit me, but I have a feeling something big happened. Steed knows what it is, and he won't tell me. My intuition tells me it's about Kenny. Otherwise, Steed would have never offered to help me with this."

"Not necessarily. He knows how obsessed you are about this, and maybe he thought telling you something shocking and hopeful would rouse you." Jackie made a sweeping motion with her hand. "It worked."

"It's more than that. During our hospital version of Thanksgiving dinner, he put up a good front of being engaging, talking sports with Daddy and complimenting Mama, but he was distracted." Darci closed her eyes, hoping to shake loose the memory resting right at the edge of her brain like a ripe apple on a tree. "I know it's something."

"It's just my opinion, but I think you should stop trying to make yourself remember. It will only keep the memory further away."

"You sound like Steed."

"I'll take that as a compliment." Jackie handed Darci the crutches. "Have you been discharged?"

"I have the copies inside my bag."

Jackie looked about the room. "You're not planning to take up horticulture, are you?" she said of the many flowers and green plants.

"Relax." Darci laughed. "I'm only taking the arrangements from my folks and Steed, and donating the rest to other patients."

"That's a relief. I'll get a nurse and your chariot and we'll be on our way."

Darci drew herself back into remembering after Jackie left. She knew Steed's case was about Kenny. So, if he promised to help her, why wasn't he telling her anything? She closed her eyes, squeezing them tighter and tighter. She had to remember. She had to know what was going on.

———— ∞ ————

"What are you saying?"

The doctor placed his glasses in the pocket of his light blue scrubs. "How can I be clearer, Detective? This is not Kenneth Warwick."

The words hadn't come as a surprise to Steed, considering the prints from the first autopsy said the same, but that didn't make them any easier to hear. Darci was right. She'd always been right. Steed eyed Dr. Josiah Horne, one of the leading forensic pathologists in the state. The answer to Steed's next question was all but a given, but he had to ask it nonetheless. "Who is the victim?"

"According to fingerprint analysis and DNA samples, this is Jason Hyde." The man brushed his hand through his balding gray hair and scratched his potbelly. "A petty criminal, did a short stint in Crider County Jail. Everything is consistent with the findings from the first autopsy, minus the identity."

"Uh-huh."

"I saw the pictures from the first autopsy. Hyde and Warwick could have been twins." Dr. Horne handed Steed the file. "Have I answered your questions?"

After several moments, Steed nodded. "Yes, Doctor, thank you." Clasping the autopsy report, Steed returned to his truck. He stared at the closed file, trying to decide whether to call Darci or Chief Rogers. Before he could choose, his cell phone rang. His gaze stayed on the file as he answered. "McGraw."

"Hi, it's me."

Steed blinked, his concentration broken by Darci's voice. "Hey." He cleared his throat. "Where are you?"

"I just got home," she said. "When are you coming over?"

"Soon. I have a couple of things to take care of first, but you'll definitely see me soon."

"Good. Steed, we have to talk."

He nodded as his eyes focused once again on the file. "Yes, we definitely do."

———≈≈≈———

Veins throbbed to near bursting at Rogers's temples as he paced around his office. "How the hell could something like this happen?" he bellowed. "Where is Warwick?"

"If I knew the answer to that, we wouldn't have anything to talk about," Steed answered.

Malena closed the file and set it on Rogers's desk. "This is unbelievable," she said.

"It is that." Steed massaged his temples. "From day one Darci had doubts. She said Warwick would never kill himself." He sighed. "She said he didn't die, and she was right."

Rogers stopped pacing long enough to fix outraged eyes on Steed. "What? Is that why you wanted the exhumation? Because of something Darci said?"

"Yes—no."

"Which is it, Steed?" Malena asked.

"Kinda both, I guess. Darci doesn't remember any of this, but we had a big blowup because Benjamin told her the case got reopened and I didn't. Right before her accident, she called and told me we were all wrong, that Warwick didn't die. She didn't get to tell me how she knew, but she mentioned the le . . ." Steed grunted. *That letter from Warwick's.* He raced to the door. "I gotta check a lead."

"McGraw!" Rogers thundered.

"I'll fill you both in later, but I . . . I have to go."

Steed phoned Carl on the way to Darci's and got the okay to ask questions, but was warned not to force memories. Steed had a feeling he wouldn't have to do much forcing. Darci was close to remembering. Every minute he spent with her said as much.

He tried not to think of her reaction as he maneuvered through the late afternoon traffic. Darci would be so angry with him, but perhaps her happiness at learning her friend was still alive would keep her from exploding. Steed reached the house, drew a breath, and stepped out of the car.

CHAPTER 20

Darci ignored the dull throbbing in her foot as she leaned into Steed's strong arms and lost herself in his tantalizing kiss. He had the most amazing lips, soft, supple, and so full of expression. From the way he smiled, to the way he kissed her, to the way she'd wanted to button them with every word he uttered when they'd first met. How fast things had changed.

"That's what I call a great hello," she said, brushing remnants of lipstick from Steed's lips.

"It was that and a welcome home." Steed helped her back to the couch. "Are you settling in okay?"

"Yeah. I've spent most of my time right here in front of the TV. I've gotten caught up in that crazy soap you watch."

He chuckled. "It keeps your mind occupied and it's a release. Makes you forget about your problems for an hour."

"For just an hour." Several quiet moments passed. "You know what I want to ask you."

Nodding, Steed sat. "Do you remember anything?"

"When I'm asleep I remember something, but when I wake up I don't. Something is going on, right?"

"Yeah. Warwick's case has been reopened."

"Did you do that?"

"No." Steed dragged his hands over his face and sat back. "I don't know how to tell you this."

Uneasiness settled in Darci's stomach. Steed was more serious than usual, and that put her more on edge. "Tell me what?" she asked.

"You were right. Warwick didn't kill himself."

Darci stared at him in disbelief, hearing the words, but not believing she'd heard them. Steed had said Kenny didn't kill himself. Was she dreaming?

"Are you going to say something, Darci?"

"How . . ."

"We're still trying to figure out the details, but we know for a fact he didn't kill himself. You said he didn't die, and you were right."

"Whoa!" She held up her hand. "I said what?"

"Darci . . ." he began.

"Don't Darci me!" Her body trembled with rage. "What did I tell you?"

Steed remained silent.

"Answer me!" she demanded.

"Right before your accident, you called and told me Warwick didn't die and you had proof. You mentioned the letter."

"The letter? The one I found at the house?"

"I imagine so. You were—you were fixated on that letter. Insistent there was something about it. Do you have any idea what it could have been? How you managed to know what the authorities didn't have a clue about?"

"If I was on my way to see you, the letter must be in my purse. Jackie told me she put it up in the closet." Darci grabbed her crutches. "I'll get it."

"I can do that for you."

She held out a crutch, halting his movement. "No, you stay here. I need a minute to calm down, and you need to prepare to answer more questions."

The time away did little to calm Darci, and the sheepish look on Steed's face when she returned didn't help.

He stood as she approached. "Is the letter in there?"

"I haven't looked." Against her better judgment, Darci accepted his assistance back to the couch. She grimaced as the weight of falling back aggravated the pain in her foot and side.

"Do you need to take your meds?" he asked.

"No. They make me groggy, and I want to keep my focus." She plundered inside the purse and pulled out two folded sheets of paper.

"What's the other sheet?"

"Gimme a second and I'll tell you!"

Steed recoiled.

Darci hated being abrupt, but was too angry to apologize. She looked from one sheet to the next and then read the words aloud. "Not dead. With Eva cop Fritz—"

"Fritz?"

"That's the one you didn't like, right?"

"Yeah. Go on."

"With Eva cop Fritz in cabin. Help." She handed Steed the page. "A hidden message was in the letter. I used our code."

"Code?"

"Something we did as kids." Darci rubbed her temples, staving off the growing ache behind her eyes. It was as if her head was in a vise and the squeeze was on. She groaned.

"You sure you're all right?"

"It's just a headache." She continued massaging her temples. "Miss Sophie reminded me of the code when I was there with Jacob." She dropped her hands and met Steed's concerned eyes. His worry made her angrier, and intensified her pain. "Jacob. He told me the case had been reopened and you didn't. Your promotion was more important than me."

"Darci, I can explain . . ."

"You always have an explanation, but I don't want to hear anymore." Darci closed her eyes as memories came flooding back. "We had a fight. We broke up."

"We were angry. You definitely had reason to be upset with me, but I want—I *need* you to see things from my point of view."

"Why should I?"

"Because I love you. Darci, I was trying to protect you. You were so . . ."

"Right! I was right, Steed."

"If you want to be technical, Darci, I was right, too."

"How do you figure?"

Steed reached for her hands, but she pulled away. The last thing she needed was his touch adding unwanted influence to whatever he was about to say.

"You insisted your friend couldn't kill himself," he said.

"And he didn't."

"But the person in the house, Jason Hyde, did. I had the body exhumed and a positive identification was made. The guy looked like Warwick. Warwick's parents thought it was him, you even thought it was him, so Eva's false identification didn't raise any flags. A lot of strings were pulled to make this happen. Kenny's message said a cop named Fritz helped Eva. If he's in cahoots with Eva . . ."

"You think she'll hurt Kenny?"

"You know her better than I do, but she allowed her parents and the whole world to think he was dead. What would she have to lose if she actually killed him? There's no telling what Fritz will do. He quit the force soon after Kenny's 'death' when Rogers wouldn't consider making him a detective."

Tension knotted the muscles in Darci's neck and the ache in her head grew stronger. As crazy as she thought Eva was, she didn't think she'd gone this far off the deep end, and Steed made this Fritz sound even worse. "You have to find Kenny."

Steed stood. "I'm going to do everything I can, Darci."

"I'm going with you." Steed opened his mouth but Darci shushed his words. "I'm going! If you had listened to me and believed in me sooner, this situation wouldn't be as dangerous as I fear it's already gotten." She grabbed her crutches and stood. "If we don't find Kenny before it's too late, it will be your fault, and I will *never* forgive you."

⚛

Fritz paced the room. Kenny had never seen him so out of sorts. If the man left, maybe he'd slip up on the outside and someone, anyone, would rescue him. He didn't know what was going on with Darci. The news report said she was conscious, but he would worry until he saw for himself she was okay.

"Damn!" Fritz smashed a glass against the wall and began an expletive-laced diatribe about Darci and what could happen to him if she talked. At the end of the final curse, his angry eyes met Kenny's. "This is your fault!" he screamed.

Kenny's gaze never wavered. He felt anger that eclipsed Fritz's a thousand times over. This man was upset about getting caught for something he did wrong, while Kenny sat locked away as his hostage.

"How do you figure this is my fault?" Kenny fired back. "I don't recall asking to be kidnapped and presumed dead, and I'm equally certain Darci didn't want to be hit by a car." He made his way to the bars, wanting to get closer to Fritz as he taunted him. "I'm glad she's okay and I hope she talks. I hope like hell the cops come looking for your rotten ass and they find out what you and my junkie sister have done."

Fritz charged over and slammed his closed fist against Kenny's mouth, rattling his teeth. The rancid taste of blood erupted on Kenny's tongue.

Fritz grabbed a handful of Kenny's hair and smashed his face to the bars. "Not another word out of you!" Fritz warned, tightening his grip on Kenny's hair. "Do you hear me?"

"Kinda hard not to with you screaming in my ear."

Fritz released the hair and shoved Kenny away. A new curse-laced tirade began.

Even with a busted lip and what felt like a patch of hair ripped from his scalp, Kenny found reason to smile. The more agitated Fritz became, the more certain he was his rescue would soon be at hand.

⁂

The station bustled with activity. Uniformed officers streamed from the detectives' office to the main computer in the communications room and back again. "You really should have stayed at your place, Darci," Steed said, pausing in his barking of orders long enough to cast concerned eyes on her. "It's been hours, and we're still gathering information. You need to be at home resting."

"I can feel just as miserable here as I can there. At least here I'll see what's going on for myself. You've proven time and again you can't be trusted to tell me the truth."

"How many times do I have to say I'm sorry? I didn't do any of this to be malicious. I was . . ."

"Looking out for me," Darci finished in a huff. "Don't remind me." The headache was gone, but her foot hurt like nobody's business. She rubbed her throbbing ankle. Maybe she should have popped one of those pain pills after all.

"You need anything?"

"No."

"Darci?"

She grunted and held up her hand, keeping him behind the desk before he approached. "Don't try to be helpful now. It's not winning you any points with me."

"Fine! Forgive me for caring." Steed swiped up a file and stormed out of the room.

Part of Darci wanted to call him back and apologize, but the proud part of her wouldn't allow it. She had every right to be angry, and it was his fault. She didn't owe him anything.

Minutes later, Malena entered the office.

"Are you all right?" Malena asked, settling on the edge of Steed's desk.

"I don't know what I am," she answered.

"Malena!" Steed approached with Rogers and whispered something to Malena.

Darci sat up. "What's going on?" Steed met her gaze but said nothing. "You might as well tell me," she said.

"We've tracked down a location for a small fishing cabin between here and Crider that Fritz had mentioned to a couple of officers. We're headed there now."

Darci reached for her crutches and pulled herself up. "Okay, let's go."

"What *let's*?"

"I'm not staying here, Steed."

"Yes, you are."

"I am not being kept out of this again."

"This could be dangerous, Darci. You'll only be in the way, and you could be hurt more than you already are. So, sit down!"

The determination in Steed's eyes proved arguing with him would be futile and a waste of valuable time. "Fine." She sat.

"Be careful," Rogers said.

"Will do." Steed looked in Darci's direction as Malena left for her car. "Chief, keep your eye on her." Steed grabbed his leather jacket. "Come on, Jackson, you're driving."

CHAPTER 21

"Dim the lights and slow down," Steed instructed Jackson and the officers following them as they approached to within a mile of the cabin. He returned the radio to the dash. With the twists and turns this case and day had taken, he had to have both end on a good note, and finding Warwick alive was the only way to do that. Steed wasn't sure if Fritz and Eva were in the cabin, but he had enough back-up to be prepared for anything. He didn't want any more slip-ups.

"I appreciate you having enough faith in me to bring me along," said Jackson, never once averting his gaze from the dark road straight ahead. "I know how important this case is."

"I trust you, Jackson," Steed said. "Yeah, you're green, but you're eager, and you're not cocky." A trait Steed had in abundance when he was a rookie, and to his detriment, held on to way too long.

"Ms. Clarke seemed pretty upset with you."

"She is beyond upset. I didn't tell her the case got reopened, and she's not happy. I don't really blame her, but the person in that house committed suicide, and the body and the prints on the gun were identified as Warwick's. I thought I was protecting her from being hurt." *I thought.* His thinking had gotten him into this mess. Darci didn't need him to think for her. She'd said that countless times. "I should have told her."

"You kept quiet because you love her. Ms. Clarke knows that, and in time she'll forgive you. My Krista and I have been together for six years, and in my experience with women and love, a little time for cooling off works wonders."

Steed blinked. "Your Krista?"

"Yes, sir, my wife."

"Wife? You're married, Jackson?"

"Yes, sir. Almost one year to my high school sweetheart."

"How come you never told me before now?"

"You never asked, sir," Jackson answered, still looking straight ahead. "I didn't have a reason to bring it up before, but now seemed to be a good time." Jackson pulled out a necklace tucked inside his shirt. "I keep her ring next to my heart, as she does mine. So even apart, we're close. Being away from Krista while I get settled here has been hard, but she'll be moving to Sterling before Christmas. That's going to make this the best holiday ever."

"That's good for you, Jackson." Steed smiled but couldn't help feeling a little jealous. Jackson wanted to learn detective work more than anything, and all Steed wanted was to have Darci in his life. "I doubt I'll ever have a Christmas like that to look forward to."

"I'm sure you will."

"I appreciate your optimism, but if we don't get Warwick out of that cabin in one piece, it won't happen."

Steed picked up the radio. "Pull over, everybody. It's time to take position."

———⟆∾⟅———

"You're really uptight, Fritz." Kenny tilted his head, grinning at the frazzled man. His mouth hurt like hell, but he couldn't give up the opportunity to twist the knife. "If I didn't know better, I'd think you were scared."

Fritz's eye twitched. "Shut the hell up!"

"Or what? You're gonna kill me?" Kenny nudged his head at Eva. Her hands swept up and down her arms and her feet tapped an erratic beat on the floor. "Eva's about to jump out of her skin. I think she needs one of your power drinks."

"Kenny, stop it!" Eva shouted, raking shaky fingers through her dark hair. "I didn't want this."

"No, you just wanted my money."

"You should have helped me."

"I tried to help you, but you didn't want my help." Kenny glanced at Fritz. Now was the time to get Eva to help him. To get her to see what a true lowlife her new love was. "You see how scared he is. What do you think is going to happen when the cops get him? You do know the cops are going to get him, right?"

Eva covered her ears. "I can't listen to this."

"You're gonna listen! When the cops nab Fritz, he's going to do any and everything he can to save himself. The authorities don't have a clue about me, but he'll give them one, and he'll make sure you take the full blame for this."

Kenny shifted on the cot as Eva dropped her hands and approached Fritz. His planted seed had taken root, and he wanted a good angle to see the fruits of his labor.

"Is what he's saying true? Are you going to sell me out?"

"No," Fritz answered in a huff. "He's playing you."

"Why would he do that?"

"So you'll turn on me."

"You ran over Darci, Fritz! She's been dating that detective, Steed McGraw. He's not going to drop this."

Kenny stared at his sister. *Steed McGraw?* He remembered meeting Steed once about a year ago when he came to record a spot on holiday safety for the evening news, and he seemed way too serious. Darci was serious, but . . . *How did she get hooked up with that guy?* She liked the suit-and-tie business type, not small-town-detective-in-denim type.

"What's this about Darci and Steed McGraw?" he asked.

His question went unanswered as the exchange between Eva and Fritz intensified.

"You're worried about nothing," Fritz said. "McGraw can't trace this back to me, so I won't have a chance to blame you."

"Which means if you got the opportunity, you'd jump on it!" Eva shot back. "I knew this suicide thing was a bad idea, but I went along with it. I let my parents think my brother was dead. I can't believe this. What have I done?" Eva turned to Kenny, and for the first time since his capture, he saw more than a flicker of remorse in her eyes. "Oh, Kenny, what have I done?"

Renewed hope filled Kenny's spirit. Eva wasn't too far gone. He could get her to let him go. He just had to be alone with her again, and he knew he could make it happen.

"Eva, don't fall for that." Fritz approached her, his hands closed around her face. "Listen to Fritz, don't I always take care of you. Don't I give you everything you need?" He kissed her. "Don't I?"

"I guess, yeah," she said softly, nodding.

"Don't guess. Trust me. I'll be back soon."

"Where are you going?" Kenny and Eva asked in unison.

"To the station. I'm going to find out just what McGraw knows about me running over Darci Clarke, if anything."

Fritz pulled open the door to find guns drawn and pointed. "I know quite a lot, Fritzano. Thanks to you," Steed said.

Fritz moved back. "McGraw."

Relief pumped through Kenny's body. *Thank you, God!*

"Take another step and it will be your last. Trust me, you don't want to give me more reason than I already have to rip your head off." Steed turned Fritz around and slapped on the cuffs. "You are under arrest!" Kenny couldn't hear what more Steed said to Fritz after reading the man his rights, but the look on Steed's face and Fritz's reaction confirmed the words weren't of a cordial nature.

Steed patted Fritz down while a young blonde officer handcuffed and arrested Eva. An attractive black woman in plain clothes and the eight uniformed officers who helped make up the rescue team escorted Fritz and Eva outside while Steed made his way to Kenny with the ring of keys he'd found in Fritz's pocket.

"You look pretty good for a dead guy, Warwick," Steed said, opening the door to the prison after trying the third key.

"How's Darci?" Kenny asked.

"She'll be doing a whole lot better once she sees you."

—◌◌◌—

"Thank you for driving me out here, Martin. I don't think I could have stayed at that police station another minute." Darci nibbled anxiously on her thumbnail as Chief Rogers drove down the long, dark country road. "Shouldn't we know something?"

"They haven't been gone that long, Darci. I promise, when there's something to know, we'll know about it." The chief's phone rang moments after he finished his sentence. "See? Rogers," he said. "Yes, McGraw, what do you have?" He paused for a while. "Really." Martin nodded. "Very good."

"What's very good?" Darci touched his forearm. "Do they have Kenny? Is he okay?"

Rogers held up his hand, silencing her words. "Yes, she got a little anxious so we started out. Okay, we'll be there soon." Chief Rogers ended the call and turned to her. "It's over. Warwick is a little bruised and bloody, but he's alive."

Darci clasped her hands together and looked up. "Thank you, Lord."

"Also, Darci, we learned it was Fritz that ran into you."

"Was all of this about Kenny's money?"

"I guess we'll know soon enough. You ready to see him?"

"Yes!"

The flip of switches on the dash transformed the dark, quiet police car to a brightly lit, siren-wailing speed-mobile. Minutes later, they pulled up to a small, secluded cabin on the end of a dirt road. Flashing lights from police cars and the ambulance provided splashes of light to the dark area, allowing Darci to spot her friend being attended to by an EMT.

"Kenny!" Leaving her crutches on the back seat, Darci hobbled over to her friend.

"Darci!" Kenny hopped off the back of the ambulance and raced over, sweeping her into his arms.

"I knew you wouldn't kill yourself, Kenny." The happiness in her heart overrode the throbbing pain in her ankle and side as she tightened her arms around him. "I knew it."

"I never had a doubt. Nobody knows me like you." Kenny lowered Darci to the ground. His hand cupped her cheek. "How are you? I heard you were hit by a car. Did that hug hurt?"

"No. All I feel right now is happiness and relief." She took a little step back and frowned. "You look horrible."

Kenny chuckled. "Ever the honest one. I could use a hot shower, shave, and a warm, soft body right about now."

"Well, I can help you with the first two things, but the last one . . ." Her voice trailed off as she cast her gaze toward the porch. Steed stood with Chief Rogers. His superior was saying something, but Steed's eyes were fixed on her.

"You and McGraw, huh? How the heck did that happen?"

"It's a long story."

"Must be. Luckily, I have lots of time to hear it."

"It doesn't matter." She turned back to Kenny. "Whatever it was, it's over now."

"Somehow I doubt that." Kenny glanced over at Steed. "The guy hasn't stopped looking at you since you hopped over to me. In fact, he looks like he's about ready to come over here and beat the hell outta me."

A little smile tickled Darci's lips. Steed was jealous. *Good!* She gave Kenny another big hug and a peck on his bruised lips. Steed's mouth tightened. He jammed his hands in his pockets. Darci smiled. Yes, he was definitely battling a green-eyed monster.

"Ouch." Kenny pulled away, grimacing as he grazed his busted lips. "I'm already battered, Darci. Are you trying to get me killed for real?"

"No. Just giving Steed McGraw something to think about."

⁓⁓

Steed watched Darci interact with her "best friend" until he could stand it no more. Feeling jealous of

Kenneth Warwick when he was a living memory Darci couldn't shake was one thing, but now . . . He took a step forward.

Chief Rogers grabbed his arm. "Where are you going?"

"I need to talk to Warwick. We need to know how this happened."

"Is that the real reason you're in such a hurry to get over there?"

"What other reason could there be?"

"I don't know, maybe the fire burning in your eyes. You're so jealous right now you can barely see straight. If you go over there, you're liable to do something you'll regret."

"I wouldn't regret it," Steed murmured under his breath.

The chief's hand closed around Steed's shoulder. "Go to the station and see what you can get out of the sister and Fritzano. I'll drive Warwick and Darci over in my car."

"Maybe I should . . ."

"Do as I say, McGraw."

Steed's feet stayed planted. He couldn't pull his eyes away from Darci. Part of him was happy, cheering her elation at being reunited with her friend. But another part of him, the possessive boyfriend, wanted to push Warwick in the path of one of the departing cruisers and get Darci to see there was another man on the premises who loved her and wanted some alone time in her arms. A man who wanted more than friendship. Darci's laughter rang in his ears. Steed groaned. He definitely needed to go.

Taking the scenic route to the station only made the situation worse, as it gave him more time to imagine Darci in the arms of a man other than him. Intellectually, he knew she and Warwick were just friends, but seeing that closeness in action . . . He didn't like it. He didn't like it at all.

"The sister is waiting in the interrogation room, and Fritz is in lockup," said Jackson when Steed walked into the station.

"Fine." Steed walked to his desk and dropped into his chair. "What is it?" he asked, feeling Jackson's gaze on him.

"Would it be okay if I tag along when you question Ms. Jasper?"

"I don't see why not." Steed stood. "Just look and listen, okay?"

Jackson smiled brightly and nodded. "Yes, sir."

Darci's entrance into the station with Kenny and Chief Rogers interrupted the trek to the interrogation room. Steed's eyes fixed on Darci. She looked a bit tired as she leaned on her crutches. He walked over. "You really should go home, Darci," he said. "How is your ankle? Are you in pain?"

She shot him a look that cut him to the quick. "You tell me." Darci touched Kenny's arm and motioned to the chairs against the wall. "I'll wait for you over there."

Rogers cleared his throat, ending the deafening quiet in the room. "McGraw, have you questioned Ms. Jasper?"

Steed pulled his gaze from Darci. "I was just on my way."

"Let it wait. Mr. Warwick wants to make his statement."

"I want this over," Kenny said. "The sooner the better."

Steed nodded. Maybe some alone time with Warwick would be a good thing. "Fine." He pointed his hand in the direction of the detectives' office. "Right this way."

Kenny walked ahead of him into the office. Steed's gaze locked with Darci's for a long moment, and then he followed her friend inside and closed the door with a resounding click.

CHAPTER 22

"You're about as bad as he is."

Darci jumped at the sound of the chief's voice. Her pre-occupation with the goings-on behind the office door distracted her from the pain in her foot. Awakened from her curious thoughts, the throbbing ache became all too real. She should have brought along some of her medication.

"I'm sorry I scared you," he said, sitting.

"You didn't—not really." Darci tore her gaze from the door. Two of the three most important men in her life were inside that office. Were they talking only about the case? The wondering drove her crazy. "What was it you said before?"

"I could have said your hair was on fire, but it wouldn't have mattered. I know you want to work out whatever this is."

"It's not that simple."

"It could be. McGraw loves you."

"I know that, but Steed's love is . . . Steed is complicated, and I don't know if I want to make up with him."

"I would almost believe that, if I hadn't seen you burning a hole through that door just now. You're angry, Darci. Anger has a way of overriding other emotions. I know you love him, too. Otherwise, you wouldn't be so upset."

Darci said nothing. She didn't know what to say. She did love Steed, but she didn't know if she'd ever be able to handle the way he expressed his love. It made her crazy and sad.

"All I'm saying is you should think long and hard before you walk away from something that will leave you with a lifetime of regret." He covered her hand. "You need anything? A cup of water, a soft drink, some coffee?"

"No, thank you."

"If you change your mind, just ask Jackson."

Darci chuckled. Poor Jackson was everything to everyone in this squad room. "I will. Thank you, Martin."

"You're welcome. You take care of yourself."

"I will." Darci returned her attention to the door when the chief left. She didn't hear any raised voices, but still . . . She sighed. *What's going on in there?*

———◈◈◈———

"So, you never knew of Jason Hyde prior to his unexpected visit to your home?"

"I didn't know this guy from Adam. I walked in to find him sitting on the couch and wearing my favorite suit. I was so pissed to see him there, looking like me but clearly not me, I didn't think to be scared." Kenny sighed. "I should have been scared. He said he'd sent me some letters, and he probably did, but I don't generally read letters from guys. Had I known he was an overzealous fan about to shoot himself in the head, I think I would have walked out as soon as I walked in."

245

"I bet." The hostility Steed felt toward Kenny had ebbed away over the last half hour. Warwick had gone through a horrible situation, and at the hands of his own sister. It was hard to envy a man who had gone through such an ordeal and still had to face the fallout. "I'm sorry about all of this."

"Why are you apologizing? You didn't cause this." Kenny released a long breath. "So, what happens to Eva now?"

"Depends on her lawyer. She's facing serious charges."

"Eva's always had problems, but she's really hit rock bottom with this Fritz. It's like he had a spell on her. He seems normal, but he's nuts. He ran over Darci and blamed her."

Steed's jaw tightened. He already couldn't stand Fritz, and it literally took everything in him not to beat the man to death after hearing what he'd done to Darci. "Well, I've had my issues with him for a while," Steed said. "How long has Eva known him?"

"I don't know. I suspect at least a couple of months. I'd never seen him with her prior to my being taken hostage. She told me they met when he stopped her for speeding."

"Speeding?"

Kenny nodded.

"Fritz was on the force a year and a half, and wanted to be detective the whole time. He quit soon after your unexpected and very tragic 'death.' I don't get how he did this to you."

"Fritz mentioned some connections, some big favors he called in, but never said names."

"Their original plan was to kidnap you?"

"Yes, when I was to fly out to Rio, but Hyde's death gave them a new twist on the plan. One that worked far better than I could have ever thought possible. The kidnapping had to have been planned for a while. You saw my accommodations. That didn't happen overnight."

"You're right. You know, I was convinced you did yourself in, but Darci never believed it."

"That's because Darci knows me. She knows me better than anyone, as I know her." Kenny sat back in his chair and folded his arms across his chest. His eyes narrowed.

Steed prepared himself to be on the receiving end of Kenny's questions.

"What's the deal with you two?" Kenny asked.

"Darci didn't tell you?"

"She hasn't said much at all, which is why I know something's up."

"Darci's not happy with me."

"That I do know. How did you two hook up? You're not exactly her type."

A frown twitched the corners of Steed's mouth. He suddenly didn't like Kenny so much. "Not her type?"

Kenny held up his hand. "There's no need to be offended. Darci has never done a lot of dating, but when she did, it was with uptown movers and shakers, not down-South detectives. I'm going to assume my case brought you two together."

"It did, but our love kept us together."

Kenny smirked.

Steed wanted to punch him. "What are you grinning about?"

"You. Darci's not in here. This rabid dog, jealous boyfriend routine is a waste of your time and energy. And you say you love her."

"I do love Darci."

"I wonder. You don't seem to know her very well."

"I know her extremely well."

"Yet you're so jealous."

"What I am is human. Darci is a beautiful woman, and best friend be damned, I don't like seeing her hanging all over another man. I don't want to lose her."

"Seems to me you've already done that. Otherwise, you wouldn't be so twisted up in knots and biting my head off for being her friend. And that's what I am, her *friend.* The one who risked his reputation in high school by buying her feminine products, and gave her a shoulder to cry on whenever she needed." Kenny stood. "If you keep this act up, you're going to lose Darci for good. I don't think you want that, and I'm pretty sure she doesn't, either. Now, are we done?"

"After you sign this." Steed pushed over Kenny's printed statement for his signature. "I'll be in touch if I have more questions."

Darci grabbed her crutches and hobbled over to the door the minute it opened. "Is everything okay?" she asked neither one in particular.

Kenny glanced at Steed and then turned to Darci with a smile. "It's fine, Darci," he answered. "You ready to go?"

"I am. Officer Jackson is going to drive us."

Steed took her arm before she could get away. Her quick intake of breath brought his hand down. Annoyance flashed in her eyes.

Steed sighed. "Can we talk first?" he asked.

"I don't think we have anything to talk about."

"I do." He frowned, not happy with having this conversation in front of Kenny. "Let's go into my office."

"I don't want to talk to you right now. It wouldn't be a good idea."

"I disagree. We have things to discuss, Darci." Steed stared at Kenny as the man's arm closed around Darci and his hand trailed up and down her arm. Steed's insides churned. She practically recoiled from his touch, but let Warwick, with his Hyde-looking self, all but molest her. "I'm sure Jackson can get your *friend* home safely," he said, unable to keep the edge out of his tone.

"I'm sure he can, too, but I want to help him all the same. I need time, Steed. Please, just give me that."

"Fine. While you're taking your time, I want you to keep in mind that everything I did was in keeping with my job, and I love you. Remember that. I love you, Darci."

Steed detected the slightest thaw in the hardness of her eyes. She hadn't written him off for good, not yet. It gave him hope.

She pulled up on her crutches and looked up at her friend. "Let's go."

Kenny nodded and opened the door for her.

Darci turned back, holding Steed's gaze for the briefest moment. He held a breath, hoping she'd drop those crutches and open her arms for him. Instead, she turned back and walked out of the station with Warwick.

Steed returned to his office and read Kenny's statement over and over. He couldn't understand how Fritz had made this happen. Who or what were these connections Warwick said Fritz used? Steed rubbed his eyes. He needed some coffee.

Just as he poured his first cup of the fresh brew, Jackson returned. Steed glanced at the wall clock. The man hadn't been gone fifteen minutes. Warwick lived just inside the city limits. At least twenty minutes one way. "Jackson, what are you doing back so soon? Having the squad car doesn't mean you should speed unnecessarily."

"I didn't, sir," Jackson answered.

"You couldn't have gotten Warwick home that fast."

"I didn't take him home. He stayed with Ms. Clarke."

Steed managed to keep a straight face from the emotional punch to his gut. "I see." He drank some coffee. Warwick was just her friend. Darci had told him that over and over again and Warwick had confirmed it.

"Is everything all right, Detective?"

"Fine." He had to squash this jealousy and find out how Fritz made the world think Kenneth Warwick killed himself. "I want you to get Paul Fritzano's personnel file. It's going to be a long night."

Kenny shrugged at Darci as he held the phone to his ear. From what she could tell, this conversation could last a while.

"Yes, Mom, I'm fine. No, you don't need to come back over. I'm just going to get some rest. Please, stop crying. Dad, get her to stop crying. Eva has her demons. You can't hold yourself responsible for what she does." There was a long pause on Kenny's end. He nodded. "No, I shouldn't have kept her addiction from you. Yes, I'm okay with that." Kenny shook his head moments later. "No, I don't hate her."

Darci hugged her warm mug of tea to her chest as she watched Kenny try to comfort his distraught parents. They hadn't lost their son to death, but it appeared they were about to lose their daughter to the judicial system. And Darci thought she had problems.

"Yes, in the morning. Good night." Kenny hung up the phone and sighed. "Maybe I should have gone home with them. They left an hour ago and have already called three times."

"They're happy, sad, scared, devastated. A lot has happened. You're alive, Kenny."

"Yes, I'm alive, and Eva is—" He shrugged and joined Darci on the couch. "Are you okay? Has your medicine kicked in?"

She shifted her injured foot, elevated on the coffee table with the help of two pillows. "I'm flying, can't you tell?"

Kenny scrunched his freshly shaven face. "Not really."

"Have you had enough to eat? You really look . . ."

"Like a blue cotton monster swallowed me," Kenny said with a laugh, tugging at the extra large T-shirt and jogging pants Darci had borrowed from her dad and decided to keep. "I'm full, clean, a little sore, but breathing. Having a pajama party with my best friend." Kenny flapped the right side of her ratty pink robe. "I thought you would have tossed this old thing by now."

"It's comfortable. Familiar."

"Familiar is good. Although, after everything I've been through, I'd think you'd want to dress in something more comfortable than a knee-length nightshirt. Hmm?" He winked.

She punched his arm, laughing. "You're still the same, you nut."

"Yes, I am. I'm great, Darci."

"Are you, really? You've been through so much."

"I have, but I made it through. I guess I should be jittery or something, but I'm just relieved and happy. I've never been one to spend a lot of time in church, but I prayed a lot while I was confined, and it helped me. It centered me. That and hoping you'd remember the code." He chuckled. "Honestly, I'm good. Worried about you."

"There's no need to be. I'm like you. I'm great."

"I wouldn't know firsthand, but from what I've heard, heartache's not so great. You haven't said so, but I know you love McGraw at least half as much as he clearly loves you. What happened? Why are you angry with him?"

She took a sip of her tea. The hot, minty beverage soothed and calmed her. She wanted to stay calm, and talking about Steed would make her angry. "I don't want to talk about it."

"I want you to. Did he cheat on you? Get frustrated with your vow of abstinence and have someone else take care of his 'needs'?" Kenny asked, making air quotes.

"No. Steed's been wonderful about that."

"That's interesting. McGraw . . ."

"What? Did he say we slept together?"

"No, he said he knew you extremely well. The way he said it made me wonder. You are aware he's jealous of me."

"Yes, and I hope it eats him alive."

"What did he do to make you like this?"

"He didn't believe in me and he didn't trust me. I kept insisting you wouldn't kill yourself, but I was the crazy one." She drew a breath to steady the anger, just thinking of this betrayal brought about. "He thought I was too close to you to accept the truth." She pressed her hand to his chest—warm, solid, real. "This is the truth. You're here, in my house, very much alive. And Steed McGraw, a man who supposedly loves me, couldn't believe in me. He couldn't be man enough to come to me and tell me there was the slightest question as to what happened to you. I can't get over that."

"Darci, he was doing his job."

"*You're* defending him? With little thanks to Steed, you are free from two twisted people who would have surely killed you. How can you be so understanding?"

"Because I am here. Darci, Steed is a cop. A detective. He can't let his emotions dictate how he does his job. If I were him, I'd think I killed myself, too."

She gasped. "Kenny!"

"You're blaming him for something he couldn't control. I'm glad you trusted in what you know of me, but it was a suicide in my house, and Fritz made it look like me.

Hyde looking so much like me didn't hurt. Your opinion as a grieving friend couldn't come into play. Besides, you were only sure I hadn't committed suicide. You thought I was dead. So, doesn't that make you wrong, too?"

Darci pulled up the lids of Kenny's eyes, staring closely. "Did Steed brainwash you?"

He scoffed and fanned her hands away. "No. I just see the way you look at him and the way your eyes light up when he walks into a room. Even with the anger, your love is clear. Steed's a part of you, and you won't be happy until you fix this."

"I can't deny I love him, but there's so much more. Steed is perplexing, Kenny."

"I think you knew this when you fell in love with him. Didn't stop you from falling, did it?"

"No, it didn't." Darci sighed. "Steed is so easy to love, but he makes it hard to want to love him."

"Nothing good comes easy." Kenny kissed her cheek. "Take a few days to be angry, then go see the man and try to work this out. I'm going to sleep." He got up from the couch. "You need help getting to bed or do you think you can make it on your own?"

"I'll be okay. You sleep well."

"In a real bed? There's no question. Good night."

Darci considered Kenny's advice as she finished her tea.

Despite of all her problems with Steed's "protection" of her, he had operated with her best interest in mind, and his jealousy was rather sweet. She smiled. Maybe one day of being angry would be enough.

CHAPTER 23

"Up and at 'em, McGraw!"

Steed's head shot up with a jerk at the chief's booming voice. He rubbed his neck, groaning as tired muscles constricted.

Rogers extended one of two steaming mugs of coffee. "Pulled an all-nighter, huh?" he said, sitting.

"Uh-huh." Steed took a big swallow of the hot liquid. "Thanks, I needed this."

"No problem." Rogers drank from his mug. "What you got?"

"Some answers as to how Fritz might've pulled this off." Steed slid his newly compiled folder to the chief.

Rogers silently reviewed the file as Steed finished his coffee. "Mona Reeves?" he said. "The lab tech?"

"Uh-huh. She's his cousin and ran the first set of prints. My guess is he came to her with a favor and she obliged."

"Has she been picked up for questioning?"

"Jackson should be bringing her in at any moment."

"Have you talked to Eva Jasper?"

"Not yet. Mr. Clayton came in last night with her parents and they talked. Seems she's ready to get help for this drug problem she has and is willing to fully cooperate with the department. The prosecutor is coming in later today, and maybe they can work out some sort of deal. After everything that family has been through, I hope they can get some peace."

"Speaking of people having peace, what about you and Darci? You talk to her yet?"

Steed tapped his empty mug on the desk. "She's not ready to talk." He grunted. "Warwick went home with her."

"Was that your reaction last night? The scorned man?"

"She went home with Warwick," Steed repeated.

"He's been like a brother to her for over twenty years."

"You said it, Chief, like a brother. There's no blood relation."

"And there will be no relationship between you two until you get over this ridiculous jealousy you have. When I told you to work on your people skills, it was for a reason. Problem is, you took it to the extreme. Darci is an independent and very strong woman. She doesn't need you to make decisions for her or handle her with kid gloves. There is a happy medium between pleasant and overbearing. You need to find it. And lose the jealousy while you're at it." Rogers smacked his hand on the desk and then grabbed his cup and left.

Steed turned his attention to the telephone. He wanted to call Darci, but he didn't want to hear Kenny's voice. He wouldn't call. The ball was in her court. She wanted time, and as hard as it was, he would give it to her.

"Detective McGraw?" Jackson entered the office, red-eyed and dead on his feet. "Ms. Reeves is in the waiting area."

"Send her in, Jackson, and then you go home. Thanks for all your help."

Jackson smiled. "You're welcome, sir. I'll see you, uh . . ."

"Tomorrow. Get some sleep, okay?"

"Yes, sir. Good-bye, sir."

Moments later Mona Reeves slinked into the office. "I was just on my way to work, Detective. Is there something wrong?"

"Could be." Steed walked over and closed the door. "Have a seat, Mona. I have some questions for you."

The short, unassuming woman sat. She'd been in the crime lab for ten years. Proficient and efficient, she did her job well and didn't kick up dust. Which, in hindsight, made her a good choice in this ploy.

"Have I done something?" Mona asked.

"You haven't heard from your cousin?"

Mona adjusted her round-rimmed glasses. "Cou—cousin?"

"Don't insult me with ignorance." Steed opened the file and pushed it forward. "We know Paul Fritzano is your cousin, and I suspect you aided him in falsifying evidence in regard to the suicide of Kenneth Warwick. A man we found very much alive last night."

The woman slumped, as if her spine had been snatched right out of her body. "I didn't want to do it, but I was afraid." Tears filled Mona's brown eyes. "Paul is my cousin, but he's . . . he's a very dangerous man, and he threatened to kill my husband if I didn't help him."

"Help him what?"

"He visited me the day this suicide happened, so when the call came in, I knew what to expect. He gave me a sample of fingerprints to 'find' on the gun."

"Why didn't you report this?"

"Report it? Paul threatened to kill my husband. Family doesn't mean anything to him. His father died in prison while serving time for a crime Paul committed."

"What crime?"

"The shooting death of a policeman. Paul didn't care about this officer or the fact his father had lost his freedom and his life for no reason. Hurting my husband or me wouldn't cause him to bat an eye."

Steed blinked. "Wait . . . wait a minute. His father was accused of killing a cop?"

"Not so much accused as he took the blame."

"How do you know this?"

"Paul told me right before he delivered his threat."

"And you believed it?"

"Yes! I was too little to remember on my own, but my family had whispered about this for years. From what I'd heard, my aunt and uncle loved each other madly, but Paul was a sore spot. He was their only child, but he was troubled. Had been from practically the time he was able to walk. At fourteen, he was a true terror. Uncle Alex wanted to send him away to a military school, somewhere to calm him, but Aunt Elena would have none of it. She almost died giving birth to him and she wanted him close. She said he just needed prayer, time, and guidance."

"What about this shooting?"

"Paul robbed an elderly neighbor at gunpoint, and the poor woman almost died from a heart attack. Once she recovered, she told Paul's parents, but was too scared to say anything to the authorities. Uncle Alex was adamant they send Paul away. He and Aunt Elena were arguing when a police officer came over. They had a store, and the officer would drop in. He'd never met Paul, but he knew Paul was the source of their trouble, so he offered to take him in for a while. Paul had been in the back of the store, and he heard this. He came out and shot the officer dead. My aunt begged Uncle Alex to save Paul from prison, and since he loved her more than anything, he did."

Steed closed his as eyes as he waged a futile battle to swallow the knot forming in his throat. *A store? Killed a cop? Uncle Alex? Alex Mancusi?* "Fritz killed a cop, let his father take the blame, and nobody said anything?"

"A cop helped cover it up. The officer's partner. Mul . . . Mulberry?"

Steed's guts twisted. This could not be happening. "Mulhaney?" he whispered.

Mona's eyes widened. "Yes! That's it. Peter Mulhaney."

"Why would the officer help cover this up?"

"Money. My aunt and uncle lived above the store and had been saving for a house. They had over ten thousand dollars, and the cop wanted it all for his silence. They gave it to him. Uncle Alex insisted my aunt and Paul move away and start fresh. After Uncle Alex died, my aunt met and married Luis Fritzano, and he adopted Paul, giving him a new name and a new start."

"Couldn't have been too good a start."

"It was a good act. Paul had been flying under the radar for years. Since none of his teen trouble resulted in arrests, when he moved back to New York years later, he was able to become a police office. I've heard rumblings he has ties to the Mafia." Mona rubbed her forehead, sighing. "I know I should have come forward when Paul approached me, but I didn't want him to harm my husband or me. If I lose my career, so be it."

"That may be the least of your problems. You might also have to face some criminal charges."

"I know."

Steed stood and pointed to the door. "Leave."

"What?"

"Go home. Not to the lab, home. Don't think of leaving the county. You'll be contacted if we need anything more."

Mona stood, her hands clasped together in sincere gratitude. "Thank you, Detective." She hurried out the door.

Steed slumped into his chair. His mind raced. The smug look Fritz always flashed burned in Steed's head, and like a healing wound having the scab ripped off, the grief he felt for the loss of his father was as fresh as if it had happened yesterday. This man who made the world think Kenneth Warwick killed himself had actually killed his father. *Fritz killed my father, and Uncle Pete knew.*

Rage dried Steed's tears, and all he could think about was wrapping his hands around Fritz's neck and squeezing every worthless breath from his body. Consumed with the need to fulfill his burning desire, Steed barreled from his desk and down the ten stairs to the male side of holding. After telling the guard to take a break, Steed made his way down the hall to the cells.

The scent of pine cleanser mingled with sweat and the misdirected urine drunken detainees had splashed on the floor. Steed arrived at Fritz's cell to find him curled on a cot with his back to the bars. He shook off the inviting opportunity to put a bullet in the man's back. That would be too easy. He wanted Fritz to see death coming. *Fritz . . . Paul Mancusi.* Steed kicked his boot against the bars. "Get up, you!"

Fritz jumped up with a start. "What the . . ." He turned toward the bars. "McGraw." The man's sinister dark eyes appraised Steed for several moments. His lips turned into a crooked grin. "So, you finally know." He sat up, chuckling. "Took you long enough, but I can't imagine you figured it out alone."

"Your cousin Mona filled me in on your past misdeeds."

"Stupid bitch. Who needs enemies when you got family?"

"You would know. The things you and Eva have done to your families defy description."

"Don't compare me to that drugged-out slut."

"You're right. Eva has an excuse for her behavior."

"Excuse? People do what they want. I didn't make my old man take the rap, he did that for my mother, but I'm not sorry he did, and I'm not sorry for anything I've done. So if you're waiting for an apology, you'll be waiting a long time."

"Why did you kill my father?"

"I felt like it," Fritz answered with a smirk. "That pig wanted me to live with him, to help my parents by straightening me out. As if he could. I straightened him out. I popped him so fast he never saw it coming. I saved my rep, your old lady hooked up with a rich guy, and Pete Mulhaney got his pockets lined pretty damn well. Everybody won."

Everybody won? Steed rubbed his inner arm against his holster, feeling the hard steel of his gun. Images of blood spilling from gaping wounds in Fritz's flesh regaled him. Blowing this bastard away would be his pleasure.

Fritz snapped his fingers, interrupting Steed's delightfully criminal thoughts. "You know, it was old Pete who made me see the many benefits of being a cop, the thrill of playing both sides. And I know how to play them. I'm in here now, but it won't stick. I'm untouchable, McGraw." Fritz snapped his finger. "You know what, I think I'm sorry about one thing. Darci. Mmm." The man's lascivious grin added an extra shot of fuel to the inferno raging through Steed's veins. "I'm sorry I didn't hit that before I hit that. I'm generally not down with the *sistas*, but that's one hot piece of . . ."

The door rattled from the force of Steed's hands wrapping around the bars. "Not . . . another . . . word!"

"C'mon, McGraw." Fritz stood, folding his arms. "How is she between the sheets? She looks a bit uptight, but I understand her kind are wildcats in the sack. Want to share some stories with an ex-fellow officer? Hmm?"

"I want to share something with you, all right." Steed pulled his gun from the holster and aimed it at Fritz's head.

Fritz eyes widened. "You wouldn't," he said.

"No?" Keeping the gun aimed, Steed unlocked the cell door.

"Help! Somebody help me!"

"I sent the guard upstairs. The other prisoners are too drunk to move, not that they would for an ex-cop like you. And no one upstairs can hear your screams. It's just you and me. McGraw and Mr. Untouchable."

Fritz backed up, falling onto the cot. He grabbed the pillow, using it as a shield as he cowered against the wall. "Okay, look, I'm sorry. I'm sorry for what I said about Darci and what I did to her and your father. I'm sorry about it all, okay? Now, put the gun down. Please, don't kill me."

Steed could only think of two things as the man pleaded for his life: his father and how a bullet had pierced his heart before he could try to reason with Fritz, and Darci and the fear she must have felt when she saw that car coming at her. Steed prayed he would feel the same lack of remorse Fritz has felt for all the hurt he'd inflicted on so many for so long.

He stepped inside, waving the gun. "Get on your knees."

"What?"

"Get on your damn knees!" Steed ordered.

Fritz hopped from the cot and fell to his knees.

"Put your hands together and beg some more."

The man trembled, his face ashen. "What?"

"Don't play deaf with me! Put your hands together and beg me not to kill your worthless ass." He pointed the gun between Fritz's eyes. "Give me one reason why I shouldn't splatter your brains all over these walls."

"Steed!"

Darci's alarmed voice provided the response Fritz would have never been able to give. Steed's gaze stayed fixed. Fritz looked almost human kneeling in prayer position, but Steed knew no humanity lived there, and the spark of satisfaction in the man's eyes and his wry grin confirmed it. Dueling emotions warred within Steed. Would he kill the love Darci still had for him if he were to murder the man who had slain his father?

Emotion squeezed Steed's throat. He knew the answer to that question. With a regretful shake of his head, he placed his gun in the holster and slammed his foot as hard as he could into Fritz's side. The man slumped to the floor, groaning in agony. Steed watched him, wanting to get pleasure in the man's pain, but none came. He didn't feel pleasure or even guilt. He felt defeated and angry, bitter and scorned, much like the hot tears sliding down his face.

Without a word, Steed backed out of the cell, locked the door, and left the holding area.

"Steed. Steed!" Darci called after him. "What was that?"

Steed continued walking. He hadn't been able to look at Darci for fear of the disappointment he'd see in her eyes, and the vulnerability he knew she'd see in his. He kept walking, clearing the final step up.

"Damn it, Steed, stop!"

The urgency in her tone as she called out to him made it clear he couldn't continue the avoidance. He stopped and turned around. Burning tears streamed down his cheeks.

"Steed." Darci hobbled up the last step and dropped a crutch when she reached him. She wiped away his tears. "What's wrong?" She dropped the other crutch and brought him into her arms. "Please, tell me what's going on with you?"

"Fritz." Steed lowered his head to Darci's shoulder and settled into her embrace. He held her closer, tighter, needing her presence, her love to protect him from the raging anger and anguished pain threatening to permeate his every pore and make him a man he didn't want to be. "That bastard killed my father."

Darci attempted to make it into Steed's house without injuring her good ankle from the obstacle course strewn clothing made on his floor. "You go to the couch and sit, and I'll put on some coffee," she said, trying not to fall flat on her face.

"No," Steed said, kicking the clothes to the side to make a clear path for her. "You sit, and I'll make the coffee. I need to think about something besides . . . besides what I'm thinking."

"We got here in one piece, that's got to say something about your powers of concentration."

"That's because I was carrying precious cargo." He took her crutches and helped her down on the couch. "You sit here, I'll be right back."

Darci looked around. Empty takeout boxes and dirty clothes covered every corner. Steed wasn't renowned for his housekeeping skills, but she'd never seen him live so much like a squatter. Now he had to deal with what Fritz had done to his father and Pete's betrayal, and she couldn't even make him a cup of coffee.

Steed returned a couple of minutes later. "It should be ready in a few minutes," he said, joining her on the couch. "I was surprised to see you."

"I wanted to see you. Kenny drove me over." Darci ignored the strained look on his face at the mention of Kenny's name. "If I hadn't come over, would you have called me?"

"I was going to, but I didn't want to push."

"If I hadn't shown up when I did, you would have . . ."

"I think I would have killed Fritz. I really wanted to. I still want to." Steed's eyes glistened with tears. "For so many years, I've missed my father, while hating the man who took him from me, and being angry with Dad for being in the position to be taken. Now, I find out my father got shot down like a rabid dog by a boy he never knew but was trying to help, and an innocent man died alone in a prison." Steed shook his head, as if trying to erase the truth from his mind. "I always knew there was something about Fritz." His hand balled into a tight fist.

"He almost killed you. He killed my father. I can't let this go."

Darci covered his hand. His body trembled, and his fist relaxed. "You have to let it go, Steed. Holding onto anger is not good for you."

His hand squeezed around hers. "But you are."

"And you are for me."

Companionable silence filled several moments. Things weren't perfect between them, but Darci had renewed hope they could be better.

"Why did you come to the station? How did you get down to holding?" Steed asked, breaking the easy quiet.

"Very slowly is how I got to holding." She chuckled. "The officer told me you were down there. Knowing Fritz was the one who ran into me, I thought I should see if everything was okay. So, when the officer went for coffee, I made my way down."

"That was quite a navigation to see if things were okay."

"I was worried about you."

"Why? It was because of my ways you walked away from me."

"I didn't walk away, I stepped back."

"You were angry with me."

"Yes, I was. When I think about it, I still am. Jackie and Kenny think I'm being too hard on you."

"Warwick?"

"He said I shouldn't fault you for doing your job. You couldn't allow my suspicions and your feelings for me to cloud your working mind." Her hands closed around his face. "Steed, you have to do the same thing for yourself. It's not your job to exact punishment on Fritz. He's in jail. The system will deal with him now."

"The system is corrupt. I did everything right with Warwick's case and it was wrong, because of a corrupt system. My father's killer has been free for almost twenty-five years, because of a corrupt system. His partner, a man I thought of as an uncle, made it happen. I always had questions about my dad's death, but I didn't fight like you did with Warwick. No, I fell victim to the system and internalized my doubts."

"It's okay, Steed."

"No, it's not. Dad's instincts were right about that couple. He didn't know Fritz, but he knew his parents were good people, and they were. Their one fault was having too much love for a son who didn't deserve it. Fritz doesn't deserve anything, but this corrupt system gave him everything."

"It's not the system that's corrupt, Steed. It's just a few bad people. There are lots of good guys. You, Chief Rogers, Malena, and Jackson. You make it work."

"Not anymore I don't."

"What do you mean?"

"I'm done!" Steed pulled off his shield and threw it against the wall with a force that frightened her. The badge remained embedded in the wall as dust and debris from the cracked sheet rock showered to the floor.

"Done?" Darci glanced from the damaged wall to Steed.

"No more following the rules. No more doing everything right. I want you to do your story, Darci. Expose the corruption in law enforcement like you said you would. The world needs to know. And while you're doing that, I'm going to take the time you said you needed."

"And do what?" The intensity in his blue eyes scared her. She saw anger. Not anger directed at her, but anger all the same. It was this unfamiliar, silent, brooding anger that scared her more than anything. "Steed?"

"Don't ask, Darci." He kissed her softly and returned to the kitchen.

CHAPTER 24

"I don't know why I listened to you."

Kenny grabbed Darci's hand and pulled her down to the couch beside him. She continued to squirm. "Darci, would you sit still!" he demanded. "You've been off those crutches for one day, and you've been doing all you can to work a trench in your living room floor. I know your foot is better, but you need to . . ."

"Be with Steed." She stopped moving. "That is what I need, Kenny. It's been three weeks."

"The man said he needed time. Besides, you talk to him."

"Two two-minute phone calls every week is not talking to him." She sighed. Every time she spoke to him, she missed him even more. She tried to talk him out of leaving, but hours after learning about Fritz, Steed took off to parts unknown. "You didn't see him. You don't know the pain he's in, and the anger he's feeling."

"Oh, I know pain and anger, Darci. I was locked up by my sister and her demented boyfriend for two months. I can school anyone on those emotions. But I can also say that time works wonders." Kenny smiled, stroking his clean-shaven face and pressing his healed lips together. "Just look at me."

Darci chuckled. Kenny was definitely his old self again. "Point taken," she said.

"Honestly, I can't imagine what Steed's feeling to learn Fritz killed his father. His upset is warranted, and he needs to deal with what he's dealing with."

"Yes, he does, but he doesn't need to do it alone. I think I know where he is, and that's comforting, but I also know he's upset. And it's what the upset is doing to him and what it could lead him to do that's driving me crazy. I should be with him, just like he was with me during my coma." She resumed her pacing. Steed's emotions were running high when he tossed his badge, but Darci knew he didn't mean that, so she talked to Chief Rogers, explained what happened, and got Steed approved for open-ended time off. He didn't seem upset when she told him, but he didn't tell her where he was or when he'd be back, either. "I should have never let him leave," she said.

"How were you going to keep him here with your bad foot?"

She gave him a pointed look. "There are ways to keep a man around."

"But not for women like you, Darci. You wouldn't lower your standards like that."

"I wouldn't be. I love Steed, and I'm so afraid for him."

"And sleeping with him is supposed to make you less afraid? Make him calm down?" Kenny's face scrunched up as it always did when he thought deeply. "Okay, it will calm him down for a little while, but until when? The next crisis comes up?"

"Weren't you the one telling me to forgive him? What's with this change in attitude?"

"It's not changed. I'm just concerned about you."

"You're concerned about me, and I'm concerned about Steed. I can't help it, Kenny. He's in so much pain, and I don't know what he's going to do."

The phone rang. Darci's heart lurched. She raced to the corner table and jammed the phone to her ear, praying she would hear Steed's voice on the other end. "Hello."

"Is this Darci Clarke?"

The Southern and very feminine voice definitely didn't belong to Steed. "Yes, it is," she answered.

"Wonderful. I'm Jean Reynolds."

"Jean Rey . . ." *Nana!* "You're Steed's grandmother."

"I am."

"Is Steed with you?"

"Yes."

Darci sighed in relief. "I thought so. How is he?"

"A lot like he was when I first met him all those years ago—angry and lost. He's only calm when he talks about you."

Darci smiled, grateful to know Steed was with people who loved him, and pleased he'd mentioned her. "He talks about me?"

"Quite often. Truth be told, you're the only girl he's ever talked about. And that's why I called. Can you come down to Fort Worth?"

She wanted to scream "Yes!" But if Steed wanted her to be with him, he would have asked himself. She'd already gotten a world of comfort knowing he wasn't alone. "I can't, Mrs. Reynolds. Steed wants time to think about things, and—"

"Steed's not thinking, he's brooding. I know he loves you, and he's too proud to tell you he needs you, but I'm not. He's so anxious, and I'm afraid he's going to do something foolish. He told us about Pete and that Fritz fellow. You can save him from himself. Please, come."

Hearing Steed's grandmother express the same worries she had about him made the decision for Darci. "I'll come."

"Lovely. I took the liberty of checking flights, and there's one leaving Crider Airport at two o'clock today. I reserved a ticket for you, and there'll be a car for you at the airport in Fort Worth."

"You were pretty sure I was going to come, huh?"

Jean laughed. "Just hopeful. I'll see you soon."

"Yes, ma'am." Sighing, Darci held the phone to her chest for a moment and then returned it to the table.

"Where are you going?" Kenny asked.

"Texas," she answered with a smile. "I'm going to Steed."

—◈—

"Who were you talking to, Nana?"

"Steed?" Jean placed the phone on the charger and approached with a brighter than usual smile. "Just a friend," she answered. "Did you enjoy your ride?"

"I did." Steed entered the den, watching Jean curiously. She was up to something. "I would have enjoyed it more if you had come along. Did you take care of your business?" he asked.

"I just finished up."

"Everything okay?"

"It's fine. You were telling me about your ride."

Steed grinned. Whatever she was up to, she wasn't going to share. "The ride was good. It gave me time to think about some things." He moved to the couch and patted the empty space beside him. "Join me."

Jean came over and sat. "Something on your mind?"

"Yeah, actually. It's time I headed out."

"Oh, no." Jean's head shook vehemently. "I disagree."

"I knew you would say that, which is why I'm not asking if you think I should go. I've been here a lot longer than I ever expected, and I have things to do."

"And people to get away from?"

"Come on now, things have been okay with Josh and me," he said, noting the change for the better in his relationship with his stepfather.

"I'm not talking about my son. Claudia called while you were out riding."

Steed groaned. "Again?" Claudia, a recently divorced old high school girlfriend, had been a thorn in his side from the moment he'd run into her in town two weeks before. Despite the numerous times he had told her he wasn't available, she wouldn't take no for an answer. *"If you're involved, why isn't she here with you?"* Claudia constantly said. *Why, indeed?*

"I guess I don't have to ask what she wanted," Steed said.

Green eyes brightened with humor. "You can't blame her for being smitten." Jean pinched his cheeks. "You're so handsome."

"And so not interested. I have a lot on my mind. And when I'm not thinking of those other things, I'm only thinking of Darci. She's the only woman I want."

"Have you told Darci this?"

"I guess." He shrugged, feeling a bit sorry for himself. "She's been preoccupied with her best friend."

"Did she say she was preoccupied?"

"She's not here."

"Did you ask her to come?"

"I couldn't do that." But he wanted to. Loving Darci scared him, but needing her scared him even more.

"Then how can you grumble about her not being here?"

Steed sighed. He hated when his grandmother stated the obvious. "Nana," he practically whined.

"Don't Nana me. You men are so . . ."

"Stubborn?"

"That works."

"I apologize for me and my species alike, but it doesn't matter. I'm leaving."

"You're going back to South Carolina?"

"Not yet. There's something—there's something I have to take care of first."

A shadow of worry darkened Jean's strong patrician features. Even in a flannel shirt and jeans, his nana was always the picture of class and elegance. She had taught him many things. Most importantly, the outside is not the measure of a person, but what they have within and allow to shine out. Steed didn't like the idea of her worrying about him, but he couldn't lie to her, either.

"I'm going to New York," he said.

"I don't think that's a good idea."

"I do." He kissed a rosy cheek and stood. "I'm going to grab some lunch, take a shower, pack, and then visit Brett and Lori before heading off to the airport."

"You can't do that!"

Her abrupt reaction got Steed's wheels to turning again. Jean was definitely up to something. "Why not?"

"It's just that . . . I really want you to stay a little longer. I can't talk you out of this trip, can I?"

Steed had wrestled with this decision for weeks, and was sure of what he had to do. He had to see Pete's face and listen to him as he tried to explain how he could take a payoff that left a murderer at large. "No, ma'am," he answered.

"May I ask a favor?"

"You can ask anything of me, Nana."

"Stay the night. I won't try to talk you out of going to New York, but maybe if you sleep on this decision one more night, you might change your mind on your own."

"I'm not going to change my mind."

"So, you should have no problem with staying. I want to spend more time with you. If you want to visit your brother and sister and say your good-byes now, that's fine, but I expect you back in time to have dinner with your old grandmother."

"You will never be old, Nana. And, for you, I'll stay until morning. But I'm leaving first thing."

"That's all I ask."

"You want to go out for dinner?"

"No, actually, I feel like cooking. I think I'll give George the night off and spend some quality time in my own kitchen for a change. I can rustle us up something rib-sticking to take the edge off these cold days and nights."

"Your chili?" Steed asked, his stomach rumbling in anticipation of Nana's divine dish. George, the family cook since forever, was a great chef, but Nana's chili was extra special.

"Why not? Chili, cornbread, and maybe bake a lemon pie."

Steed rubbed his stomach. "That's reason to stay."

"Josh and Beth have that fund-raiser, so it'll just be us."

"I couldn't think of a better date to share this evening."

"Somehow, I think you could." She shooed him off. "You go on and shower and then do your visiting. I'll see you later."

Steed crossed his arms. "You tryin' to get rid of me? I know you're up to something. Is a man coming over?" he teased. "I think I saw old man Jessup giving you the eye the other day."

"Jessup is cross-eyed. It looks like he's giving everyone the eye."

Steed laughed. That man could give a headache to anyone who looked at him too long.

"Besides, I've lived enough years where I don't have to hide anything I do," Jean finished.

She didn't have to hide anything, yet Steed knew she was hiding something. Maybe she would share at dinner.

"Whatever you say, Nana." He kissed her cheek. "See you later."

———

"There's nothing I can say to make you stay, Steed?"

Steed stared at Claudia Preston in disbelief. This woman could inspire many a blonde joke. She had accosted him in the driveway of the ranch the moment he returned from visiting his siblings, and he'd spent the last several minutes trying to get rid of her.

"No, there's absolutely nothing you can do." Claudia's two hands felt like ten, moving from his hair to his back to his bottom in a continual motion. The disappointed pout on her overly made-up face did nothing to soothe Steed's growing irritation. He put up a valiant fight to keep the woman's paws at bay, but he was losing the battle. "Why are you here?"

"I wanted to say good-bye. It's going to be dark soon." She blew in his ear. "I give great good-byes."

Claudia pinched his bottom. Steed jumped. "Hey!" he yelped. "I said good-bye to you weeks ago."

Her phony high-pitched laugh rang in his ears. "Oh, Steed, you're such a kidder."

"Who's kidding?" He continued to fight her advances. "I've told you I'm not interested or available. Why won't you get that?"

"Because the only woman I ever see you around is your grandma, and she likes me."

Steed frowned. Could Claudia be that something Nana was keeping to herself? He shuddered at the thought. She wouldn't do that to him. "Nana likes every-body," he said. "It's a blessing and a curse."

"Did your time in South Carolina turn you into such a sourpuss? You used to be so much fun."

"I grew up and learned life isn't all about fun."

"You're such a cop, Steed." Claudia draped her arms around his neck, stabbing his shoulders and collarbone with her pointy elbows. "Loosen up."

Claudia's eager lips covered his mouth. Steed pressed his lips together, fighting to keep the woman's seeking tongue from entering his mouth. He continued his struggle to push Claudia away, working feverishly to pull her spindly arms from his neck, and snake-like leg from around his waist.

"Steed!"

His body froze. He'd dreamed of hearing that voice, so real and close, but never in a nightmarish situation like this. Released from Claudia's grip, he turned to find his worst fears realized in the shiny pools filling the dark eyes he loved so much. His heart dropped to his stomach. This was bad.

"Darci." Steed approached, brushing his hands over his mouth and swallowing the knot forming in his throat. "I can explain," he said. "This is . . ."

"Not what it looks like?" Darci finished.

He nodded. "Yes."

"This woman is your secret love, Steed?" Claudia gave Darci a cursory glance. "No wonder you kept quiet."

"Shut up, you!" Steed fired back. Taking a tentative step forward, he reached for Darci's hand. She quickly snatched it away. The look in her eyes cut him like a knife. "Please, let me explain."

"I don't want to hear it." Darci wiped away her tears. "I shouldn't have come here."

She raced off into the rapidly darkening night. Steed called to her, begging her to return, but she kept on running, never once turning back.

CHAPTER 25

Darci ran and ran. To what, she didn't know. She wanted to be wherever Steed wasn't. Who was she kidding? She could run forever and never get away from Steed. He was in heart, and he had stomped all over it.

"Darci! Darci!"

The sound of Steed's voice thrust her into high gear. She didn't want to talk to him, much less look at him. The chilly wind whipped at her face, her lungs burned, and her newly healed ankle tingled from the unexpected workout. Refusing to stop or turn around, Darci ran on until she couldn't slow herself down. She felt herself tumbling forward, but before the plush grass could meet her, a hand wrapped around her arm pulling her back.

"Darci, stop! Please, stop!" Steed held her against him, his strong arms tight around her, but not punishing. "Calm down," he urged.

She battled against him. Hair flew about her face. "Let me go, Steed! Let me go!"

"Never! Darci, what you saw . . ."

She stopped abruptly and met his gaze. "Was some gorgeous blonde all over you!"

"Yes, *she* was all over *me*, while I was trying to push her away. I don't want any part of her. You must know that."

"I know what I saw, and that was your hands all over her."

He raised his hands in surrender. "You know what, you're right. How can I ask you to deny what you've seen with your own two eyes?"

"Indeed!"

"But isn't that what you asked of me? To ignore what the evidence said in Warwick's case and believe and trust in you?"

"That's different."

"No, it's not. Because in both instances, what we saw wasn't what it appeared to be. I knew Claudia years ago, but it meant nothing. She showed up here tonight and kissed me. I was trying to get away from her when you came up, Darci. I swear."

Steed hesitated whenever he had to think of the right thing to say, but there was none of that this time. He held her gaze and had his say. Darci felt relieved and the slightest bit foolish. He was telling the truth. "She went after you, huh?"

"Like a woman possessed."

Darci chuckled. "I guess it's that animal magnetism."

"You believe me?"

"Yes. I'm sorry I jumped to the wrong conclusions."

"Don't apologize. I'm just glad you believe me." His finger trailed along her cheek, a simple touch she felt from the tip of toes to the roots of her hair. "When I first heard your voice, I thought I was dreaming. But with Claudia groping me, it felt like a nightmare. I was afraid I had lost you forever." His thumb brushed her lower lip, and her whole body tingled. "Now, with you standing right here, so real and so beautiful. Oh, Darci, I just . . ."

Steed pulled her in his arms, crushing his lips to hers. Darci willingly surrendered to his charms, losing herself in the movement of Steed's tongue against her, and his strong, yet, gentle, touch on her body. She'd missed his kisses and the feel of his scratchy whiskers against her face. She'd missed his arms being around her. She'd missed him. And she wanted him—badly.

The feelings of need, want, and desire Steed stirred in her scared Darci to death. Would giving up her vow to wait be so bad when she was giving herself to the man she loved so much? Wanting something that felt so right couldn't be wrong.

Steed held her tighter. His every touch, kiss, and caress said things mere words could never convey. Darci's inner conflict continued. If Steed's hard, warm body said one more yes, there was no way she could say no.

"Ahem!"

The unexpected sound broke the kiss and ended the fierce battle Darci's body and heart waged with her head to give in to feelings and urges that defied her once-unflagging mindset. Maybe this exaggerated cough was a sign. Although at present, she wasn't sure how good a sign it was.

"I'm sorry to interrupt," said the smiling older woman.

Steed waved over the lady Darci knew to be his beloved grandmother. "Nana, there's someone special I want you to meet," he said, resting his arm around Darci's waist.

"If the special someone isn't Ms. Darci Clarke, you're going to have a whole lot of explaining to do."

Steed chuckled. "Fear not, Nana, this is the lady herself." A sense of pride washed over Darci as Steed hugged her close to him. "Darci, this is my nana, Jean Reynolds."

Darci extended her hand, feeling a nervousness she hadn't experienced since her first on-air interview. "Mrs. Reynolds, I'm so happy to finally meet you." She smiled.

"It's Nana, and what's this with a handshake?" Jean pulled Darci into a hug. "That's a down-home welcome," she said, pulling back. "I'm so glad you're here. How was your flight? Was everything comfortable for you?"

"It was wonderful. Thank you."

"Fine. That's real fine."

Steed looked from Darci to his grandmother. "Am I missing something?" he said.

"Your grandmother called me," Darci answered. "She was as worried about you as I was, and asked me to come down."

"I knew you were up to something." Steed kissed his grandmother's cheek. "I owe you one."

"Seeing that big smile is all the gratitude I need. You two look so happy. I hope this means whatever problems you had have all been worked out."

"I think we're fine," Darci said, "but I suspect Steed is still wrestling with something." Her hand moved up and down his arm. "Your time away hasn't helped much, huh?"

"It has," he said. "I told Nana earlier I'm leaving here to deal with some things."

Jean shook her head. Worry etched her wrinkled face. She touched the hand Darci had wrapped around Steed's arm. "Try to reason with him. I've done all I can do." She rubbed her hands up and down her arms. "I don't have anyone out here to keep me warm, so I'm going back inside. You two take as much time as you need, and when you get hungry there'll be some supper in the kitchen. Your bags are already inside, Darci, and Steed can help you get settled in whenever you're ready. I'll see you young people later."

Darci kept her eyes on the woman until she disappeared in the distance. She frowned at Steed. "Do you want to have your grandmother so worried?"

"Of course not, but Nana knows . . ."

"She knows you're about to do something foolish, and she doesn't want you to do it. Neither do I."

Steed groaned. "Darci, I have to do this."

"What is 'this'?"

"I'm going to New York. I have to talk to Pete. I need to see if there's the slightest bit of guilt in him when he learns I know what he did."

Determination filled Steed's eyes. Darci pressed her hand to his cheek. "This is very important to you?"

"Essential."

"Okay, I won't try to stop you."

"Thank you."

"I'm just going to go with you."

————❦————

"It's been a while since I enjoyed a leisurely evening stroll, but that one I really needed," Darci said, patting her flat stomach as she entered her bedroom. "Your grandmother is a terrific cook."

Steed followed Darci into the bedroom and joined her on the bench at the bay window. She'd been yapping a mile a minute about everything but what he needed them to talk about—this decision she'd made to accompany him to New York.

Darci stared out at the starry sky. "It's such a beautiful night. This ranch is absolutely gorgeous, Steed. I'm still amazed at how green everything . . ."

He pressed his finger to her lips. "I don't want to talk about the ranch or Nana and her cooking ability."

"So let's talk about your mom and Josh. They are very nice. You know, you have your mother's smile. Too bad you don't use it as often as she does."

"Darci, you are not going to New York with me," he managed to slip in before she started talking about his sister and brother who had completed the unexpected family reunion.

"Yes, I am." She moved to the bed.

"Why are you being so stubborn?"

She laughed. "That's funny coming from you."

"I'm serious."

"I know that, too."

Steed sat beside her, groaning. "Why won't you hear me out?"

"I hear you. I'm just not listening to you. It's pointless to argue, because I'm not going to walk away from you when I know you need me."

Her squared jaw and steadfast pout dared him to fight her on this. Steed was too touched to try. It was strange and wonderful to have somebody care about him so much. Somebody he loved so much. "Fine, you win."

"I knew I would." Scooting widthwise on the bed, Darci reclined on her elbows. "Nana told me I'm the first girl you ever talked about." She smiled.

That explained her determination. Nana had shared all his secrets, just like she'd shared his mother's album of his baby pictures. He shuddered at the memory of Darci cooing at his toothless grin and bare bottom. Steed flipped to his stomach and propped a pillow under his chin. "Nana talks too much."

Darci laughed softly. "No, just enough. Your whole family showed up tonight. I feel honored."

"I think the honor was theirs, meeting *the* Darci Clarke. I'm glad my family met you."

"Me, too. I was a little nervous at first, but Nana made me feel right at home. Everybody's so nice. Nothing like the guy I met in Sterling three and a half months ago."

"Back then I had this pushy lady all over my back. I'd say we've both come a long way since then."

An easy silence filled the room. Darci's intoxicating scent worked its magic, and all that mattered in that moment was having her in his arms. He leaned over her, practically tasting her sweetness before their lips met.

"What time does the flight leave tomorrow?"

Steed pulled back, confused and a little surprised by her question when their lips hovered mere inches apart. "Six."

Darci looked over his shoulder toward the alarm clock. "It's eleven now." She toyed with the loosened top buttons of his shirt and then slowly unfastened the others while trailing hot kisses along his chest. The soft touch of her fingertips felt like down feathers against his taut nipples, driving him crazy and turning him on. "We should get some rest."

"Yeah, we should," he said, making quick work of the buttons on her blouse and sliding the silk material off her shoulders and to the floor. "But I'm not sleepy."

"Me, either."

Steed claimed Darci's lips in a desperate, starving kiss as their bodies fell to the softness of the bed. Eager tongues advanced and retreated, while busy hands explored. Three weeks without her kisses, her touch, and her nearness had felt like a million years, but one moment in her arms made up for the torture he'd endured from being without her for so long.

His lips left hers, traveling along her neck, down to the valley of her perfect breasts. Steed cupped the firm, heavy mounds through the satin and lace of her bra. Her nipples hardened against his hands, and her blissful cries increased. Sliding the material aside, he divided his attention between each aroused tip, suckling like a starving babe.

Darci lips grazed his shoulders. The gentle, yet fiery touch of her fingers trailed a slow path across the planes of his back, to his denim-covered backside where they squeezed and caressed, and back again. He grew harder against her. A deep moan rumbled in his throat. Soft, tender, passionate, and intense, Darci's motions on his body were as dynamic as the woman herself. She was everything he wanted, and more than he could ever dream possible.

Visions of Darci's beautiful nude body writhing in orgasmic pleasure from the many ways he would love her, please her, and taste her raced through Steed's mind. The bulge in his jeans tightened.

Darci moaned softly, deeply. "Steed," she murmured.

A shiver raced down his spine at the emotion in Darci's voice. A thousand, a million times he'd heard his name called, but never like that. *Take me. I'm yours. I want you. I need you. I love you.* He gazed into her eyes to find every emotion that breathed life into the simple utterance staring back at him. In that instant her name became indelibly seared to his heart. He belonged to her, and he only wanted her to belong to him. "Say that again," he said.

"What?"

"My name. Say my name."

Her brows stitched into a curious line. "Guys really say that?"

Boisterous laughter shook Steed's body. "Oh, my beautiful Darci." He smacked her lips and pulled her up. "Yes, guys really say that, but I didn't mean it like that. I wanted to hear my name again because I loved the way you said it."

"You never asked me to do that before."

"You've never said my name like that before."

Darci curled her arms around his neck, bringing him to rest on top of her. "Steed," she said with a kiss.

"Steed." She kissed him again. "Steed." She gazed deeply in his eyes, softly stroking his hair. "I love you."

"And I love you. So very much." He pulled away and handed Darci her shirt. "That's why we have to stop."

"What?" She shot up. "Stop?"

"Yes." Steed couldn't believe he'd said the words, and neither could his throbbing erection, but he meant them. He stood and pulled on his shirt. "It's not time yet."

"It feels like time to me." Her eyes drifted to the zipper of his jeans. "It definitely looks like time."

"Maybe for now, but I remember what you said before. You want to be married, and you should have that. You deserve to have that." And after tonight, he had every intention of making sure she had it—with him. Steed checked his watch. "We both need to get some rest."

Darci patted the space beside her. "You can rest here."

Steed glanced at the knot in his pants. "No, I can't," he said, buttoning the shirt and allowing the long tails to conceal his aroused state.

"You're not going to try to leave without me, are you?"

"I've thought about it, but I won't." He bussed her cheek. "Good night, Darci."

His mind on a very cold shower, Steed left the room to find his mother turning the corner toward him. "Mom?" The house had over twenty bedrooms, and his mother's was clear on the other side. "What are you doing over here?"

"I was on my way to your room. Is everything okay?" Beth tightened the belt of her housecoat as she looked over his shoulder toward Darci's door. "You two didn't have a fight?"

"No, Mom, we didn't have a fight. Why would you ask that?"

She shrugged. "It's been a while since you've seen her. I just figured you'd—"

"Mom . . ."

"Hey, it's none of my business. I can tell she's special to you, and I think she's wonderful. You've never shown this much interest in anyone, and the way you are with Darci, the way you look at her . . ." She smiled. "Your father used to look at me the same way."

"You've been thinking about Dad?"

"I always think of Matthew. I loved him, and I always carry a part of him in my heart." Beth pressed her hand to Steed's cheek. "I know you've had your issues believing that because I married Josh."

"I'm sorry about that. I was . . ."

"A sad and very angry teenager. You've grown so much, Steed, and best of all, you've found someone to love. You always kept your heart so secure, and since your father died, you've never said more to me than you had to."

Steed lowered his head. He'd spent a lot of years angry at his father for dying and angry with her for marrying Josh and giving him a child. An overpowering emotion that blinded him to any and everything else. How many times could he say he was sorry? "Mom . . ."

"I'm not trying to make you feel guilty, Steed. I just never had the opportunity to do this, and now that I do, I want to do it right."

"Do what?"

"I was on my way to your room to leave this." She reached into her pocket and extended a red jewelry box. "Open it."

Steed lifted the lid to find the one and a half carat diamond engagement ring his father had given his mother almost forty years before. The same ring his grandfather had given his grandmother, and his father before him. "Mom?"

"I'm sure Matt would want you to have it." Beth smiled. "I have a strong feeling it will be put to use very soon, and I'm so grateful, because I was afraid the name your father gave you would become a curse. I've wanted you to have someone special in your life for so long. Someone who could tame that restless spirit in you. You're almost there, Steed. Don't let whatever is leading you to New York destroy what you've found with Darci. Don't go back, son. Go forward."

"That's what I plan to do, Mom." Steed pocketed the ring. "That's exactly what I plan to do."

CHAPTER 26

"Get outta the way, moron!"

Steed and Darci exchanged looks as their taxi driver, who looked like Santa Claus right down to the unlit pipe held tight between his teeth, played a speedy version of dodge car through the late morning New York traffic. Christmas was over a week away, but the man drove as if he had billions of stops to make before the day ended. The snow falling and covering the street didn't slow him down one bit.

Steed inched closer to Darci as they bounced around like bobblehead dolls in the back seat of the car. "You should have stayed at the hotel," he said. "It would have been okay."

"And leave you to take care of your 'business' without me?" Darci shook her head. "No way."

"And this is so much more fun." Steed gave her free hand a supportive squeeze. "I'm sorry."

"Even with the years I've lived here, I never got used to these taxi rides. And I didn't drive in the city, so I've had plenty of them." She groaned. "Roller coasters are less scary."

The driver cleared his throat and glared into the rearview mirror at them.

"But I'd go through anything to be here for you," Darci said.

"That means a lot to me." Steed thought of the precious ring tucked safely away at the hotel. Visions of white picket fences and giggling brown-skinned, dark-haired children danced in his head. "You mean a lot to me."

The taxi came to an abrupt stop as he leaned over to kiss her. "That'll be seven fifty-five," Santa Hack said.

Not having correct change, Steed reluctantly handed the man ten dollars and suggested he slow it down. The man grumbled something under his breath as Steed ushered Darci into Pete's apartment building.

The former cop lived on the fifth floor of a luxury high-rise. Steed had never wondered how an ex-cop could live so well. Now he felt foolish that he didn't. He drew a deep breath and rang the doorbell.

Darci's hand slid into his. "You okay?" she asked.

"I'll know when I finish talking to Pete."

Moments later a young, pretty brunette in a blue satin robe opened the door. She smiled brightly at Steed. "Hiya, honey," said the woman with a Queens accent as thick as the frosty gloss coating her lips. "You lost?"

"We must be," said Darci, stepping forward and wrapping her arm around Steed's in a show of possessiveness that brought a smile to his lips. "We thought Pete Mulhaney lived here."

"He does. You all friends of his?"

"My father was," answered Steed. "Is Pete around?"

"He's in the shower." The woman stepped aside. "Come in and sit. I'll go get him for ya."

They took a seat on the couch while the barefoot brunette padded down the hall.

"I take it that's not his daughter," Darci said.

"Only in the context of his being her sugar daddy." Steed looked around. The sight of ill-gotten gain turned his stomach. How would Pete lie his way out of this? Would he try?

Darci jiggled his hand. "What are you thinking?"

"I don't know. What I'm going to say. Maybe wondering why I didn't call the cops to meet me over here."

"You know why I think you should have done that."

"Yes, I know," he said, remembering her displeasure when he'd tucked a gun in his waistband. "Don't worry, I won't shoot him." He kissed her cheek. "I promise."

"Steed!" Pete entered the room wearing a sunshine yellow knee-length bathrobe and rubbing a light blue towel through his damp hair. At sixty-two, Pete looked like a retired football player, stocky but a bit worn out. "Angie told me I had company, but I never imagined it was you." He smiled at Darci. "You look familiar." Pete snapped his fingers. "You did the news. Clarke, right?"

"Yes. Darci," she said.

"That's right." He gave Steed a broad smile. "I didn't know you knew her, but it's always nice to see a pretty lady." Pete sat in the wing chair across from them, showing way more of his pasty pale thighs than Steed wanted to see. "So, what brings you to town?"

"I have some questions about the man who killed my father."

Pete's pursed his lips and draped the towel around his neck. "I don't know what more I can tell you. He died in prison many years ago."

Steed's jaw clenched. He wanted to toss Pete out of the windows offering a stunning view of the city. As if sensing his growing ire, Darci gave his hand a gentle squeeze, and like magic, he calmed. Steed kept his gaze on Pete, hoping his previous emotional battle didn't show on his face. "And you don't know anything else about the man who killed Dad?" he said.

"You know everything I know."

"Indeed I do, you despicable bastard!" Steed erupted, unable to keep up the friendly façade a moment longer.

"What are you—"

"Don't even try to deny it!" Steed sucked in breath and lowered his tone. "I know the whole story. The boy who killed my father is now a man in the Sterling jail." Pete's eyes widened. "That's right. He's being held on numerous charges. Ironically, he falsified a death."

Pete's face grew ashen. He lowered his head. "Steed . . ."

"I can't believe you!" Steed shot off the couch. "I looked up to you and trusted you, and you did this to my mother, my sister, and to me. For money!" He waved his hand about the room. "Was it worth it?"

"Not taking the money wouldn't have brought Matt back. Those folks were desperate to save their son, and that boy was troubled. He needed help he couldn't get behind bars."

"So you were being magnanimous? You can't clean this up, Pete. That boy didn't get any help. None! You committed a crime, several of them, and you will pay."

"You saying you want a cut?"

"Don't insult me."

"Then what?"

"What do you think? I don't want your blood money, Pete. I want you to spend what's left of your miserable life in the prison the man-child that killed my father should have been in. Put on some clothes, we're taking a trip."

"A trip to where?"

"Downtown. You're about to make a confession."

"I . . . I can't do that. You know what they do to cops in prison, and I'm an old man now." Pete managed to squeeze out a single tear.

Steed grunted. Pete made him sick.

"Please, don't do this. Son, I'm pleading with you."

Anger engulfed Steed's body with a speed and intensity that scared him. He pointed a quivering finger. "Don't you dare call me son!" he said through gritted teeth. "Now, either you're going to walk out of here under your own steam, or I'm going to drag your ass outta here." He pulled out the gun. "One way or another, you will go to jail." He waved the gun. "Start walking."

From the corner of his eye, Steed saw Darci approach. She touched his back. "Steed, is this really . . ."

"Don't worry, Darci," he assured her. "It's okay."

Pete laughed. "You bet it's okay, sweet thing." He left the chair and moseyed over to the fireplace. "You won't shoot me, Steed," he sneered, propping his elbows on the dark marble mantle, relaxing as if he had not a care in the world. "You care too much. You don't have the balls to shoot me."

Without a word, Steed raised the gun and fired a single shot. The bullet whizzed by Pete's ear before breaking the vase directly behind him.

Darci gasped, wide-eyed.

Angie rushed into the room, her robe replaced with a red wrap dress. "What's going—" Her words ceased when she saw Steed, his gun, and the frightened, hunched-over Pete.

"That shot missed you on purpose," Steed explained. "If there is another, I promise I won't miss. And then we'll see who has the balls around here." He jutted his head at the brunette. "You're free to go."

"Petey?" she murmured.

"Don't you worry, Angie. I'll be fine."

Steed clicked his tongue. "I wouldn't lie to her if I were you, Pete. Extortion, obstruction of justice, tampering with evidence, and that's just the beginning. Take a long hard look at him, Angie. I suspect the next time you see him there'll be steel bars between you."

Angie hustled to the door and waved. "It's been swell, Petey. Bye."

Steed made a call to the police station and then walked over to Darci and kissed her cheek. "You okay?"

"You said you wouldn't use the gun."

"No, I said I wouldn't shoot Pete. I shot the vase."

"Semantics."

Steed took a long look at the weeping man. "I could almost feel sorry for him. The charges for the crimes against my father probably won't stick because of the statute of limitations, but he's nervous for a reason. I'm certain he's done these same crimes and many others several times over, so something will stick. He's getting what he deserves."

"Yes, he deserves this, but you're really not going to let him walk out in twenty-degree weather wearing just a yellow bathrobe, are you?"

"It'll serve him right. A yellow robe for a yellow bastard."

"Steed, it's freezing out."

"Don't pout, Darci." He pecked her lips and gave her a smile. "He doesn't deserve your kindness."

"It's not so much kindness as it is a public service." Darci frowned as she looked at Pete's pale and very hairy legs.

Steed chuckled. "Point taken. I'll let him get dressed. The citizens of New York don't need to be subjected to that." He gave her cheek a soft caress. "Consider that request the first of many presents coming your way today."

―⚬⚬⚬―

The slamming of Pete's cell door played like sweet music to Steed's ears. He learned the D.A.'s office had been investigating Pete for a couple of years in connection with racketeering charges against a local crime lord; a crime lord who also had connections with Fritz. Extradition papers for Fritz were in the works, as was the promise of a lifetime or two in prison. For the first time in years, Steed didn't have what felt like the weight of the world on his shoulders. He had closure, answers, and most importantly, justice for his father. It felt good, and it made him want to do something he'd put off for way too long.

Steed hailed a taxi when he and Darci stepped out of the precinct. "I want us to make one stop before we head back to the hotel," he said, helping her into the car.

Darci nodded. "Okay. Where are we going?"

"A family reunion."

Minutes later, the cab pulled up at West Hill Cemetery. "Here we are," Steed said, escorting Darci out of the car.

Steed stopped as he approached the entrance. He hadn't been inside the cemetery since the day of his father's funeral. He'd passed the gates many times, but overwhelming emotions kept him from going in. Today, he wanted and needed to walk through those gates with the woman he loved. He continued on.

Darci squeezed his hand as they approached the family marker. "Are you okay?" she asked. "It's been a long time."

"I don't remember ever being more okay in my life." His finger brushed her cool cheek. "I feel good, Darci, and though it might sound weird, I want to introduce you to him."

She smiled. "It's not weird at all. Come on."

~∾∾~

Fifth Avenue bustled with activity. Carefree shoppers carrying bags of brightly wrapped gifts and nine-to-fivers just ending their day's work kept the flow of pedestrian traffic going. Darci missed this part of New York. The twinkling lights and festive decorations, the smiles on usually dour faces, and the feeling of clean the freshly-fallen snow gave the city. Christmas in New York. This was her favorite time of year, and walking hand in hand with Steed in the middle of it all made it even more special. If she'd worn on a heavier coat, this moment would be perfect. Her teeth chattered.

"Darci." Steed took off his jacket and wrapped it around her shoulders. "Why didn't you tell me you were cold?"

"You wanted to walk after we left the cemetery, and I wasn't that cold then. I've been enjoying the walk. It's just the temperature is starting to get to me."

"We're less than a block from the hotel, so you'll be toasty warm in no time."

"That being the case, what's this about more presents coming my way?"

Steed chuckled. "You're direct, aren't you?"

"I try to be when I can. Do these presents have anything to do with all those calls you were making earlier? The calls you had to make in private?"

"Sorry, no hints. You'll have to wait and see."

"I don't think I've ever seen you so laid back."

"It's closure, Darci. It works wonders on a person," he said, guiding her inside the hotel.

After a brief clandestine meeting with the concierge, Steed directed Darci to the elevator.

"I guess it's pointless to ask what that was all about," she said, stepping into the car.

Mischief shined in his eyes. "I love your perception."

Darci groaned. "Steed, what are you up to?"

"You'll find out soon enough." Steed said nothing more on the short ride to the ninth floor. Grinning like a Cheshire cat, he blocked the door when they reached the suite. "You sure you want to know what's going on?"

"Yes!" she answered emphatically.

Steed laughed. "Okay, okay." He inserted the key card and moved aside. "Your wait is over."

Darci stepped into their luxurious two-bedroom suite to discover a beautiful world of flowers, music, and lights. Dozens of roses of every color filled crystal vases and fragranced the air with their delicate scent. Candlelight cast a soft glow over an elegantly set round table for two. A huge Christmas tree, decorated with bright bulbs of red, yellow, green, and blue, added a splash of color, and the high-tech stereo system filled the room with jazz sax songs of the season. Darci's mouth opened, but no words came.

Steed closed his hands over her shoulders and kissed the back of her head. "Darci Clarke speechless," he said with a laugh. "I think this is a first."

"I knew you were up to something, but I never dreamed . . . It's beautiful, Steed." She kissed his cheek. "Thank you."

"You're welcome." He pecked her lips and pointed at the tree centered perfectly against the large picture windows boasting the spectacular city skyline. "I believe there's a little something for you over there."

Darci spotted a huge brightly wrapped box beneath the thick fir branches. "That's a *little* something?" She walked over to the rectangular box and gave it a shake. "What's in here?"

"You'll have to open it to see. Go on, you don't have to wait until Christmas for this one." He motioned toward her bedroom. "Open it in there."

"Why?"

"Because it's something I want you to wear tonight."

Darci gave the box another shake. It felt a little too heavy to be a negligee, but if by some chance the "something" fell along those lines, she didn't see the point in making him wait to see what she felt strongly he'd be looking at long before the night was over. "Why don't you come in with me." She tucked the box under one arm and took his hand. "I might need some help with this something." She winked.

"Nah, I don't think you'll need any help."

Her shoulders slumped. "Steed."

"Darci, humor me. I took the liberty of having the maid service run a hot bubble bath for you. Take a few minutes for yourself, and I'll see you back in here in," he checked his watch, "at least half an hour. Please, indulge me."

Feeling more bold and brazen than she had in her life, Darci trailed her finger along the buttons of his shirt, stopping only when she reached the button of his jeans. "I'm trying to indulge you right now." She dropped the box to the couch, and leaned into him. His masculine scent was like a drugging, invisible fog, the side effects being an increased heart rate, a rise in body temperature, and a huge spike in libido. Darci combed her fingers through his hair. The melted snow sparkled like diamonds against his thick raven locks. She kissed his neck. "I've reconsidered everything, Steed. I want . . ."

His warm, supple lips shushed her. His arms so strong, yet so gentle, tightened around her, holding her against his stirring manhood. His tongue danced with hers, showing it all the things she wanted his body to show hers. "I want, too, Darci. I want so many things." He took a couple of steps back. "Right now, I want you to go into that room and enjoy yourself."

Darci brushed her tongue against her lips, savoring Steed's kisses. "I think I'd enjoy myself more with some company."

Steed whimpered. "Please, Darci." He handed over the box.

"Okay, okay. I'll see you in thirty minutes."

"At least thirty minutes."

"Right." Darci made her way to the room, taking slow deliberate strides, adding a bit more sway to her hips with the feel of Steed's eyes on her and his deep grunts of appreciation. She turned back with a wide grin. "You sure . . ."

"Yes, I'm sure. I'm sure."

She laughed. "Just checking."

CHAPTER 27

Twenty-eight minutes later, Steed took a final look around the room. Thanks to the very capable hotel staff, everything had come together to his exact specifications. He had never wanted to take advantage of his unlimited access to money, but today provided an exception. Many years before, Nana insisted he have a little something set aside for a rainy day, but from the many numbers in his bank balance, the rainy day was more like a monsoon. There was no question money made things happen, as did love, and he'd finally arrived at a point in his life where those two things came together.

Steed moved to the mirror and adjusted his bow tie. Generally, he wouldn't be caught dead in a monkey suit. The only other time he'd worn one was when he gave his mother away at her wedding. Yet, here he was, willingly dressed like a penguin, counting the minutes before he would propose marriage to the woman of his dreams.

The woman of his dreams. He could scarcely believe it. Many women had crossed his path and warmed his bed, but none of them left a lasting impression. Darci Clarke was another story. His body craved her for sure, but his heart and mind needed her like he needed air to breathe.

No woman had ever affected him like Darci. She knew him, pushed him, stood toe to toe with him and didn't step back. She loved him even when he made it impossible, and she'd offered her whole self to him, the man she'd called an ass on several occasions. They had come such a long way, and he'd come even further to decline the offer of her virginity. Was he crazy?

"Steed, I can't believe this dress. You've . . . Wow!"

The sound of Darci's beautiful voice answered Steed's question. He wasn't crazy, just in love. And he wanted her to have everything her heart desired. Hopefully her heart would desire him in her life for the rest of his life. He turned to her with a smile, and in the instant he saw her, every word he wanted to say disappeared from his mind.

"Steed McGraw speechless? It must be a first." Darci grinned. "Like you in a tuxedo."

He shook his head and put up two fingers. "Second time for the tux." He reached out and stroked her cheek. The black dress exceeded his expectations, and with her thick, dark hair piled high atop her head, she personified a dream walking. "Do you have any idea how beautiful you are?"

"If the look on your face is any indication, I think I have a clue." Her gaze darted about the room. "I still can't believe what you've done." She took his hand, eyeing him from head to toe. "You're in a tuxedo. If I wasn't already impressed with the dress and its complementing accessories, the sight of you right now would definitely do it."

Steed couldn't keep his eyes off her. "You look stunning, Darci." The backless dress hugged her body like a second skin. Silver sequins trailed the spaghetti straps along her shoulders to the dark fabric along the fullness of her breasts, and a high split midway up her left thigh gave him a wonderful eyeful of a luscious, long leg.

"Steed, what is all of this?"

He extended a single, thorn-free, long-stemmed red rose. "This, lovely lady, is all for you." Steed escorted her to the table and poured two glasses of champagne. "A toast," he said, handing her a glass. "To new beginnings."

Darci clicked his glass and smiled. "To new beginnings," she said, taking a drink.

Steed reached for her hand. "Let's dance."

Taking to the floor, they swayed to the soft music. Steed drew Darci close, breathing in her sweet scent, and enjoying her soft, womanly curves. Like any red-blooded male, he couldn't help responding to the gyrations of their bodies.

Darci lifted her head from the crook of his neck, and with a knowing smile met his lips in a kiss. She opened herself to him as his tongue sought hers. Steed moaned deeply as he pulled her tongue further into his mouth, suckling her, enjoying the taste of her. Darci's soft sighs, the motion of her fingers threading his hair, and the sway of her hips against his fueled the white-hot need burning through his body. If this continued much longer, his every hope for this evening would go up in smoke. He couldn't let that happen, no matter how much his flesh wanted him to.

Finding strength he didn't know he had, Steed broke the kiss. Darci blinked, her face a picture of confusion, but one he had to ignore. "I bet you're hungry," he said, escorting her back to the table.

"Actually, I am starving, but . . ."

"Great. It's your favorite—filet mignon. Prepared just how you like it."

Darci's eyes narrowed. "What's going on with you?"

Steed shrugged as he sat. "I don't know what you mean."

"You don't?"

"No." He cut a small piece of the slightly pink meat and brought it to her lips. "I'm just trying to feed you."

Her unblinking eyes stayed on him as she chewed.

"What?"

Darci dabbed her lips with the linen napkin. "You're making me nervous, Steed."

"Nervous?"

"Something's going on behind those sparkling blue eyes."

"A feast of fancy. They're dining on you."

"I'd like to be dining on you, but you keep diverting me."

Steed drank some champagne. "You know why," he said.

"No, I don't."

"I remember our close call at your house, and what you said that night. I never forgot."

"Neither have I." Darci dropped the napkin to the table and moved over to his lap. The barely settled stirring in his loins flared up with a vengeance. She snaked her arms around his neck. Her smooth cheek brushed against his freshly shaven one. A deep moan rumbled in Steed's throat. Darci was making this way too difficult. "I also said things could change." She brushed her lips against his neck. "Things have changed."

"Darci . . ."

She pressed her finger to his lips. "I said I wanted to wait because I didn't want regrets. I won't have a single regret about making love to you, about giving you the greatest gift I have. I love you, Steed."

"And I love you." A precious love that now drove him crazy with need, and had brought him to this crucial moment in his life. "Will you marry me, Darci?"

She blinked. "What?"

"Will you marry me?" he repeated, his gaze unflinching, but his heart pounding like a jackhammer in his chest. Darci looked surprised, but he couldn't read any other emotion in those gorgeous dark eyes. Would she make him the happiest man in the world, or cause him to crash and burn. "Are you going to give me an answer?"

"Uh, this is a bit extreme to get to home base, don't you think? Steed, I want to be with you, and you don't have to . . ."

"I want to." Steed settled her on the chair, and dropped to one knee. "I know this seems sudden and unexpected, but I've never been more sure of anything. Darci, I love you. I want a houseful of beautiful little girls who look just like you, and to be honest, a little boy, too. I want to wake up every morning with you by my side. I want to grow old and toothless with a woman I know will be the hottest granny in the world. I want to spend my life with you. I want to be your husband. Please, tell me you want me to be. Say yes."

She smiled. "Yes."

His eyes widened. "Yes? Really?"

Darci shrugged. "Why not? Keep in mind I can only spare about sixty years or so, okay? I'm a busy woman." She grinned.

Steed laughed. "Of course." He pulled the ring out of his pocket and slipped it on her finger. "I hope you like it."

Darci held out her hand, admiring the sparking jewel. "Steed, it's beautiful. It looks like an heirloom."

"It is. Passed down through four generations of McGraw men to the ladies of their hearts." His knuckles gently grazed her cheek. "I've been in love with you longer than I think I want to admit to myself, but last night I knew without question I wanted you in my life forever. Soon after I left your room, I ran into Mom, and she gave me this ring. She knew what was in my heart, too." Steed kissed her adorned finger and stood. "It's a perfect fit. Meant to be."

Darci leapt into his arms, squealing like a teen at a rock concert. "I can't believe we're getting married!"

Steed laughed. "I take it you're happy about this."

"Ecstatic!" She curled her arms around his neck. "After the way we got started, it's a miracle we're together."

"Darci, you are my miracle. When you walked into that office, my world changed. Love was something I never entertained, but you—you were a force of nature. A beautiful, dynamic, exaspe . . ."

Darci stifled his words with a kiss that immediately took on a mind of its own. Steed clasped his hands around her waist and lowered them to her bottom as her hips rolled against his. Steed's skin was on fire, and Darci lowering his jacket to the floor as her tongue left a trail of tingling chills along his neck did little to squelch the flame.

Moans of pleasure rumbled in his throat while renewed memories of Darci's confession rattled in his head. *"I'm a virgin, Steed, and I plan to stay one until I'm married."* They couldn't make love yet. He silently screamed an expletive. Trying to do the right thing would be his death. "Darci, sweetheart—"

"Let's take this to the bedroom," she murmured against his lips. Active fingers worked on his bow tie, studs from his shirt flew here and there. "I want you as much as I know you want me." Her hand moved down his torso, stopping at the bulge in his pants. "I know you want me, Steed." Her fingers caressed the mound in his slacks while fiery hot kisses dusted his chest. "I can feel how much you do."

Steed moaned. "I do," he answered, reveling in her amazing touch. "I really do. But . . ." He closed his eyes. Even with his pants between them, the power of her caress defied all description. He enjoyed another moment of pleasure and then said the words he truly meant, but could barely force off his tongue. "Darci, I want us to wait."

Darci's fingers and lips stopped moving. He opened his eyes to see her pull back, staring in wide-eyed amazement. "Are you serious?"

"Yes, Darci, I am very serious." He gave her shoulder a little pat, not trusting himself to touch her more intimately. "We're going to wait."

"Steed, I don't even want to wait anymore."

He nodded. "Yes, you do. See, you're a virgin, so what you're feeling now is something you're not used to. It's blind lust, unbridled passion. I promise, it'll pass." He eased into the chair and drew a cleansing breath. "Let's eat."

Darci stayed still as a statue, continuing her stare.

Steed took a bite of steak. "Your food is getting cold."

"And I'm getting hot!" Darci pulled the pins from her hair and slid the straps of her evening dress off her shoulders. Her dark tresses tumbled to her shoulders and her gown to the floor.

Steed nearly choked as she stood before him in a lacy black bra and panty set. He thought his zipper would break from the force of his arousal. "You're not playing fair," he said, hungrily drinking in every glorious inch of this provocative side of her.

"And you're not playing at all. We're alone in a beautiful hotel room, engaged, and madly in love. We don't have to wait, Steed. You're not really going to make me wait, are you?" she cooed, closing the short distance between them.

"Darci, don't take another step closer," Steed said in a desperate rush. Her lips turned into a seductive smile. He grabbed his glass of champagne and drained it in one swallow. It didn't help. Snatching his glass of water, he doused the icy drink over his face. The shock of the chill startled his senses and gratefully took some of the edge off the fire down below. "Making love to you is something I want to do so much, but as much as we want each other right now, think of how much better it will be when we're husband and wife."

"Steed?"

"I have been with more than my share of women, and it's always just been sex. A warm body in my bed. When we finally come together, it won't only be your first time making love, but it will be mine, too. Yes, we could be together tonight, and it would be incredible, but on our wedding night it will be even more special. You can't disagree with that, can you?"

Darci sighed. "No." She walked over to her dress. "When did you become such a romantic?"

"When I fell in love with you," he answered with a smile.

"You know, that's all well and good, but I sure hope you don't believe in long engagements." She slipped back into the dress. "I think I might die from anticipation."

Steed laughed. "In our case, I don't. I want Santa to bring me a wife." He made his way over and enfolded her in his arms. "How does December twenty-fourth sound to you?"

"If you mean the one eight days from now, it sounds great."

"Then we'd better get cracking." He kissed her nose. "We've got a wedding to plan."

CHAPTER 28

"Finally, a moment alone with Mrs. Steed McGraw." Kenny slid into Steed's empty chair at the bridal party table and took Darci's hand. "Tell me, friend, are you as happy as you look?"

"Kenny, I don't think my outside can show how happy I feel on the inside," Darci answered. Her cheeks hurt from smiling so much, but she couldn't stop. "This day has been even more incredible than I ever imagined it could be. *I'm married.* Married to a guy whose neck I wanted to break a few months ago." She looked onto the dance floor where Steed boogied with Nana and Miss Sophie. "A guy I couldn't love more if I tried. He's everything to me, Kenny. He makes me crazy, he makes angry, and he makes me so incredibly happy. My life with Steed will definitely not be boring."

"If your wedding is any clue of what's to come, it will be very interesting. You guys get engaged one week and married the next. His grandma is the best person, and the gorgeous *moi* is the person of honor." Kenny chuckled. "I can safely say I've never been to a wedding quite like this."

"And that's really funny considering Steed and I are both so traditional. We had a beautiful church wedding, I'm wearing my mother's dress, he gave me his great-grandmother's engagement ring, and you know about my status. This dress isn't white for nothing."

"No doubt." He nudged her shoulder. "When I first heard you were seeing McGraw, I couldn't believe it. Then I saw how miserable you were without him, and I couldn't believe that. He completes you, Darci, and I'm very happy for you. Even though I am a little sad for myself."

"Sad? Why? You and Steed are getting along better."

"Yeah, he's a cool guy, but things aren't going to be the same for us. I won't be able to talk to you and see you like I used to. Everything's gonna be different."

"Kenny, my being married won't change us." She paused for a moment. Devilish thoughts of what tonight promised brought a smile to her lips. "Okay, maybe you won't be able to call me at all hours of the night anymore, because I'll probably be otherwise engaged, but aside from that . . ." She laughed.

Kenny rolled his eyes in exaggerated annoyance. "Good grief," he grumbled.

Darci laughed. "Seriously, we're going to be anchoring the news together, so we'll see each other every day. And even without that, you are my closest friend in the world, and you'll never be rid of me. If it wasn't for your 'death,' I wouldn't have met Steed."

"You'll find the rainbow in a bad situation, won't you?"

"What happened to you was bad, but a lot of good came from it. Steed finally freed himself of the weight he'd been carrying around since he lost his father, he got his promotion, and Fritz is finally behind bars where he belongs."

"Along with my sister," Kenny added.

"Eva is getting the help she needs in prison. In a few years, she'll be out and ready to have a better life. She called me the other day, and she sounded good. Clear and contrite."

Kenny nodded. "I told her about your wedding. She's been clean for over a month, and my parents and I are supporting her. Who knew there was such a good drug treatment program in prison? She's already stronger, and she'll make it this time."

"See, there is a lot of good. My folks are moving back to Sterling, and look at Jackson on the dance floor with his wife." Darci giggled as the young officer and his sweetheart tried to keep up with Steed and his dance partners. "Steed told me Lucas could make detective in a couple more years."

"Looks like my 'death' was a good thing."

"The best thing is you're alive, and you'll be alive for a very long time, keeping me abreast of your latest conquests."

Kenny bobbed his head. "Yeah, there is that," he agreed. "Just don't go returning the favor, okay? Blech!" He shuddered as they broke into more laughter.

"You two will have to save this laugh-fest for another time, because it's time to cut the cake," said Jackie, ending the friendly catch-up.

Kenny nudged her shoulder. "You'd better get going."

Darci leaned over and gave him a hug. "Thank you for everything, Kenny." Their embrace tightened. "Thank you for being the best friend a girl could have."

"Don't hold back, Darci." Kenny kissed her cheek and flashed his widest grin. "I'm the best everything a girl can have."

Darci gave Kenny's arm a sportive punch and made her way to Steed. Thankful for all the wonderful changes in her life, but grateful some things stayed the same.

―――∾∾∾―――

Steed swooped Darci into his arms, eliciting a jovial laugh from her. He could listen to her laughter all day. "There was a time I could barely get a smile out of you," he said.

"You've put your best foot forward since then. I've been walking on air from the moment you shared your choice for our wedding day. Who knew you would make that feeling so literal."

"Just following a tradition, Mrs. McGraw." He brought her into the room and slowly turned around. As planned, the room was set up exactly as they'd left it. "What do you think?"

"It's identical to our last night here, except on this evening things are going to end a whole lot differently."

"So very differently." His lips brushed hers. "Darci, I've spent the last seven nights dreaming of this day. The way you would look as your father escorted you down the aisle to me, and the way I would feel when we exchanged vows. But nothing I dreamed was as wonderful as the reality."

"Our wedding was incredible, wasn't it?"

"It was perfect." Steed held Darci's gaze as he carried her into the bedroom. "Just like this night will be."

"I really hope you think so."

"It will be."

"You, uh, you gave me thirty minutes I didn't want the last time we were here. I want you to take ten, while I go into the bathroom and slip into something more comfortable."

Steed agreed, having a couple of ideas for setting the mood in mind. "Okay, I think I can be without you for ten minutes." He lowered her feet to the floor. "But just ten minutes."

"Nine and a half." Darci gave him a quick kiss, grabbed the small carry-on the bellhop had brought in earlier, and disappeared behind the bathroom door.

Steed stripped down to his black boxer briefs, and then went about setting the scene. With the last of a dozen candles lit, Darci returned. Her compliment on the room barely registered as all of his attention had remained fixed on the slinky white ensemble barely covering her incredible body.

"You look so beautiful, Darci." Steed trailed his finger along her cheek. She trembled ever so slightly, but enough for him to notice. "Don't be afraid." He brought her hands to his lips and then held them to his chest. "I'll take care of you."

"I know. I'm not scared, Steed." She glanced at the bulge in his briefs. "A little nervous, maybe."

"You don't think I'm nervous?"

"You? No."

"Well, I am. An anxious, sorta excited kinda nervous. You're a virgin with expectations I'm expected to meet or exceed. That's pressure."

Her gaze swept over his body again. "Sorry. Doesn't look like you're feeling any pressure to me."

Steed laughed. "Sometimes looks can be deceiving. You turn me on, Darci, and I want you so much, but it doesn't mean I don't have a little stress. I think that's what you're feeling."

She nodded. "Yeah."

"I'm going to be very gentle with you, but if you feel uncomfortable with anything at all—"

She pressed a finger to his lips. The warmth of her touch and the look in her eyes stopped him cold. His breath caught, and the stirring in his loins intensified.

"I know there's going to be some discomfort, but I trust you, Steed, and I love you." She kissed him softly. "I think we've done enough talking." Darci slid the super-short sheer robe of the skimpy ensemble off her shoulders and onto the floor.

Steed caught her hands as she went for the straps of her gown. "Let me do that." He slipped his forefingers underneath the thin strips of cloth and dragged them down her arms. "I want to enjoy unwrapping the best Christmas present I ever got."

Transfixed, Steed watched as second by second, inch by inch, the soft material fell away, introducing his new bride's beautiful body to his approving eyes. His gaze traveled slowly, taking in all the places he'd only dreamt about before. "I want to pinch myself to see if I'm dreaming. Beauty like this can't be real."

"Pinch me." Darci stepped forward. "Feel how real I am."

Following her instruction, Steed eagerly took possession of her mouth while his probing hands squeezed and caressed every inch they could. He rolled his hips and pushed against her, letting her feel just how much he needed her.

Darci's soft sighs grew deeper with the trail of his lips along her neck, across her shoulders and down to her breasts. His tongue flicked the taut nubs. Darci's blissful sighs rippled through him when he slid his hand between their meshed bodies and buried it at the apex of her thighs.

She cried out in sweet pleasure as his fingers moved against her sensitive little bud. He released her breast from the suction of his lips and slowly removed his hand. The look of passionate need in her eyes fueled his desire for her. Steed's briefs grew tight, too tight. He feared at any moment his pulsating erection would burst unexpectedly out of his briefs like a demented jack-in-the-box and pop straight into Darci's heat.

As if sensing his need for relief, Darci slid her hands into the back of his briefs and slowly pulled the cotton material off his body. Freed from its restricting confines, his liberated manhood shot out like a butterfly breaking from its cocoon. Darci's sharp intake of breath was unmistakable.

A curious, shaky hand took possession of him, slowly moving up and down his length. Steed closed his eyes and surrendered to her incredible touch. Silky hair brushed the path her sensual kisses created from his neck to his shoulders to his hard, achy nipples. A deep, guttural moan, emanating from a place inside him he didn't know existed, reverberated in his throat as Darci continued to stroke, kiss, and caress him. He wondered how she could ever feel insecure. Every demonstration of her love for him pleased him more than the last, and left him wanting more and more of her.

Reclaiming Darci's sweet lips, Steed led her to the bed. They fell atop the softness without breaking their kiss. The feel of her writhing body beneath him, hot and aroused, left Steed aching to spread her thighs and stroke her to submission, but he knew she wasn't ready. Getting her ready would be his pleasure.

With whisper-soft kisses, Steed dusted Darci's forehead and worked his way down her radiant bronze skin. His lips slid along her breasts and across her flat tummy. His tongue darted inside her navel and then continued on a downward path. He lifted her knees and parted her thighs.

"Steed?" she whimpered, her breasts rising and falling from the rapid beat of her heart.

"Trust me," he said, before engaging her in the most sensual of kisses. His lips and tongue possessed her. Darci's cries grew louder at his every encounter with her tiny bud. Her body thrashed on the bed and her knees trembled about his head, but he never broke his concentration. He was lost in her. Breathing in her scent, drowning in the taste of her, in the pleasure he gave her.

His erection pulsated and jerked, bouncing off the cool linen like a springboard after a dive, searching for but not finding that tight, warm space it needed to rest. She was so wet, so hot. But was she ready?

Still savoring her sweetness, he slipped a finger inside. Her hips responded. Fingers threaded his hair, holding him closer. Her moans increased. Spurred by her reaction, he eased another further still and encountered her barrier. Her soft grunt paused him for several seconds, but then her velvety walls closed around his fingers, urging them to go further, deeper. He willingly obliged as her hips rose and fell with the motion of his fingers. She was ready.

Steed raised himself above her spread thighs and slowly pushed forward. Her hot tightness enveloped him immediately, welcoming him inside. He continued on and encountered her virgin wall. Darci grimaced. Her hands gripped his upper arms.

"You okay?" he asked, near delirious from the incredible feel of her, but intent on being aware of her needs.

She nodded.

"Am I hurting you?"

"No, you're loving me." She nipped his lips. "Love me."

She'd said the right words, but her discomfort was all too real, and Steed knew that. "Darci, I . . ."

"Love me."

Pulling almost completely out of her, Steed again raised up before plunging forward in one swift motion. Darci cried out as he broke through her maidenhead, filling her completely.

Neither moved. Darci's eyes stayed closed and her hands stayed tight around his arms.

Steed fought the blinding urge to thrust inside her. Never had he felt anything as incredible as Darci's love. But he knew she hurt, and even buried deep and throbbing to near explosion inside her, he couldn't think of himself. Darci, his wife, his love, was who mattered, and he would be a statue for however long it took. Sweat trailed down his face. *Please, God, don't let it take too long.*

Even with her eyes closed, Darci could feel Steed's gaze on her. His warm breath caressed her, and his words of love comforted her. How his lower half could remain so still defied comprehension. Many men in this same position would be thinking of one thing, and staying still wasn't it. But not Steed.

He'd been considerate of her all night. The way he touched her . . . The feel of his soft lips and hot tongue between her thighs, eliciting urges and desires in her she didn't know she had. A delightful tingle awakened in her core with the sensual memories. Guttural moans rumbled in her throat. He made her feel so good. So wanted. So loved.

Steed throbbed inside her, seemingly expanding with every passing moment. The feel of him in her hands could never prepare her for the feel of him inside her, as if warm satin and steel mated and produced the force that filled her so completely. There was pain, but in the context of everything, the most heavenly pain.

She opened her eyes. Steed's finger brushed her cheek. "How do you feel?" he asked, his voice strained with need and filled with concern.

"Besides a little guilty for making my brand-new husband test the bounds of patience and restraint by remaining stark still in what has to be the dream location for any other red-blooded heterosexual man, I feel a little sore." She eased up and kissed him ever so softly. "But just a little." Curling her legs around his waist, she undulated her hips. "I'm ready."

Steed groaned. "You sure, Darci? I don't want to . . ."

She silenced him with a deeper kiss, and his once-stationary hips joined hers in a gentle sway. Their tongues met, twisting and sliding in a tempo mimicking the motions of their gyrating hips. Her arms closed tightly around him, and he took the lead in their lover's dance.

Exalting the heaven he'd found between her thighs, Steed pushed inside her like a slow-moving piston, advancing and retreating. Wondrous pressure built deep inside Darci, and the earlier pain became a distant memory.

Steed's words, his movements, and his touch made real all the feelings she'd heard about but wondered if she would ever experience. She dragged her feet against the back of his legs. The silky hairs tickled her feet. His moans grew deeper. This was real. She buried her face in his shoulder, nipping him, tasting the salt of his skin. Steed whispered her name. The emotional timber in his voice made her body tremble. He was so real. Her husband. The man she loved.

Darci arched her back, bringing Steed closer to the firestorm he'd created in her. His thrusts grew deeper, faster. Her legs tightened around him. The spice of their joined bodies perfumed the room, drugging her, thrilling her. The delicious pressure grew more intense. Darci clung to him. Her body stiffened.

"Look at me, Darci," Steed directed, his breaths heavy and his heart pounding against her chest as he continued his frenzied motions. "I want to look into your heart, see your very soul when I take you there."

He pushed deep inside her and then ceased his movements. Darci cried out. Her body convulsed and trembled in release. Keeping her eyes open became impossible as wave after wave shook her. She thought of her first taste of expensive chocolate, and how she swore sex couldn't be as good. Her cries grew louder as Steed called her name, jerking against her, filling her womb with his seed. Chocolate could not compare. She'd never been happier about being proven wrong.

Steed rolled over on his back, bringing Darci's head to rest on his chest. He kissed her forehead. "So there's no question in your mind, let me tell you, Mrs. Steed McGraw, you did not disappoint," he said breathlessly, draping a cool sheet around their entwined bodies.

Darci smiled. She didn't have to hear those words, but she enjoyed them nonetheless. The feel of him inside her, the way he'd said her name at the height of his pleasure . . . Her smile widened. Oh, she definitely knew.

"You kinda let me know already." She rolled her hips. "But I appreciate your verbal confirmation."

His fingers combed her hair. "How do you feel?"

She propped her chin on his chest. "You keep asking me that."

"Because I always want to know you're okay."

"I'm better than okay. I'm absolutely fantastic."

"And how!" Steed grinned. "Was it everything you expected?"

She kissed his chest. "No, it was *way* better."

Steed smiled broadly. "I aim to please."

"You did." Her finger circled his nipple. "I'm not sorry I waited, but I can't believe what I've been missing."

"On a purely selfish note, I'm glad you found out what you've been missing with me." He took her hand, brushing his thumb against her adorned finger. "I've come to appreciate the close relationship you share with Warwick, but since I didn't have the pleasure of meeting you first, I'm glad I got this significant first with you. And I gotta tell you, it was definitely a first for me, too, because I've never experienced anything like what you and I just shared. I guess it's what love and marriage will do." Steed blew out a breath. "We're married."

"And the activity we just indulged in sealed the deal."

"Uh-huh. It means you're stuck with me forever."

"Ugh. That long?" She smirked.

"Hey." He gave her shoulder a playful scolding tap.

Darci laughed. "Seriously, I'm looking forward to spending forever with you." Her fingers splayed in the silky, dark hairs on his chest, enjoying the feel of the soft, damp hair and rock-hard muscles beneath her hands. "Meeting you made me want something I never gave much thought to—domesticity. Before I came back to Sterling, I was caught up in my career. I dated, but waiting wasn't hard, because love and commitment weren't issues. Now, the idea of somebody calling me 'Mommy' is a bigger thrill than getting the impossible interview. And you did that."

"Even when we butted heads, I'd find myself grinning and daydreaming of chasing you and a parcel of giggling children around a big house with a white picket fence and a carpet of green grass." He chuckled. "I guess that's the American dream."

"A dream a lot of the world might see as a nightmare." She twined her fingers with his. Noting the striking contrast in their coloring. "We never really talked about our differences."

"Because we don't have any. I'm not unaware of the narrow minds of the world, but I'm not big on what other people think, and I know we're stronger than anything out there."

"Me, too."

"You know, we got along like oil and water in the beginning because we're so much alike. Stubborn, hard-headed, and never wrong. And if we're never wrong, it must mean we're right."

Darci snuggled against him. Happy, content, and ready for whatever lay ahead. "Yeah. Just right."

THE END

ABOUT THE AUTHOR

A native of Denmark, South Carolina, Tammy Williams is a graduate of Denmark Technical College and Voorhees College. She is a member of Romance Writers of America and Lowcountry Romance Writers of America. *Not Quite Right* is her third novel.

Visit Tammy's website at TammyWilliams Online.com, send an email at *TamWllms@aol.com*, or write to her at P.O. Box 84, Denmark, South Carolina 29042. She always enjoys hearing from readers.

2010 Mass Market Titles

January

Show Me The Sun
Miriam Shumba
ISBN: 978-158571-405-6
$6.99

Promises of Forever
Celya Bowers
ISBN: 978-1-58571-380-6
$6.99

February

Love Out Of Order
Nicole Green
ISBN: 978-1-58571-381-3
$6.99

Unclear and Present Danger
Michele Cameron
ISBN: 978-158571-408-7
$6.99

March

Stolen Jewels
Michele Sudler
ISBN: 978-158571-409-4
$6.99

Not Quite Right
Tammy Williams
ISBN: 978-158571-410-0
$6.99

April

Oak Bluffs
Joan Early
ISBN: 978-1-58571-379-0
$6.99

Crossing The Line
Bernice Layton
ISBN: 978-158571-412-4
$6.99

How To Kill Your Husband
Keith Walker
ISBN: 978-158571-421-6
$6.99

May

The Business of Love
Cheris F. Hodges
ISBN: 978-158571-373-8
$6.99

Wayward Dreams
Gail McFarland
ISBN: 978-158571-422-3
$6.99

June

The Doctor's Wife
Mildred Riley
ISBN: 978-158571-424-7
$6.99

Mixed Reality
Chamein Canton
ISBN: 978-158571-423-0
$6.99

2010 Mass Market Titles (continued)
July

Blue Interlude
Keisha Mennefee
ISBN: 978-158571-378-3
$6.99

Always You
Crystal Hubbard
ISBN: 978-158571-371-4
$6.99

Unbeweavable
Katrina Spencer
ISBN: 978-158571-426-1
$6.99

August

Small Sensations
Crystal V. Rhodes
ISBN: 978-158571-376-9
$6.99

Let's Get It On
Dyanne Davis
ISBN: 978-158571-416-2
$6.99

September

Unconditional
A.C. Arthur
ISBN: 978-158571-413-1
$6.99

Swan
Africa Fine
ISBN: 978-158571-377-6
$6.99$6.99

October

Friends in Need
Joan Early
ISBN:978-1-58571-428-5
$6.99

Against the Wind
Gwynne Forster
ISBN:978-158571-429-2
$6.99

That Which Has Horns
Miriam Shumba
ISBN:978-1-58571-430-8
$6.99

November

A Good Dude
Keith Walker
ISBN:978-1-58571-431-5
$6.99

Reye's Gold
Ruthie Robinson
ISBN:978-1-58571-432-2
$6.99

December

Still Waters…
Crystal V. Rhodes
ISBN:978-1-58571-433-9
$6.99

Burn
Crystal Hubbard
ISBN: 978-1-58571-406-3
$6.99

Other Genesis Press, Inc. Titles

Other Genesis Press, Inc. Titles (continued)

Other Genesis Press, Inc. Titles (continued)

Other Genesis Press, Inc. Titles (continued)

Indigo After Dark Vol. IV	Cassandra Colt/	$14.95
Indigo After Dark Vol. V	Delilah Dawson	$14.95
Indiscretions	Donna Hill	$8.95
Intentional Mistakes	Michele Sudler	$9.95
Interlude	Donna Hill	$8.95
Intimate Intentions	Angie Daniels	$8.95
It's in the Rhythm	Sammie Ward	$6.99
It's Not Over Yet	J.J. Michael	$9.95
Jolie's Surrender	Edwina Martin-Arnold	$8.95
Kiss or Keep	Debra Phillips	$8.95
Lace	Giselle Carmichael	$9.95
Lady Preacher	K.T. Richey	$6.99
Last Train to Memphis	Elsa Cook	$12.95
Lasting Valor	Ken Olsen	$24.95
Let Us Prey	Hunter Lundy	$25.95
Lies Too Long	Pamela Ridley	$13.95
Life Is Never As It Seems	J.J. Michael	$12.95
Lighter Shade of Brown	Vicki Andrews	$8.95
Look Both Ways	Joan Early	$6.99
Looking for Lily	Africa Fine	$6.99
Love Always	Mildred E. Riley	$10.95
Love Doesn't Come Easy	Charlyne Dickerson	$8.95
Love Unveiled	Gloria Greene	$10.95
Love's Deception	Charlene Berry	$10.95
Love's Destiny	M. Loui Quezada	$8.95
Love's Secrets	Yolanda McVey	$6.99
Mae's Promise	Melody Walcott	$8.95
Magnolia Sunset	Giselle Carmichael	$8.95
Many Shades of Gray	Dyanne Davis	$6.99
Matters of Life and Death	Lesego Malepe, Ph.D.	$15.95
Meant to Be	Jeanne Sumerix	$8.95
Midnight Clear	Leslie Esdaile	$10.95
(Anthology)	Gwynne Forster	
	Carmen Green	
	Monica Jackson	
Midnight Magic	Gwynne Forster	$8.95
Midnight Peril	Vicki Andrews	$10.95
Misconceptions	Pamela Leigh Starr	$9.95
Moments of Clarity	Michele Cameron	$6.99
Montgomery's Children	Richard Perry	$14.95
Mr. Fix-It	Crystal Hubbard	$6.99
My Buffalo Soldier	Barbara B.K. Reeves	$8.95

Other Genesis Press, Inc. Titles (continued)

Other Genesis Press, Inc. Titles (continued)

Other Genesis Press, Inc. Titles (continued)

ESCAPE WITH INDIGO !!!!

Join Indigo Book Club©
It's simple, easy and secure.

Sign up and receive the new
releases
every month + Free shipping
and
20% off the cover price.

Visit us online at
www.genesis-press.com or
call 1-888-INDIGO-1

Order Form

Mail to: Genesis Press, Inc.
P.O. Box 101
Columbus, MS 39703

Name _____

Address _____

City/State _____ Zip _____

Telephone _____

Ship to (if different from above)

Name _____

Address _____

City/State _____ Zip _____

Telephone _____

Credit Card Information

Credit Card # _____ ☐ Visa ☐ Mastercard

Expiration Date (mm/yy) _____ ☐ AmEx ☐ Discover

Qty.	Author	Title	Price	Total

Use this order form, or call 1-888-INDIGO-1	Total for books _____
	Shipping and handling: $5 first two books, $1 each additional book _____
	Total S & H _____
	Total amount enclosed _____
	Mississippi residents add 7% sales tax

Visit www.genesis-press.com for latest releases and excerpts.